Anthony Gilbert and The Murder Room

>>> This title is part of The Murder Room, our series dedicated to making available out-of-print or hard-to-find titles by classic crime writers.

Crime fiction has always held up a mirror to society. The Victorians were fascinated by sensational murder and the emerging science of detection; now we are obsessed with the forensic detail of violent death. And no other genre has so captivated and enthralled readers.

Vast troves of classic crime writing have for a long time been unavailable to all but the most dedicated frequenters of second-hand bookshops. The advent of digital publishing means that we are now able to bring you the backlists of a huge range of titles by classic and contemporary crime writers, some of which have been out of print for decades.

From the genteel amateur private eyes of the Golden Age and the femmes fatales of pulp fiction, to the morally ambiguous hard-boiled detectives of mid twentieth-century America and their descendants who walk our twenty-first century streets, The Murder Room has it all. **>>>**

The Murder Room
Where Criminal Minds Meet

themurderroom.com

T0352202

Anthony Gilbert (1899–1973)

Anthony Gilbert was the pen name of Lucy Beatrice Malleson. Born in London, she spent all her life there, and her affection for the city is clear from the strong sense of character and place in evidence in her work. She published 69 crime novels, 51 of which featured her best known character, Arthur Crook, a vulgar London lawyer totally (and deliberately) unlike the aristocratic detectives, such as Lord Peter Wimsey, who dominated the mystery field at the time. She also wrote more than 25 radio plays, which were broadcast in Great Britain and overseas. Her thriller *The Woman in Red* (1941) was broadcast in the United States by CBS and made into a film in 1945 under the title *My Name is Julia Ross*. She was an early member of the British Detection Club, which, along with Dorothy L. Sayers, she prevented from disintegrating during World War II. Malleson published her autobiography, *Three-a-Penny*, in 1940, and wrote numerous short stories, which were published in several anthologies and in such periodicals as *Ellery Queen's Mystery Magazine* and *The Saint*. The short story 'You Can't Hang Twice' received a Queens award in 1946. She never married, and evidence of her feminism is elegantly expressed in much of her work.

By Anthony Gilbert

Scott Egerton series
Tragedy at Freyne (1927)
The Murder of Mrs
  Davenport (1928)
Death at Four Corners
  (1929)
The Mystery of the Open
  Window (1929)
The Night of the Fog (1930)
The Body on the Beam
  (1932)
The Long Shadow (1932)
The Musical Comedy
  Crime (1933)
An Old Lady Dies (1934)
The Man Who Was Too
  Clever (1935)

**Mr Crook Murder
  Mystery series**
Murder by Experts (1936)
The Man Who Wasn't
  There (1937)
Murder Has No Tongue
  (1937)
Treason in My Breast (1938)
The Bell of Death (1939)

Dear Dead Woman (1940)
  aka *Death Takes a
  Redhead*
The Vanishing Corpse (1941)
  aka *She Vanished in the
  Dawn*
The Woman in Red (1941)
  aka *The Mystery of the
  Woman in Red*
Death in the Blackout (1942)
  aka *The Case of the Tea-
  Cosy's Aunt*
Something Nasty in the
  Woodshed (1942)
  aka *Mystery in the
  Woodshed*
The Mouse Who Wouldn't
  Play Ball (1943)
  aka *30 Days to Live*
He Came by Night (1944)
  aka *Death at the Door*
The Scarlet Button (1944)
  aka *Murder Is Cheap*
A Spy for Mr Crook (1944)
The Black Stage (1945)
  aka *Murder Cheats the
  Bride*

Don't Open the Door (1945)
 aka *Death Lifts the Latch*
Lift Up the Lid (1945)
 aka *The Innocent Bottle*
The Spinster's Secret (1946)
 aka *By Hook or by Crook*
Death in the Wrong Room
 (1947)
Die in the Dark (1947)
 aka *The Missing Widow*
Death Knocks Three Times
 (1949)
Murder Comes Home (1950)
A Nice Cup of Tea (1950)
 aka *The Wrong Body*
Lady-Killer (1951)
Miss Pinnegar Disappears
 (1952)
 aka *A Case for Mr Crook*
Footsteps Behind Me (1953)
 aka *Black Death*
Snake in the Grass (1954)
 aka *Death Won't Wait*
Is She Dead Too? (1955)
 aka *A Question of Murder*
And Death Came Too (1956)
Riddle of a Lady (1956)
Give Death a Name (1957)

Death Against the Clock
 (1958)
Death Takes a Wife (1959)
 aka *Death Casts a Long
 Shadow*
Third Crime Lucky (1959)
 aka *Prelude to Murder*
Out for the Kill (1960)
She Shall Die (1961)
 aka *After the Verdict*
Uncertain Death (1961)
No Dust in the Attic (1962)
Ring for a Noose (1963)
The Fingerprint (1964)
Knock, Knock! Who's
 There? (1964)
 aka *The Voice*
Passenger to Nowhere (1965)
The Looking Glass Murder
 (1966)
The Visitor (1967)
Night Encounter (1968)
 aka *Murder Anonymous*
Missing from Her Home
 (1969)
Death Wears a Mask (1970)
 aka *Mr Crook Lifts the
 Mask*

The Scarlet Button

Anthony Gilbert

An Orion book

Copyright © Lucy Beatrice Malleson 1944

The right of Lucy Beatrice Malleson to be identified as the author of this work has been asserted in accordance with the Copyright, Designs and Patents Act 1988.

This edition published by
The Orion Publishing Group Ltd
Orion House
5 Upper St Martin's Lane
London WC2H 9EA

An Hachette UK company
A CIP catalogue record for this book is available from the British Library

ISBN 978 1 4719 0980 1

www.orionbooks.co.uk

CHAPTER ONE

I

BESS CARTER sat at the triple-winged mirror in her room at "The Case Is Altered," arranging a scarlet silk snood over her incredibly golden hair. She was wearing a short black woollen frock and a little scarlet coat with buttons shaped like dolphins. She painted her mouth, put mascara under her eyes and curled up her long lashes with a minute brush. Then she ran out of her room into the passage, where she almost cannoned against a tall dark young man with a haggard face and an air of being perpetually on guard. He put out a hand and caught her arm.

"One of these days you're going to turn your ankle, wearing those ridiculous shoes," he said, soberly.

She looked down at the shiny black shoes with their absurd red heels and laughed.

"My shoes know my feet," she said. "Where are you going to-night, Ken?"

The young man stared at something she couldn't see and said, "Oh, nowhere special."

"Don't lie to Momma, darling," said Bess encouragingly. "Nice clean shirt, best suit—passing Bess up? Is that it?"

He shook his head as though she were some stinging insect exasperating him beyond endurance.

"For God's sake, Bess."

"Whyn't you join Tony and the others in the bar?" she suggested.

"You know damn well what happens when I join Tony in the bar."

"Well, but, ducks, you don't have to drink too much, do you? Though if it takes your mind off things . . ."

He pressed her arm. "You're a sweet thing, Bess. God knows why you should bother over me and my foul temper."

"You're all right. Everyone gets under the weather sometimes. What is it, Ken? Not—not money?"

"I suppose you think I'd take that from you as well as everything else."

"Beats me," said honest Bess, "why men make such a fuss about taking money from women when they take everything else like the divine right of kings. Well, I must be going down again. I only popped up to powder my nose during the news. These Russian names get me down."

1

He said abruptly, " I wish you didn't do this sort of work. All those fellows trying to paw you."

She exclaimed, genuinely surprised. " They're only boys, want a bit of something before they go out. You know."

He knew. He had enough flying hours to his credit to know better than she could guess. All the same, though being a pilot wasn't all jam, there were worse things on terra firma—far worse. He wished he could tell Bess. But there are some things you can't tell any woman, even if she is the kind that can't be shocked and wouldn't call herself a lady anyhow.

She turned and straightened his tie. " Wherever you go," she said, " have a good time. Your trouble is you're too young."

" Now you're going to spring that old chestnut on me about all women being naturally ten years older than men, I suppose."

" All those girl kids who were born in the *Times* this morning are older than you," she told him—and hesitated. " All women aren't too good," she said as though it was something to be ashamed of. " You want to watch out."

" Don't worry about me," he said in a constrained voice. He walked away from her to look out of the landing window. The bombers were going out in terrific force to-night. You could hear them roaring overhead. Not so very long since he'd been with them, before he'd made that pancake landing and done something to his knee. When he joined the Air Force he'd thought, " God, a new beginning. Good-bye to all the old muddle," but he knew now that you never say good-bye to your past. You can run like the hare in the fable, but when you get to the winning-post the tortoise is waiting for you. It's been there all the time you were kidding yourself you'd left it behind. It was a dull sort of night—might be snow later, he thought, though not likely before midnight. He wished he were with those chaps, though it might mean a crash—was bound to mean a crash for some of them. A force that size never came home intact. But it was better than what he had to do to-night.

Bess came across and suddenly put her arms round his neck. " For God's sake don't spoil my make-up," she said, " but be good to yourself. You owe yourself something."

Then she had gone with a final wave of her hand with its phoney rings, gone leaving only the scent of her powder and the echo of her gay laugh. It wasn't surprising the men made passes at her; she was what you wanted in a war, someone who laughed and had a drink with you and made the present so cheerful you didn't think about the future.

The passage seemed very cold and dark now she'd left it. He looked at the watch on his wrist. Not too much time to go.

He went up to his room, limping a little and got his coat. There was a heavy stick standing in the corner and he took that, too. He hated to walk with a stick, hated to emphasise the lameness he loathed, but he had a walk to-night and a stick would be useful. He caught a glimpse of himself in the mirror, a tall haunted young man with a white face and a smudge of black moustache and dark eyes that saw more than was good for them. He stared hard at the reflection. He didn't look in the least like the traditional young pilot of twenty-five : but then he wasn't. He'd stepped out of the ranks a long time ago and Heaven only knew if he'd ever be able to step back. It was a good thing his people were dead ; he might know Bess had a heart of gold but to his father she'd be merely the barmaid at " The Case Is Altered," a bit meretricious for all her sincerity, and much too old in experience as well as years for him.

Outside he was glad of the darkness ; the bombers were still roaring past and the roads were deserted. He walked fast as lame men often do, thinking of what lay ahead. His objective was a tall old-fashioned house as dark as the grave. The words came instinctively to mind and he tried to thrust them out. Above all things he didn't want to think of graves to-night. Without any warning the snow he'd anticipated began to fall ; it came down as suddenly as though someone had just turned a jug upside down. It soaked into his shoulders and the sleeves of his coat ; big flakes melted between his socks and the rim of his shoes. He cursed softly but after all it would keep the roads empty and that might be important.

When he reached The Crescent there wasn't a soul in sight. Most of these big houses had been adapted as offices or taken over by the authorities as emergency rest-centres in case of raids ; he felt to-night he'd be glad to see even those forbidden gleams of light that are usually visible like ribbons of gold from the pavement. It would have established his contact with a living world. But still, perhaps it was better so. The house he wanted was No. 32. The basement had been strutted up as an air-raid shelter ; the front door stood ajar to afford protection of a sort for those unfortunate enough to be caught out-of-doors when the sirens sounded.

He went quickly up the steps and taking off his hat shook the snow from it. He looked rapidly in both directions but the place seemed deserted. No one, then, had seen him come, and even Bess didn't know his plans, had never so much as heard of James Chigwell, Chigwell the human spider who fattened on the blood of other men, on their misfortunes, on their mistakes. Oh, only a fool believed the past could die.

3

He went softly up the long uncarpeted stairs. He'd been here before ; he knew where the wood creaked and where you had to step on the painted border if you didn't want to advertise your coming. Chigwell was on the second floor. The first floor was the workroom of a beauty parlour, what they called a beautician in America. They shut down smartly at five o'clock, but even now a faint scent of powder and cream came through the locked doors, reminding him of Bess. Suddenly he wished the whole horrible business was over, that he'd never come, in short, but was back at " The Case Is Altered," with Bess warm and laughing beside him, Bess who laughed at ill-luck, laughed at poverty, laughed at danger, would one of these days laugh at death. There it was again—the forbidden word. He shivered. On the second floor he stopped, listening intently. There wasn't a sound from within. He bent double and looked under the door. No light in the hall, no movement, no murmur of voices. So Chigwell was alone. He was here, of course. Rumour said he never left the place, even sleeping on the premises. From his pocket Kenneth Jardine took a key. Heaven send it would fit the lock, go in smoothly, not betray him. It was of the essence of his scheme that he should take Chigwell by surprise. The key went into the lock like a hot knife into butter. The door opened noiselessly and now he stood in the narrow dark hall. He was shaking from head to foot ; it seemed to him the stairs were creaking as though an army of ghosts, ghosts of all the poor devils who'd come stealing to this house of dishonour after dark as he'd done, waited there, encouraging him, cheering him on. He put his hand to his forehead. He mustn't get excited now. A pulse beat furiously in his temple ; he felt his heart pumping. Very gently he closed the front door. The room he wanted was on the right. There was a golden gleam under the door and he stood a moment, sweating like a nervous horse, trying to get himself in hand for what lay just ahead. There were great double doors to this room, painted white and never washed ; the handles were tarnished gilt. As you opened the right-hand door—the left one was permanently bolted—you saw yourself in a long mirror on the wall. Chigwell had put that mirror there and had his desk in a place that enabled him to see the reflection of every new-comer. A man who lived as he did couldn't be too careful.

Kenneth opened the door a crack and waited. Still there wasn't a sound. It was possible that Chigwell hadn't noticed. He thought of the terrible story of " The Tell-Tale Heart," of the watcher pausing an hour in the darkness to make sure that his victim slept. His (Kenneth's) nerves would stand no such strain. He gave the door a sudden push, thrust in his hand and switched off the light. Chigwell always arranged the lights so that he and his desk were in gloom ; a man with a business like his couldn't afford unnecessary risks.

He rather expected Chigwell to speak, to turn on another light, to pick up the telephone. But nothing happened. He began to talk in a loud voice that was almost a shout.

" This is Kenneth Jardine, Chigwell. I've come for the papers of mine you've got. I haven't brought the hundred pounds you asked for. I haven't got a hundred pounds. I'm not worth so much to anyone in the world. So I've come to take them for nothing. You see ? You'd better give them to me. I'm desperate. I shan't draw the line anywhere, Chigwell, not anywhere. And I'm armed."

Still that heavy brooding silence, full of threats. He turned on the light and at the same instant hurled himself forward at the big man sitting at the desk.

2

It wasn't very long, after all, before he was standing, sweating and retching, in the little narrow hall. It didn't matter how much noise he made now, Chigwell wouldn't hear him. No sense walking back while he looked like this. You never knew when you mightn't cannon into a bobby or some fellow who'd recognise you, and then when the news got out to-morrow he'd remember he saw you in the neighbourhood and you were obviously rattled. All the same, he'd give a good deal not to be able to remember what he'd left behind in the darkened room. Suddenly he jerked upright. There was a new sound, easily distinguishable from the various sounds that pealed only in his own brain. In the room of death a telephone had begun to ring. It rang and rang and he stood there hypnotised. He wanted to lift his head and shout, " You bloody fool, what's the good of hanging on ? He's not going to answer, he's never going to answer anyone again. Except the Recording Angel." Knowing Chigwell you'd wonder if he mightn't have some answer even for him. It seemed to Kenneth the whole world must hear that pealing bell. At any minute footsteps would sound on the stairs, hands thunder at the door. Then a new thought came to him. Suppose this was Fate giving him a last chance ? He'd learned that you can't trust Fate, but he knew, too, that miracles do happen. Steeling himself to re-enter that awful room he took the receiver from the hook. " Yes," he said, and if his voice didn't sound like James Chigwell it didn't sound like Kenneth Jardine either.

" Mr. Chigwell," said a desperate voice at the other end of the line, " this is Mrs. Amherst. You've got to give me another week, just a week, Mr. Chigwell. Money doesn't grow on trees, and I can't ask Jim. You know I can't ask Jim. Please, Mr. Chigwell." He couldn't stand any more. He knew too well what it was like to hold on to a receiver with shaking hands and a burning heart and plead for mercy from something that couldn't spell the word. He laid down the receiver very gently and someone went on talking to nothingness. He thought he couldn't stand any more of this. His watch said ten o'clock. Surely he'd established the fact that Chigwell was alive then. His muddled brain couldn't tell him how that would help him, but it seemed somehow important. He came back into the hall ; in a few minutes now he'd be back with Bess, with warmth and light and a courage that a hundred Chigwells couldn't daunt. He tried to forget that woman's voice, to tell himself that by to-morrow she'd know she could stop being afraid. It didn't occur to him that when the murder was discovered she might not give her testimony because she wouldn't want the unknown Jim to know of her connection with the dead man.

He was about to open the front door when a second and far worse shock staggered him. This new development was something he'd never contemplated. Someone was ringing the electric bell of the flat ! He had been so much occupied with the telephone he hadn't been listening for sounds from outside. Now he was caught like a rat in a trap. Because that door wasn't going to be opened, and that would be proof, in spite of half a hundred telephone calls, that Chigwell had been dead when the visitor came. The new-comer, he assumed, had an appointment at ten o'clock, and when they found the body next morning he'd come forward with his evidence. The bell shrilled again ; Kenneth stood absolutely motionless. Go away, his heart was imploring, go away and let me get out. But suppose whoever it was went to the police, suppose something aroused his suspicions ? He, Kenneth Jardine, might be found on the premises and what defence could he conceivably offer ? His only hope was that the man on the farther side of the door wouldn't be anxious to advertise his whereabouts. Most of Chigwell's clients came by stealth and went with shame. The police were the last people they wanted to meet.

He seemed to have waited a long time. Now everything was quiet. The visitor must have crept away. No one surely would remain so long outside an unopened door. Then he remembered Chigwell's unpleasant habit of keeping his victims hanging about to show his own power over them, and decided to wait another five minutes. And it was as well that he did so. For a minute later the letter-flap was pushed back and under Kenneth's fascinated, horrified eyes something came wavering through the slit. The man on the other side was leaving a note—a note for a dead man. Kenneth put his hands over his mouth so that he shouldn't laugh out loud. There was a wire cage nailed on the door and this was padlocked, but there was a narrow space between it and the door and the strip of paper slipped down and lay on the mat. After another agonised minute Kenneth heard the steps going downstairs, firm assured steps they sounded. He wondered how his would sound to a stranger. He'd go down on tiptoe expecting voices to speak to him out of the dark, hands to reach out to detain him. He hadn't the consciousness of innocence, actual and intended, that makes it possible for a man to face even his accusers with courage. Slipping through into the hall, not daring to put on the light but using a small electric torch, he picked up the bit of paper. It was a sheet from a diary and read :

" Came at 10 o'clock as agreed by 'phone to-night ; no reply. Will 'phone to-morrow.—R. B."

Even now he didn't dare open the door and come out ; the fellow might be sheltering in the entrance. Or he might even come back. But though he stayed where he was for another fifteen minutes there was no further disturbance of the silence. He stole back into the room and lifted a corner of the heavy black-out. There was no one to be seen ; the snow was still coming down steadily.

He came away at last ; he thought there might be another visitor and his shattered nerves wouldn't be able to bear it. In the hall he hesitated again over the slip of paper. Should he leave it where it was or destroy it ? His instinct now was solely one of self-preservation. He had no thought any longer for the man who had left the message or for the Thing sprawled over the big desk in the living-room. Eventually, still not sure that he was acting wisely, he dropped the paper back on the floor and slipped out. The door had a self-closing mechanism and shut without a sound. He edged his way down the stairs step by step, and came softly out into the street. He had often heard that men lose the throw because they don't see far enough ahead, don't take the long view. He tried to cast his thoughts forward to to-morrow and the day after but it was no good. His brain was paralysed.

7

3

He reached his room at " The Case Is Altered " without encountering anyone. He had a shock when he saw his own face ; it was hardly recognisable.

" Just as well," he said aloud, with a sound that was meant for dispassionate comment and ended alarmingly in a smothered giggle. " Don't want to be recognised. Can't afford to be recognised."

He dropped into a chair. Oh, God, why had he gone to that flat to-night ? His chin dropped to his chest. He'd been tired before, tired when he was in the Air Force, but never tired like this. He'd been afraid, too, as most men were one time or another—lame-ducking home, not sure if you'd make it or come down in the cold dirty sea. But that wasn't this new sort of fear. This was craven, despicable. The awful thing was that he couldn't bear the burden of his knowledge. He wanted to go down to the brightly-lighted bar packed with men, all laughing with Bess, chaffing her, getting saucy repartees. He wanted to tell them what had happened, what was awaiting discovery at No. 32 The Crescent. He got to his feet, then halted, panic-stricken. That was the one thing he must never say.

He shivered and realised that he was soaked through. He'd better change before he got pneumonia and babbled all his secrets on a bed of delirium. He pulled off his clothes, flung them down anyhow, the way he always did.

" Anyone 'ud know you were a bachelor," Bess used to say.

He got into another suit, lighted the gas-fire and crouched over it. If only he could stop shaking, lose this sense of numbing cold. Even the snow wouldn't wholly account for that. If he went around looking like this in the morning a blind man would know something was wrong. He looked again at his watch. 10.50. Only thirty minutes ago he'd been stealing like a thief out of Chigwell's flat. An hour and a half ago he'd been in the room he occupied now, with this evening's history still unwritten, his share of it, at all events.

" Oh God ! " he exclaimed in desperation. " Help me to put up a good show when Bess comes up."

Because he knew that if he didn't go down she'd come looking for him. It was one of the ironies of fate that she, who brimmed over with the maternal instinct, would probably never have children of her own.

He sat there, lighting cigarettes and pitching them away till his case was empty. He looked at his watch again. Eleven o'clock. He found an odd cigarette in his coat-pocket and lighted that but it tasted dry, bitter. Two or three puffs were all he could manage of that.

Bess came up a quarter of an hour later ; he heard her footsteps stop at his door.

" You back, Ken ? "

" I'm back." He came quickly to meet her. Perhaps in the half-dark passage she wouldn't notice anything strange.

" Wouldn't she look at you ? " taunted Bess. And her hand touched his shoulder. It was like a finger of flame. He must have been mad to think he could keep a secret from her.

" I meant to come down for a drink," he lied, flinching away from that kind hand. " God, it's cold out to-night."

" I suppose you got soaked through," she said severely.

" A bit. I've changed, though, and I've been roasting in front of the fire."

" Let's come in and have a warm for a minute."

She seemed so blessedly normal, so alive and fearless ; it was like meeting someone from a sunlit world. He had moved among nightmares and shadows for so long the sunshine dazzled him. She picked up the coat he'd flung anyhow on a chair, carried it across the room to the wardrobe. She stooped for his discarded trousers, then his shirt. He said something casual, because silence was the one thing he couldn't bear, but she didn't reply. He turned to look at her and saw that she had his shirt in her hand, was staring at it.

" Hullo ! " he exclaimed. " What's the matter ? Another button gone ? "

It seemed a long time before Bess answered. She was like that creature beloved of the novelist, a woman turned to stone. His eyes left her face, followed her rigid gaze. He started.

" What's that ? " For on the sleeve of the shirt was a dark unmistakable stain.

" What do you think ? " demanded Bess. " What does it look like ? "

He said in a voice that matched hers, " It looks like blood."

" It is blood," confirmed Bess. " Ken, what have you been doing ? "

He exclaimed sharply, " It'll wash out, won't it ? " cursing himself for that inattentiveness to detail that might do for him yet.

" It'll wash all right," she agreed. " What I want to know is —how did it get there ? "

He stammered. " I don't know—I didn't see—that is, I can't tell you."

9

" Lucky for you I saw it before anyone else did. Ken, what in Heaven's name have you been up to ? "

" I don't know what you mean," he said in a rough voice. " I've—just been out. God, I wish I had a drink."

She took no notice of that. She rolled the shirt up to take away. Then she looked at him ; he was afraid when he saw the storm of feeling in her candid eyes. No man living, he thought, had a chance with a woman once her mind was made up.

" You'd much better tell me," she urged. Then she paused. " Or maybe you're right not to say anything. Maybe no one should know."

CHAPTER TWO

I

IT WAS a charwoman who found the horribly battered thing that had been James Chigwell soon after seven o'clock the next morning. She came in with her pail and brush and her bit of matting as she did every morning and groped her way over to the window, because the room was in complete darkness. Sometimes he was up already, peering at her in a way that would have given a more sensitive woman the creeps. She liked it better when he lay late. She never cared much about doing for Mr. Chigwell ; he never gave you anything, only sometimes left coins lying about. Marked coins. She knew. She'd looked at them under the light. She had a son in the Middle East. It seemed a crushing shame he should be fighting to preserve men like that. When she'd pulled back the curtains she turned and saw him. She screamed automatically and went on screaming as she blundered her way across the room and into the hall. She was screaming as she came on to the stairway and screamed all the way down the stairs. An auxiliary fireman coming down the street heard her and caught her arm.

" What's the matter with you that you're screaming blue murder ? " he demanded.

And she went on screaming, " That's just what it is—murder. Murder—but not blue. Red—red everywhere. Up there." She waggled her finger towards the building she had left.

" Look here," said the fireman, " what you want's a cup of tea." He led her to a canteen across the street. " Now, what's this story of yours ? "

She told him in long strangling gasps. " You stay here, ma," said the fireman. " I'll look after this."

He went up to the second floor of No. 32. He wasn't surprised she'd screamed. James Chigwell lay forward over his desk with the back of his head caved in. Whoever did that had put all his force behind the blow. He didn't stop longer than he had to. Whoever was responsible had hated the old coot good and proper. Air raids hardened you to a lot of things, but a sight like that before you'd had your breakfast was enough to make your stomach turn over.

The news was all round the place within the hour. The midday papers carried it, mostly in small paragraphs—Man Dead in a Flat. And all over the county and sometimes farther afield people's hearts stirred in their breasts with incredulous relief that one of the dead man's victims should have reached the end of his tether and saved them all. But if the unknown murderer was a hero to them, to the authorities he was just a criminal to be identified and arrested and tried and—doubtless—hanged.

The milkman brought the tale to " The Case Is Altered." When Bess heard it she said, " Who do they think did it ? Do they know ? "

" Give 'em a chance," said the milkman. " It only happened last night."

" So they know that much." With an effort she pulled herself together. It didn't do to let your imagination run away with you. It was silly to go fancying things. " Any idea what time ? "

" I'm delivering milk," said the man pointedly. " Not acting as a special constable."

" I wonder if they know who saw him last," persisted Bess.

" You women are all the same," opined the milkman. " You love a murder. My missus now . . . "

" How was it done ? " She couldn't help asking that question.

" Someone battered his brains out and they don't think it could have been a woman or an old man, because of the strength used. He was a big chap—must have been someone he knew, because they think he must have let the murderer in.' '

" Strikes me it isn't only women who're interested in murder," put in someone else.

" Well, things don't happen much these days," said the milkman, sublimely ignoring the fact that the whole civilised world was being battered to bits. " Anyway, they'll probably find the weapon—the police always do—if it isn't at the bottom of the river by now."

The talk turned on murder and motive. Familiar names were bandied, names that had been front-page news in the

11

evening papers in the good old days when the press reported murder cases in full. Bess didn't stop and listen. She was a fool, she told herself, making mountains out of molehills, but she couldn't forget Ken's white face, the blood-stained shirt, his shaking hands. She remembered about the heavy stick, too. When she got a chance she slipped up to his room to look for it and knew an almost unbearable relief when she saw it in its usual corner. She took it up with hands that trembled and carried it over to the light. There was a darkish mark on the knob, and nervously she wetted her finger and rubbed the place. A reddish stain showed on her skin. She remembered the blood-stained shirt, Kenneth's attitude, his defiance before he went and the stark fear he held in leash as a man may hold a wild beast on a chain, on his return. She took the stick into the bathroom and scrubbed the top till she scrubbed off some of the varnish. There wasn't any blood now, but it was obvious that the stick had been washed. On the whole, she wondered whether she hadn't made things worse. In panic she took the stick out with her and dropped it in the river. There was no need to tie a stone round it or anything ; it sank of its own deadly weight. She hoped Kenneth wouldn't notice its disappearance, but of course he did. The first thing he looked at every time he went into his room was that stick.

The night it wasn't there he knew at once what had happened. He went to find her, raw with impatience and dread.

" Seen my stick, Bess ? "

" Oh, Ken, I meant to tell you. I took it out and I—I must have left it somewhere. I'm ever so sorry."

" Where did you go ? "

" Well—just the shops, you know."

" Perhaps you left it at one of them."

" No, no. I've asked." Whatever happened he mustn't be allowed to go round making enquiries, drawing attention to himself.

" It must be somewhere. Did you take it to the pictures ? "

" I took it on the bus," she lied desperately. " I must have left it there."

" Then it ought to turn up at the Lost Property Office."

" I'll ask," she said quickly. " It has to be the one that lost it. That's the rule. But you know things you lose on buses never do seem to come back."

" Not often," he agreed wryly. He knew well enough this wasn't coming back. He could make a pretty good guess where it was. He was torn between anger at her interference, that was, in fact, to have more serious consequences than either of them appreciated at the time, and tenderness for her loyalty. You'd never get Bess to say what she thought. Wild horses wouldn't wring it out of her. She might think he'd done it, most likely did, but her attitude towards him didn't change. There was a profound humanity about her that made her painted finger-nails, her pillar-box red mouth and her brilliant hair matters of small account. Bess watched him anxiously. His face had begun to shut up. She wanted to speak but there was nothing she could say and nothing he could tell her. If he'd done this frightful thing how could he make her an accessory after the crime ? and if he hadn't—well, would she believe him whatever he might say ? For her sake he would be bound to deny it through thick and thin.

The police were hotfoot on the trail. Their first enquiries were directed into discovering the approximate time of death. They were helped here by a diary they found in the dead man's pocket, in which were noted a number of appointments, each signified by an initial. Against 8 o'clock on the fatal night were the three letters F. M. A. Against 9 o'clock R. B.

Mr. Francis Maurice Ainwright, F.R.C.S., was at breakfast when the police came to call on him. He'd heard the news the day before, and had been trembling in his shoes ever since. It did a doctor no good to be mixed up in a murder case, even if he were simply the man who'd found the body, and if, as in this instance, he could be dragged into the limelight and some disgraceful scandal started, it spelt sheer ruin. He thought of his wife and two young daughters ; he thought of his reputation and realised that the patient of the moment was eying him oddly. He pulled himself together and she decided she'd been mistaken. After she had gone he said to himself over and over again, Nobody knows I went there. Nobody knows. Even if the police find the papers that doesn't mean anything. As the day passed and he received no summons hope began to flower again in his breast. Let this pass and he was safe, safe for the rest of his days. Once he knew they weren't going to track him down he could yield to the sense of relief that burned in him like a flame. But the police found him in their stolid patient way, and one of them came walking up the steps and ringing the door bell too early to be a patient. Besides, patients didn't come to his private address.

" Dr. Ainwright ? " said the policeman. " I believe you knew the late Mr. Chigwell."

He'd have denied it if he could, but he knew that was worse than useless. He said tonelessly, " Yes."

" And I believe you saw him shortly before his death ? "

He wondered if that were a bow drawn at a venture, if it would be safe to deny it, then remembered that the police don't go round doing fancy target practice. He said quickly, " I had an appointment at eight o'clock. I left at eight-twenty. He was all right then."

" What time did you get back, sir ? "

" In time for the nine o'clock news."

" He didn't speak of any other visitors he was expecting ? "

" He'd hardly confide in me."

" And you didn't meet anyone on the way out ? "

" Not a soul. Look here, you're not trying to pin this on me, are you ? If I'd had anything to do with it do you think I'd have used anything as clumsy as our friend, the anonymous blunt instrument ? A doctor has opportunities. . . . "

" Well, that might be why," said the official slowly. " I mean, anyone can get hold of a stick, but if it had been poison, say, well, then you'd start looking for a doctor or a chemist."

He admitted the reasonableness of that. " Whoever put this chap's light out did a service to the community," he added recklessly. " He did more harm than a dozen murderers."

" You had your remedy," said the official, sober and unimpressed. " You could have come to us."

But Ainwright shook his head. Just as there were things you couldn't explain to wives, so there were things you couldn't explain to policemen. If you were a doctor you couldn't afford risks and one mistake was one too many, as he'd found to his own cost.

" If we had real justice," said Inspector Marlowe, who was in charge of the case, " a man like Ainwright would be regarded as an accessory. It's just because people don't trust the police that these murders happen. And it's not the first, by a long chalk. I'd be prepared to bet quite a number of people have taken an overdose of sleeping-draught or jumped in front of a train because they couldn't face what Chigwell offered them. All the same," he added, " we know someone saw Chigwell after 9.20, which is when the snow started, because there are wet marks on the carpet, obviously made by feet. And this chap's got his alibi for nine o'clock."

An air-raid warden called Bairstowe read about the murder in the *Morning Record* and exclaimed aloud.

" Holy Smoke ! "

" What's the matter, Ray ? " demanded his wife, who cultivated acidity as some people cultivate roses. " Your bacon's getting cold."

" Why on earth didn't I tumble to it yesterday that this was the chap they found dead in his office ? I heard the report, but— well, well."

" What are you talking about ? " Mrs. Bairstowe demanded.

" This fellow, Chigwell. Why, I saw him just before nine o'clock. There was a gap in his black-out and I went up to warn him. I didn't know who he was, but there was a light showing and since the heavy raids have started again you have to be fussy. I thought at the time there was something fishy about him."

" You always think that afterwards," said Mrs. Bairstowe after the manner of wives.

" It was just before the nine o'clock news. I thought I'd get round to the Post in time to hear how many more salutes Stalin had fired to celebrate victories. I went up and rang the bell and at first no one came. Well, you get used to that. They guess it's a warden and go round putting out all the lights they know aren't properly screened, and then they come and look at you like a lot of brooding cows and say it must have been the house next-door. Or else they just hope if you don't get an answer you'll go away. I was just going to ring again when the door opened. The chap who opened it didn't even look at me. He said, ' I'm not ready for you yet. It's not nine,' and began walking away. I said, ' It'll be nine o'clock at Bow Street if you don't look after your black-out better.' I never saw a chap switch over so quickly. You'd have thought I'd brought him a cheque."

" People like that simply ask to be murdered," observed Mrs. Bairstowe after the manner of women.

" He asked me to show him where the curtain was wrong and offered me a drink. I didn't hear the news, after all."

" It was just the same as it always is," said Mrs. Bairstowe.

" I suppose I'd better go and see the police," reflected her husband.

" You don't want to go getting yourself mixed up with the police," she snapped. " The neighbours'll start thinking things."

" It'll make a change for the neighbours," said Bairstowe.

" Besides, you don't know anything," she insisted.

" I know he was alive at nine o'clock."

" You don't know who he was expecting."

" He told me it was an ex-employee who was always badgering him."

Mrs. Bairstowe sniffed. " Funny hour to call."

" He might be working late."

" If he was working, what did he want help for ? "

" Well, I don't suppose it was an employee really. He just said that to put me off."

" Anyhow, there's no sense your taking that sort of story to the police."

" Funny if anyone happened to see me coming out of the place—see anyone in warden's uniform, that is—that night and happen to remark on it. Police 'ud be down on me like a cartload of bricks. Why hadn't I told them ? "

The police were polite and interested, but they'd have been a lot better pleased if he had remembered seeing someone come along the road as he came out. They asked if the snow had started when he left and he said " No, it hadn't." They didn't ask him anything after that.

All the evidence they had was the damp patches on the carpet and the message that had been found on the floor of the hall. Sheer ill-luck, from an official point of view, made this piece of evidence of much less value than might have been anticipated. Had it been found inside the letter-box it could have been tested for fingerprints since, the box being locked, it could have been handled only by the person who left it there. As, however, it had slipped through on to the mat it had been trodden on first by the agitated charwoman, who hadn't noticed it and then by the N.F.S. man, who had seen a scrap of paper on the floor but hadn't supposed it to be of any value. Then it had been picked up by the policeman and the original finger-prints were quite indecipherable, since the fireman had worn rubber boots which were damp from the street and had left a large footprint right across the face of the paper.

Nevertheless, this slip was destined to play a great part in the solving of the mystery.

2

Mr. Rupert Burke, the author of the message in question, was a long lean creature of two-and-forty, with a tendency to dress in a way that stockbrokers of an earlier age would have called Bohemian. He had made a profession of dabbling, having tried art, the stage, writing, and finally a year in the Middle East, whence he had been invalided back to England and now held a position in the local branch of the Ministry of Goods and Chattels. Ever since the discovery of the body he could think of nothing but the slip of paper he had pushed through the letter-box in the fatal flat. His main concern was whether he had acted wisely or the reverse in leaving in that place of death anything that could link him up with the crime. Over and over again, like a dormouse turning its wheel, he argued the pros and cons of the situation.

" Suppose I'd left nothing," he'd argue, " and suppose they'd found out I was in Chigwell's power." He didn't know a great deal about the police, but he presumed they would check up on all the dead man's victims. He might then be asked to explain his movements on the fatal night, and he had no alibi at all. Surely (he hoped) the fact that he had left a message, fortunately mentioning the time, and this message would be found by the authorities in the locked letter-box, would be proof that he hadn't been able to gain admission. On the other hand, suppose this action had merely succeeded in drawing attention to himself ? He gave it up after a time, realising that one of the most exasperating factors in life is that you can never be sure if you've done the right thing or not. Sometimes the after-trend of events justifies or derides your choice, but as often as not you go to your grave without being sure.

Every time the telephone rang, either at his office or at his flat, he repressed a start. In the office he tried to seem indifferent or impatient ; at home he moved cautiously over to it, rather like a cat stalking a mouse, took off the receiver and answered in his usual voice, or as near his usual voice as he could contrive. Fate, like a cat with a mouse, played with him for twenty-four hours until, like Ainwright, he began to wonder if he was going to be let off. Then when he came back from his office on the second evening he found a scrawled message beside the telephone. He had a small service flat, being to all intents and purposes unmarried and without inconvenient female relations anxious to keep house for him, spend his money and devour his rations.

" A policeman called to-day," the message ran, " he will call again to-night."

He supposed that any man in his shoes would feel as he did. If he heard another man tell his own story, what would his reaction be ? He might have killed Chigwell, slipped out and pushed the message through the letter-box. He wondered if the police would think of that, then reflected that if it occurred to him, the amateur, the possibility wouldn't be ignored by them. He repressed an inclination to pick up the telephone and offer to come down to the station. There was always the chance that they wanted to see him about something else. though he didn't really believe this. And if it was about Chigwell's death, mightn't they think it queer that he should be in such a hurry ? He tried to read—it was the latest Mr. Moto story—but it couldn't hold his attention. He walked over to the window and looked down at the street, replaced the curtain and wandered back into the room.

" Of course you're safe," he told himself. " They're just checking up on everything."

But he had the same feeling about the police as women he knew had about the Ministry of Labour, that they were all-powerful and that you had no chance against them, in spite of what people said about fair play and British justice. The clock moved slowly, the telephone rang once but it was a wrong number, there was broiled rabbit for dinner but he couldn't touch it, and at last the visitor arrived. It was Marlowe himself and he introduced the name of James Chigwell at once. He showed Burke the slip of paper and asked if it conveyed anything to him, and Burke said quickly that he'd written it the night before last. He'd had an appointment but he couldn't get any reply.

" And that surprised you ? "

" Not just at first, because Chigwell liked to make you wriggle like a worm on a hook. But when he didn't come after about five minutes I wrote that note and pushed it through the letter-box. I wanted him to know I had turned up."

" An urgent matter ? " suggested Marlowe.

Burke shot him a quick look. " If you've been through his safe you know what his profession was, and you probably know the hold he had over me. Well, I rang twice but nothing happened so I wrote the note and pushed it into the box."

Marlowe said woodenly, " It wasn't in the box."

Burke stared. " Not in the box ? Then where . . . ? "

" It was found on the mat."

" But—— " suddenly he saw his danger ; he was like a man in a boat close to shore that is suddenly swept out on a current, that carries away the oars. He spun helplessly for a moment. " I pushed it through the flap, I tell you. I don't see how it could have been on the mat." His voice was stupid with surprise. This was something no one could have foreseen. " Someone must have taken it out. There were people on the premises before the police arrived, weren't there ? "

" There were," Marlowe agreed, " but it doesn't make sense all the same. Why should anyone take that slip of paper out of the box ? There was a charwoman and a fireman. That's all. And the box was locked."

He threw up his hands. " I give it up. All I can tell you is I pushed it through the flap on the other side of the door."

Well, thought Marlowe charitably, so he might. There was just a chance the thing had slipped between the box and the wood, and in a case like this you had to give your suspect all the benefits of the doubt there were.

Still, they knew Chigwell was alive at nine, and they hadn't traced anyone who had come in after the snow started—except this man who swore he hadn't entered the flat. And from the evidence they'd taken out of the safe he had reason enough to want the blackmailer out of the way. He'd been slowly bleeding to death if the figures in Chigwell's book were anything to go by. The doctors weren't going to tie themselves down to the time of death within an hour ; he might easily have been killed at ten. And what actual proof was there that the note was true so far as time went at all events ?

" He was killed with a stick, wasn't he ? " demanded Burke. " Well, you can hunt the place out. You'll find nothing that would kill a man here. As a matter of fact I never use a stick. I have an umbrella, a plain crook-handled affair. I hadn't even got that with me, though. I didn't anticipate the snow."

" I see," said Marlowe. " After leaving the note did you come straight home ? "

" Yes. I don't live ten minutes away. But if you want to know when I arrived I can't tell you. I live alone. There's a caretaker in the basement, but she wasn't about. I didn't see anyone. But look for the stick. I promise you you won't find one."

" I wouldn't expect to," said Marlowe.

" You mean—my God ! " He sounded appalled.

" I don't suppose whoever is responsible has still got the weapon whatever it may have been on the premises," Marlowe continued.

" I see. You think I did it, don't you ? Don't you ? "

" You don't have to say things like that," the Inspector assured him.

Burke said, " I suppose you've never been in my shoes. You don't know what it feels like. I tell you, I know nothing about Chigwell's death, that I couldn't get into the flat that night. But I can't prove it. And the official view will be that someone got in and why not me ? "

" Do you generally make your appointments by 'phone ? " Marlowe asked unemotionally.

" I had been going to see him at nine, but I had a long specification to do for the Ministry and I was working on it in my flat. It was urgent and I had to get it done, and I knew I couldn't keep my appointment with Chigwell. So I telephoned and asked whether I could come a bit later. He told me I could risk coming round at ten, if I liked. Well, I live a bare quarter-hour from Chigwell and I'd got to see him, so I said I'd make it. As a matter of fact, I only just did it as it was."

" You didn't see anyone coming away from the house when you arrived ? "

" No one."

" And when you didn't get any reply, you didn't think there might be something wrong ? "

" I thought it was one more instance of his petty tyranny. I'd changed an appointment ; he was going to show me I couldn't do that sort of thing lightly. It would amuse him to think of me coming out at the end of the day's work and not getting admitted when I arrived. He had a warped sense of humour. . . . "

" He must have done," agreed Marlowe, drily. " How long did you stay ? "

" Oh, five minutes, possibly a little longer. I did think at first he might be just keeping me waiting. That's a favourite trick of his. After a little I rang again, but nothing happened and I went away. When I got back to my flat I telephoned, because he generally did answer the telephone, but though I could hear it ringing there wasn't any reply, and then I thought he might have gone out. After all—I hadn't thought of it before —but perhaps even he wasn't altogether a free agent."

" What does that mean ? " asked Marlowe sharply.

" You know the saying—Big fleas have little fleas—and every blackmailer is blackmailed in his turn. Perhaps some chap had made him turn out in the snow."

Marlowe was non-committal. After he'd gone Burke tried to visualise his probable reaction. He didn't really believe they'd arrest him, because you don't believe things like that about yourself, even though you may fear them. When they came round and told him he was wanted on a charge of murder and had best not commit himself in speech he was dumbfounded. And even after he found himself in a prison cell he couldn't actually believe it. Other men are tried and found guilty and hanged—but not oneself, never oneself. The police would discover they'd blundered. They'd decide—what in Heaven's name would they decide ? He was being a fool, a romantic, a victim of wishful thinking. The police don't arrest men for fun, they don't arrest them unless they believe they've got a pretty good case. And how in fortune's name was Rupert Burke to prove his innocence ? He tried to console himself with the thought that they had to prove his guilt, but presumably they thought they could do that or he wouldn't be here now.

When he realised the desperation of his position he fought fear like a wild thing, then, utterly exhausted, tried to think how he could provide proof, inalienable proof, that he couldn't have done the thing of which he was accused. But if it's hard to prove a fellow's guilt it must be even harder to prove his innocence.

Even alibis are suspect, and anyway he had no alibi. He couldn't produce a single person to swear he was in his flat when Chigwell was struck down. He couldn't prove his story. He couldn't. He couldn't. And so—and so he'd be found guilty. **Guilty.** And hang.

CHAPTER THREE

WHEN BESS saw that they'd taken a man called Rupert Burke for the Chigwell murder she knew such a rush of relief that it was all she could do to prevent herself tearing up to Kenneth and thrusting the paper in his face. Common-sense, however, warned her to desist. To betray just how deep that relief was would be to reveal how poignant had been her dread that he was himself the guilty man. She realised now that all along she'd feared he had done it. The stick, the blood-stained shirt, Kenneth's air of shrinking, his blind silence when the news was made public, all these were the marks of a guilty man. She anticipated that he'd speak, but he didn't and for some reason that frightened her. At last she found a paper that gave the fullest account of the murder and subsequent arrest and left it in his room. Now surely he must say something. It was just possible, though not remotely likely, that he hadn't heard. She had been told that men in great danger deliberately avoid places and people where that danger may be a subject of comment. When she saw him again he had the paper in his hand. The look on his face, the tone of his voice, were anything but reassuring.

" Did you leave this in my room ? " he said.

" I expect so. I don't want it anyway."

" You wanted to be sure I saw it, didn't you ? "

" Well. . . . " She didn't lie convincingly, though you'd have thought her life had given her experience enough.

Kenneth took her face in his hands. " You thought I'd done for him, didn't you, Bess ? Come on, let's hear you say it."

" I didn't know," she told him frankly. " You acted so queer. And there were other things . . . "

He knew what she had in mind. " You mean the stick ? Ah, yes, they'll want to know where that is. You might as well tell me where you put it."

" I told you—I lost it. . . . "

" Where ? You'd better tell me. Otherwise they'll come to you."

" They ? "

" The police."

21

She choked back a cry. " Ken ! You're never going to the police."

" I've got to. Surely you can see that."

" But they've got the man that did it."

" They've got the man who didn't do it. Though I'm probably the one person living who can prove that. If I'd had any guts I'd have gone to them right away. As it is, the poor devil's been suffering the torments of the damned. Well, Bess ? "

She said in a low voice, " I put it in the river."

His crooked mirthless smile frightened her. " It only wanted that."

" Oh, Ken ! " She held on to his arm. It was like holding the arm of a corpse. " I only wanted to help you." He laughed then. It was like hearing a dead man laugh.

" That's what the modern woman's always doing, trying to do a man's job and do it better than he could do it himself. The Victorians had more sense."

She didn't argue that. She'd been brought up in a hard-boiled world to stand on her own feet. If she'd waited around for men to help her Heaven only knew where she might be now.

" Well, thanks for telling me," he said. " It'll save time and trouble."

But even now she wouldn't let him go. " Tell me, Ken, why are you going to the police ? What do you know ? You knew him, I suppose."

He nodded. " Oh yes. I knew him."

" And—you were there that night ? "

" Right again."

" But you didn't kill him ? Ken, you didn't." He was silent and she said in a new low tone, " Or—did you, Ken ? No, don't tell me. I don't want to—trap you."

He drew himself free. " I'll tell you who didn't kill him," he said, " and that's Rupert Burke. He couldn't have killed him because you see, he was dead when Burke arrived."

The police showed less enthusiasm over his confession than Kenneth had anticipated. For a minute he got the idea that they didn't believe him, and he had to choke back an hysterical desire to laugh.

" Do you think I'd be telling you this story if I could help myself ? " he demanded.

Marlowe—he'd insisted on seeing Marlowe—answered mildly, " You'd be surprised, sir, the number of confessions we get with every murder, and half the time the people who make 'em weren't in the same county when it happened."

" I wasn't there when it happened," said Kenneth harshly,

22

" but I was there when Burke arrived. I saw that message come through the letter-flap."

" Yes, sir. And you read it ? "

" I read it. It slipped through the crack on to the floor. I don't mind admitting I thought of destroying it—might have done Burke a good turn if I had, though it wasn't Burke I was thinking of. I just wanted to save my own skin. I could see what it would look like, my being found there with him, and how was I going to prove I hadn't done it ? "

" Quite so, sir." You couldn't move Marlowe. " Do you remember what the bit of paper looked like ? "

" It looked like a page out of a diary, one of those pages they put in the beginning and you never fill in. Telephone number, dog licence, registration number—you know the kind of thing."

Marlowe metaphorically pricked up his ears. Up till now he hadn't been sure his visitor wasn't one more of these unbalanced young men who, having suffered from excessive nervous strain in war service (Marlowe had a son of his own in the R.A.F. and he knew what flying, night flying in particular, could do to the most stolid youngster) go headlong for the limelight for no reason at all except that they feel out of things and have to force a way into the picture somehow. But here was the confirmation he sought. There had been a certain amount of publicity about the message, but no actual description of the paper. Now it was obvious that Kenneth was telling the truth in this particular at all events, and must have been in the flat. That, obviously, changed the entire situation.

" What time was your appointment with Chigwell ? " Marlowe wanted to know.

" I hadn't got an appointment. He'd no idea I was coming. I had a key that fitted the lock, and I meant to take him unawares. On the way up it seemed to me the stairs themselves were against me. I'll swear they never made so much row before. I thought he must hear, till I got into the flat and realised he'd never hear anything again."

Marlowe looked thoughtful. " How long had you had the key ? "

" About a fortnight. But I'd never used it before."

" I take it it wasn't a friendly visit."

" Would you be friendly with a black mamba ? " asked Kenneth in bitter tones.

" So—he had something on you ? "

" A fool of a job I did five years ago. There was a girl and I wanted money—and there was somebody else's cheque-book handy—and I was mad and . . . "

23

Marlowe nodded. It was an old story to him. He'd heard it a thousand times.

"We didn't find—anything to connect you with his affairs among his papers."

Ken's face twisted. "I saw to that."

"You mean, you ransacked the safe? With him there?"

"Yes. I'd meant to get that paper at all costs. I meant to get it from him, by violence if necessary. . . . "

Marlowe put up his hand. "If you didn't use violence there's no need to say that. Go on, Mr. Jardine. You found him dead and—how did you get hold of the keys?"

"The safe was open, with the keys in the lock."

"Did he generally keep his safe open?"

"As a rule he guarded those keys as the saints guard their immortal souls. He kept the safe behind a picture of Whistler's 'Mother.' He said every time he looked at it it reminded him he'd got to provide for his old age. He liked to open it now and again just to let you see how much power he had."

"But that night the safe was open?"

"Yes. Someone else wasn't taking any chances either."

"You didn't think of closing it?"

"It played my game much better to leave it as I found it. Besides, I couldn't have put the keys back in his pocket. I never meant," again that harsh unmusical laugh, "anyone to know I'd been there."

"It didn't occur to you to call the police when you found him?"

"It's been done too often. Guilty man gives alarm."

"There's medical evidence," Marlowe reminded him. "It's known that he was alive at nine o'clock. What time did you arrive?"

"About half-past."

"You must have been wet."

"Drenching. The snow came so suddenly."

"It was running it fine, but if you'd telephoned us at once the doctor could have told if death had taken place within ten minutes."

Kenneth said thoughtfully, "I can only just have missed the chap. If I'd got there a few minutes earlier." He broke off. "What's the use? It's easy to see why so few men make murder their career. It needs practice and so few of them get a second chance."

"Not if we can help it," Marlowe agreed pleasantly. "By the way, what weapon did you take?"

"Weapon?"

" You said you were prepared to use violence, and—you'll forgive my mentioning it—but a lame man doesn't stand much chance against a bull like Chigwell if he's unarmed."

" I—had a stick."

" Ah, yes. You didn't bring it with you ? "

" No. I—er—lost it. Must have left it somewhere."

" Perhaps if you thought a bit longer, Mr. Jardine, you could tell us where."

He threw back his head with a sudden gesture of impotence. " All right, you win. I took it with me and I meant to threaten him. I don't know if I'd have killed him, perhaps I would, but if so, I'd not have come back myself. However, that's just words to you. You don't have to believe it and I don't suppose you will."

Marlowe supposed it was as good a story as you could expect and better than a more practised hand would have offered. There was a take-it-or-leave-it quality about it that defied argument. Kenneth didn't pretend there had been a quarrel and Chigwell had threatened him or tried to get the police or anything like that. He just said the fellow was dead ; and the police couldn't prove he wasn't.

He said, " About that stick, Mr. Jardine," and Kenneth replied, " It's in the river. When I heard you were hunting for a weapon I got nervous. I thought if you found out about me—there was a mark on the stick where it fell against him—I couldn't get it out—and I took a chance. I didn't see why you should ever find out I'd been there that night. Well." Again that wry dreadful smile. " You've called my bluff. That's all."

Marlowe had no comment to make on that. Instead, he asked in a voice by no means unsympathetic, " Can you remember what time you got back ? "

" I stayed about ten minutes after the note came through the door. It would take about twenty minutes to get back."

" You didn't meet anyone on the way ? "

" I didn't see anyone except Bess—Bess Carter—she helps at ' The Case Is Altered '—after I came in. She came up when I'd been in half an hour or so. She might remember the time. It would be after eleven anyway. They shut the bar at eleven."

" I see," said Marlowe slowly.

" You probably see a lot that doesn't exist," retorted Kenneth. " She doesn't know anything. You needn't try and drag her into it."

" That's all right," said Marlowe. " Now, are you prepared to make out a statement and sign it, embodying what you've just told me ? "

25

Kenneth smiled. "That's a nice question. As if I've any choice!"

His nerves were like wires. Hasn't told us everything, Marlowe reflected. Well, they never did, always too much or too little. He handed the young man over to a subordinate and went down to "The Case Is Altered." When he saw Bess he realised that he was up against another tough proposition. At the mention of Kenneth's name she hardened and he knew she'd lie like a trooper if she thought it would help and she could get away with it.

She said she'd never heard of Chigwell before the murder, that Kenneth hadn't told her where he was going that night and it would have conveyed nothing to her if he had. She hadn't heard him come in and she hadn't seen him till after eleven o'clock.

"You didn't happen to notice if he brought the stick back with him? He tells me he took a stick out that night."

"He brought that back," said Bess, quickly. "It was in his room next day."

"It's not there now."

"No," flashed Bess, "it's not. And I'll tell you why. I suppose you think it was funny about the stick disappearing when he was an innocent man, but it wasn't Mr. Jardine who put the stick in the river—it was me."

"What made you do that?" Marlowe gave the impression that a choir of angels couldn't surprise him.

"I was frightened—for him. I was mad, of course, but I lost my head. He was so queer that night."

"I think you said you didn't know where he was going."

"No, but I could see he was all strung up. I could see it was important."

"Perhaps he told you . . ."

"He didn't tell me anything. Why, I'd never heard of the man till it was all over the papers."

"And then he told you?"

"No," repeated Bess furiously. "He never said a word. Why, he didn't even know I'd taken the stick till he missed it, and then he asked if I'd seen it."

"And so you told him?"

"I told him I'd taken it out and lost it. Afterwards I told him where it really was."

"I see. You had some reason for hiding the stick, of course."

"When I read in the paper that the man had been killed, probably with a stick—and Ken's was one of those heavy things you could lay a man out with . . ."

" And perhaps there were reasons why it should be connected with the crime ? Traces, perhaps . . . "

" There was a mark—it might have been blood. I don't know. But like I told you, I lost my head and put it in the river. I see now it was a daft thing to do and didn't help Ken a bit."

" I'm still not sure I altogether understand," confessed Marlowe. " You say Mr. Jardine didn't tell you about Mr. Chigwell either that night or subsequently, but as soon as you heard of the murder you associated him with it. Why was that ? "

Bess bit her lip. " He was so queer that night. I could see something was wrong." She began to wish she hadn't spoken at all. Marlowe got it all out of her, the bloodstain on the shirt, Kenneth's preoccupation, his reaction when he heard about Burke's arrest. It was difficult. It always was difficult getting information from women like that; she'd have no scruples about lying if she could sustain a lie. He came away heavy with doubt.

" Of course, we'll have to free Burke," he told his subordinate. " Well, that's just a matter of fulfilling certain formalities. Point is, do we take Jardine for the crime ? We can't afford to take the wrong man twice. On the other hand, it's significant that this girl was immediately convinced that he'd been to see Chigwell and that in spite of the fact that she swears she'd never heard his name before. There's the bit about the bloodstain, and there may have been a lot more to the stick than she'll acknowledge. Pity it's been in the river all these days. It's not likely to be much use to us by this time."

" It's going to be a tight fit to find anyone else who got to the office between 9 and 9.30, had a row, committed a murder, rifled the safe and got off the premises without being seen. Jardine says there wasn't a soul in the road. He stopped particularly to look. Didn't want it to be generally known where he was visiting that night."

" It looks black," Marlowe agreed. " It looks damned black. He can't even show what time he really got back to the pub. And we can't trace anyone else at the time that matters."

He told his subordinate to detail a man to keep an eye on Kenneth. " We don't want him following his precious stick into the river," he observed grimly, " and a lot of men in his shoes would rather drown than hang."

Not that you could prevent a fellow taking the easy way out, he reminded himself wryly. There are plenty of means. But if Kenneth had considered that solution he had very little time to put it into effect, because twenty-four hours after Burke was released they arrested the young ex-pilot in his place.

CHAPTER FOUR

THE MURDERER of James Chigwell sat by his fireside staring into the electric flames. The rapid move of events since the night of the crime had been bewildering. He had passed from amazement at his own madness, through anguished anxiety to a sense of comparative security. The replacement of Rupert Burke by Kenneth Jardine was a development no one could have foreseen. At one time it had appeared to him practically impossible that he could escape the noose, but now he felt that, bar something else equally unpredictable, he was safe. For the young man now in prison and innocent of the crime for which he was committed he had no thought but a kind of contemptuous gratitude. It was not in him to understand a temperament that would go to almost certain death for the sake of a code of behaviour. Such a fellow could hardly expect Providence to take any further interest in his concerns if, having been offered so magnificent a let-off, he deliberately signed his own death-warrant. The danger now was that the real criminal would become restive ; he would want to put up obstacles all round himself to ensure his own safety. He remembered Crook, that wily fox among lawyers, saying that a masterly policy of inactivity was the criminal's best defence.

" Don't give the police anything to work on," he said. " Give a copper a couple of facts and he'll build Buckingham Palace on 'em. I wasn't there, I don't remember, everything went blank. Those are the foolproof defences—only most criminals won't believe it." The murderer lighted a cigarette with hands that shook a little.

" The police won't acknowledge themselves wrong twice," he argued. " Besides, I'm covered absolutely. This chap can't get out. The circumstantial evidence is too damning."

It occurred to him presently that he could do with a drink ; besides, in a pub you heard what people were saying. Committing a murder gave you the oddest feeling. You didn't cease to be a human being, but you felt as though people only had to look at you to see the mark of Cain on your forehead.

" Keep your mouth shut and your ears open," he adjured himself. " That's all you've got to do."

It was one of those things that sound so simple and are in fact harder than murder itself.

Rupert Burke was down at " The Case Is Altered." He had

come to see Bess. There were a good many people in the bar, but he picked her out at once from the newspaper description and photograph. For the Chigwell case had leaped from a rather bored obscurity—in the heart of a world war with the flower of England and her Allies dying all over the world there were no tears to spare for a man who had died as most people believed he deserved to die—to positive notoriety. You could thank Kenneth for that. He had all the limelight now. Chigwell didn't matter and Rupert Burke was just a dilettante no one had ever heard of, but Kenneth became a sort of hero to the masses, who are inclined to prefer courage to virtue. In any case his staggering confession had caught the public imagination. There were pictures in the papers ; reporters came swarming down to see Bess and got precious little for their pains, not even a drink. But that didn't discourage the reporters. They'd had all the answers ready before they arrived. The pictures were in all the popular papers. Mr. Burke. Mr. Jardine. Miss Carter. It was even mentioned by a reasonably celebrated divine in an evening sermon.

Burke felt anxious. His own position was obviously enormously improved ; but he couldn't leave the matter at that. The public imagination had been caught by Kenneth Jardine's quixotry and in consequence quite a number of addle-pated people were saying that a man capable of such an act couldn't possibly have committed a murder. Burke could understand that attitude, but he knew it wasn't the one the police would adopt. Not even the reporters had been able to unearth a frail old mother or a father with whom the accused man had quarrelled ; in fact, there was no mention of relatives at all. Kenneth's only friend seemed to be the mysterious Bess Carter and you could think what you liked so far as she was concerned. Bess wouldn't care and it might be true, anyhow. So Burke came down to " The Case Is Altered " to see Bess. She, sensible creature that she was, saw no romance about the situation. She had never had the sort of mother that tells fairy-tales and she didn't attempt to hide from herself the fact that by monkeying with the stick she had put the final touch to the case against Kenneth Jardine.

When Burke, a little awkwardly, introduced himself, she said in a blunt, bitter voice, " Are you another relation ? "

He stared. " I beg your pardon ? "

" There's been one along already to make sure we didn't pinch anything Ken might have left in his room. An uncle by marriage, he said he was, come to collect anything going. Go right ahead, I told him. Between you and the police you won't

29

leave the poor lad a stitch to his back. A lawyer he called himself," she added vindictively.

" I'm Burke," said her visitor. " Rupert Burke."

" Oh ? " It was her turn to stare. " That Burke."

" Yes. I don't know if you'll think it queer my butting in but I owe that lad a lot. It took guts to do what he did, and I wondered if I could help anyhow. But if the uncle's a lawyer . . . "

" Uncle by marriage," corrected Bess. " And if you think he's going to do anything to help Ken you're wrong. He's a churchwarden he told me, and I bet you he's on his knees in his church this minute thanking God it's not the same name."

" Didn't he speak of it ? " Burke sounded puzzled.

" He said his firm didn't deal in that class of business, and he understood that Ken had a little money of his own. You can't explain to that sort of porpoise that young men in the Air Force don't save. They don't see any sense in it."

" No. He doesn't seem helpful. Look here, I don't know how far you're implicated . . . " He broke off. He was doing this very badly.

" That's what the uncle said, ' I wasn't aware my wife's nephew was engaged.' Well, of course he isn't. If he has any luck, if this thing doesn't break him, one of these days Ken will marry a girl of his own sort, someone who won't be connected with any of this, and won't know which side of the counter a barmaid stands. But in the meantime he wants someone to— to look after him. . . . "

" And you're filling the gap ? You're pretty fond of him, aren't you ? "

Bess coloured under her paint. " That's my affair."

" I'm sorry. I say, please don't take offence. It's just—I can't get the thing out of my mind. You know, I wouldn't have stood a chance if he hadn't come forward, and if he hadn't no one would have known."

" Oh, yes." Bess sounded surprised. " Ken would have known."

" Yes," agreed Burke slowly. " But I wonder if he realised what it was going to feel like to be in a cell faced with a trial for murder, knowing that it might not be possible to get out . . . "

" Don't ! " said Bess, sharply.

" I've had first-hand experience," the man reminded her. " I feel I owe that chap something. I had to come over. Of course, if his own people were backing him there'd be nothing for me to do, but I just had to be sure. I mean . . . " he hesitated, and candid Bess filled in the blank for him.

" You mean money ? "

" You said yourself these Air Force chaps don't save. And you can't blame 'em."

" And you're here to help ? "

He replied soberly, " I owe young Jardine a life. And he's going to need a damn good counsel to persuade thirteen perfect strangers that he didn't do it. I've been where he is now, and I tell you, you feel as helpless as if you were bound to a stake and saw the man approaching with the burning brand."

She didn't find the simile extravagant ; probably because she had an extravagant nature herself. Certainly she'd never been able to safeguard anything—not money, not her own feelings, not her security.

" Do you suppose I don't think of it ? " she whispered. " I don't think of anything else."

" No," he agreed, " you wouldn't. Not even of yourself."

" Oh, me ! " She sketched a gesture of disdain. " Now don't go jumping through any hoops. I don't mean a thing to Ken. When he falls in love it'll be with someone whose brother went to his sort of school. And if I thought she'd be good to him I couldn't fade out fast enough. I wouldn't want to hold him back or make him feel grateful. Men don't like having to be grateful to women. I know."

" You know a hell of a lot."

" Your wife would tell you the same," Bess assured him.

" I haven't got a wife—not any longer. Look here, could you regard me as a sort of partner in this show ? I mean, you can say what you like about yourself, but young Jardine's never going to have a better friend than you all his life long."

" Everybody isn't going to believe he's guilty," she exclaimed.

" Maybe not, but you—you don't care if he did do it, do you, so long as he gets off. Now look here, this isn't going to be just chicken-feed. You remember what Marshall Hall used to say, that a man with a bad case needs a good counsel, the best there is. That's the sort of chap we've got to find, a chap who won't mind risking an adverse verdict."

" No." Bess's mouth set in stubborn lines. " We don't want a man who can even think of losing his case."

" Do you know of one like that ? "

" I was asking the boys. They get about, you know. They say the man we want is Arthur Crook. His motto is : ' My clients are always innocent.' "

" You want someone with a good reputation." Burke sounded doubtful.

" His reputation can stink like a rotten egg for me," returned

31

Bess inelegantly, " provided he gets Ken off. I expect," she added thoughtfully, " he's pretty expensive. Teddy—he's the one who told me about him—says he doesn't sit back and spin himself a cocoon of red tape like a lot of lawyers. He gets down and does things himself."

" Wonder how popular he is in the profession," murmured Burke.

" If you're rich enough you don't have to worry about being popular," returned worldly-wise Bess. " Of course, if he won't take Ken's case on I must find someone else. That uncle by marriage isn't any good and no one else seems to care."

" Are you going to write to the fellow ?" Burke enquired.

" Me ? I hardly know which end of a pen to put in the ink. No, I'll go and see him: Want to be sure he's all right for Ken," she added explanatorily. She hesitated a moment, then went on : " That's another thing in his favour—he doesn't care. He doesn't care about anything but getting his man off. But I expect you have to pay for it. As Teddy says, you're buying his conscience as well as his wits."

" As far as money's concerned, within reason, you can count on me. Look here, would it be any help if I came up to town with you ? "

" To see Crook ? " Bess considered. " No, I don't think so. For one thing, I haven't got any scruples where Ken's concerned and if he's the man I hope he is he won't have any either. But you're something in the Government. It's different for you." (He found that a bit touching.) " Besides," she added shrewdly, " it'll be more expensive if you come the first time."

" You think of everyone, don't you, except yourself ? " He came closer and took her hand gently.

" I don't think of anyone but Ken," said Bess simply.

" One of these days," suggested Burke, " you might find it nice to have someone think of you."

Bess laughed. He didn't know what to read into that laugh but it was clear she intended to change the conversation. They went back to the bar where a stranger was matching darts against Bairstowe. He was pretty good ; a ring of admirers stood round watching the match. Afterwards they all got together and the winner, who gave his name as Clarke, paid for a round of drinks. You'd never have guessed, seeing them there so easy, so friendly, that one of them was a murderer.

Bess Carter didn't let the grass grow under her feet. Within twenty-four hours of her talk with Rupert Burke she was wearing her quietest suit and was in the train en route for London.

The train, like all trains in 1944, was packed ; she arrived five minutes before it started and managed to get hauled up to stand in a corridor with numbers of young men in uniform, speaking every language in Europe. By the time they separated at Paddington she had learned a lot about their mothers, wives, kids, sweethearts and ambitions ; she had refused a number of invitations, saying, ' I'll be seeing you,' as she swung off the train. There was a queue of people waiting for taxis, and porters ran up and down carrying baggage. Bess walked into the street, jumped a bus that halted by the traffic lights and presently boarded another, which put her down at Bloomsbury. Here she made for 123 Bloomsbury High Street, and rode up in the lift to the top floor where Arthur Crook had his office. It wasn't necessary for Crook to advertise his existence, and although his office was shabby and he himself anything but the general conception of a lawyer. He had been known to observe, with truth, that he had one of the most highly paid practices in the country. Like Bess, He had his own code, and it was one that suited a lot of men who had drifted on to the windy side of the law, and didn't find it too easy to get reliable representation in court. For Crook, despite the oddity of his appearance and his code, was reliable. There was quite a number of people going about who would have worn rope neckties long ago but for him.

He always said he hadn't any use for women and didn't under-stand them ; he said any man who worked with a jane was a fool ; but he said, too, that it was the fools who kept his practice going. When he saw Bess he sized her up at once. Her suit was trim and looked new, but she hadn't paid a packet for it ; he saw her bright hair, her long lashes, her painted finger-nails, her high heels, her big pillar-box red mouth ; he knew she was generous, shrewd, reckless and, like himself, had an individual moral code. He knew she wouldn't be easily foxed or frightened. He wondered what she was going to ask him to do.

Trained to earn a living and knowing the value of time she came to the point at once.

" Boy-friend in a jam ? " asked Crook sympathetically. You could see it wasn't her jam, because if it had been she wouldn't be asking his help, and you could see, too, that she was the sort that will have boy-friends from cradle to grave.

" That's it. Kenneth Jardine. You'll have heard of the case. I expect you've got a point of view."

Mr. Crook said No, he hadn't. Why should he ? It wasn't, to date, anything to do with him. And he made it a rule to preserve an open mind in such circumstances in case he should later become involved.

"Well, he says he didn't do it," explained Bess.

"And you believe him?"

"I don't know about that," she acknowledged.

His heart warmed to her unexpectedly. "But you want me to prove he didn't."

"That's it. Mind you, I don't know a thing about it. I didn't even know he knew the man and if I had it wouldn't have meant anything. But he may have a chance in spite of everything if you'll take the job on."

"You know, you know your onions," Crook congratulated her candidly. "By the way, you betrothed or anything like that?"

Her surprise at the question was the genuine thing. "Me and Ken? Well, of course not. He's—well . . ." She cast about in her mind for a synonym for the old-fashioned word gentleman. "He went to Eton," she said at last, as though that clinched the matter.

"Maybe when we get these new schools they're talking about they'll teach the boys to do without their nurses," said Crook, reflecting that when they do that girls like Bess will lose half their jobs. She was born to hold some man's hand, soothe some man's fears, drive out the bogeys. . . .

"Then you know how it is," she went on. "He came a purler—well, it's bad luck for him being young and not having a job, and it sort of preyed on his mind, I think." She frowned. She'd seen Ken's look on the faces of other young men, a look they shouldn't know in their early twenties; in fact, she spent two-thirds of her time ironing that look out. "Him and me—well, we're just good friends. Just that. You know."

Crook knew. "Well—you thought you'd do him a good turn and chucked the stick away?" He reflected it was typical of women, an action like that; if anyone paved the road to hell with good intentions, it wasn't men.

"Mind you, I don't say he didn't do it. I wouldn't know. But—there was a case about ten years back, I should think, when they took a fellow for murder—found his girl's body all tucked up cosy in his trunk—and he got off because someone had seen three men going into the house after he'd left it. Mind you, no one knows if they were visiting her, but he got the benefit of the doubt. Now it seemed to me that Chigwell was expecting someone at nine o'clock when he was knocked up by the warden. And he wasn't expecting Ken."

"So our murderer is the man who called at nine?"

"Doesn't it seem that way to you?" she demanded.

"It could be," Crook acknowledged, "it could be. Only the jury may think your friend was the one he was expecting."

" But Ken didn't leave ' The Case Is Altered ' till after nine and he didn't get there till after the snow began. And if Chigwell had been expecting him he'd have been listening and he'd have heard the stairs creak. Ken said they seemed to creak loud enough to wake the dead. He thought an army must be marching down to meet him."

" Guilty conscience," nodded Crook. But he liked the girl better. She had her head screwed on all right, and she didn't beg him to do his best. She just took it for granted he was going to win. Crook took it for granted, too.

She explained about the money and Crook said, " Very generous of the chap, but in the circumstances understandable enough. Any idea how generous he can afford to be ? "

" You could ask him," suggested Bess, and he said, " Why, so I could. The things you think of."

She stood up, picking up her shiny red bag that Ken had given her.

" Any time you want me I'll be at ' The Case Is Altered,' " she said.

" Then you're pretty sure to see me," Crook told her. " There's only one thing, and you tell this to your friend, too." His thick red brows gathered across his face like a hedge. " Amateurs and pros. don't mix. They don't mix on the stage and they don't mix anywhere else. If I take on this job you leave it to me—see ? If you think you've found a wonderful clue don't put it in a cage and feed it groundsel—bring it to me right away. I'll tell you if it's any good. Got that ? "

" What do you think I am ? " demanded Bess. " Lady Molly of Scotland Yard ? I've got a living to get."

She went. " There's a fizzer for you," observed Crook to Bill. " If she'd done the chap in it 'ud be a real pleasure for me to get her off."

When Bess got back to " The Case Is Altered " she rang up Rupert Burke. " It's all right," she said. " Thought you'd like to know."

" Was he any good ? " enquired Mr. Burke.

" If you were asked what he was, a lawyer's about the last thing you'd suggest. More like a bookie's tout or one of these chaps in charge of Fun Fairs. But he's going to get Ken off."

" How can you be sure ? "

Bess considered. " That's funny. I don't know really. But he says he will."

She spoke as if that were an end of the matter.

35

CHAPTER FIVE

WHEN they told Kenneth Jardine that he had a visitor he said sharply, " Who is it ? " for he had a terror of Bess turning up without warning, and he didn't want Bess at the prison. He liked to remember her as she had been, sturdily untouched by all the misery of existence, shining like a candle. He knew she blamed herself for the matter of the stick, but he was honest enough to acknowledge that even without that he wouldn't have stood a dog's chance once he'd told the truth. When they said, " A gentleman," he relaxed and said, " Oh, bring him in." It then occurred to him that it might be a parson but the man who rolled cheerfully past the warder had never been in Holy Orders ; they have burked at that even on the music-hall stage. Kenneth had been told that he could have free legal advice if he asked for it, but he'd felt altogether too confused and wretched to take any active steps. Sub-consciously he anticipated that the uncle by marriage would do something, and indeed he supposed that the visitor would be the unpleasant Mr. Howard Neville. But Mr. Neville would have been outraged at the suggestion that he and Mr. Crook belonged to the same profession, and indeed Crook called it his trade. He sold his services with the same efficiency as he'd have sold fried fish.

Crook introduced himself and said, " Now let's hear your yarn. Never mind that you've told it to the police already. The police and me don't always see eye to eye. Besides, it's natural that they should pick on the details that fit their story and I want to know what they are, and then I'll pick out whatever helps me and serve it up with parsley round the dish, the mixture as before, precisely as Mother made, and you can stop worrying."

He listened to the story without interruptions. At the end he asked one or two questions but he didn't exclaim, as Kenneth had vaguely hoped, " Well, that makes it perfectly clear. Now I know who killed Chigwell." Only when Kenneth said, " I think I knew that night what people mean when they talk about seeing red," he leaned forward to observe impressively, " Now look here, you and me, we're partners in this, and partners have to hang together—no pun intended—if they ain't going bankrupt. When you're in the witness-box, supposing this thing gets as far as a witness-box, don't say things like that. It's going to put ideas into the jury's head, and there's always plenty of room in a jury's head for ideas. See ? "

" I see. What I really meant was that I was so enraged at the thought of all he'd done to wreck not only myself but all those other brutes who'd been crazy enough to get into his power that I didn't see him till I was practically on top of him. Then—then—did you see him, by the way ? "

Crook shook his head. " No, but I dare say he didn't look any different from all the other chaps who've had their brains bashed in. Well ? "

" That's all," said Kenneth. " Except—it was queer about the safe, you know. He used to say no one would ever get at that except over his dead body."

" They do sometimes tell the truth, the clever ones," Crook reassured him. " It's more confusing for the other side. It looks to me as though Chigwell had been interrupted."

" He wouldn't have sat down at his table and left the keys in the lock. I'm sure of that. Besides, the safe was open. And he must have been sitting down when whoever it was hit him."

" Did you get the idea that he was hit from behind ? "

" He never let anyone get behind him. Too dangerous. There were plenty of people out for his blood. He used to say so himself. He'd say to me, ' You'd like to see me dead, wouldn't you ? What are we waiting for, then ? I'm alone. You're a young man and I'm not armed.' "

" And I suppose they'd still call it murder, not suicide. Ah, well, it was coming to him some time."

" It's a pity it didn't come a long time ago," said Kenneth in a voice so full of a cold hate that Crook wondered if he were really fighting for a murderer.

" Now follow up what you've just said," continued Crook in business-like tones. " The safe was open with the keys in the lock ; Chigwell was sitting at his table and he was struck from the front. Is that what you meant ? "

" Someone had caught him a terrific blow on the back of the head. The bone had just splintered and—I tell you, it was driven into the brain. There were blood all over the table. He always sat at a very wide table to put as much space as possible between him and his visitors. I suppose that's why it wasn't all over the floor, too. You know, I've thought of something else. This chap who killed him must have got a lot of blood on him, mustn't he ? "

" He could have worn a mackintosh and washed it afterwards. It was a brute of a night."

" But the snow didn't start till 9.20," urged Kenneth, " and then it was unexpected."

" If you were going to commit a murder you might wear a

mackintosh in a heat wave," Crook suggested. " Now the
obvious thing would have been for X to re-lock the safe. . . . "

" How did he open it ? Chigwell kept the keys in his pocket."

" Then I suppose X took the keys out of his pocket."

" Robbing a dead man ? " Kenneth shivered.

" You mustn't be squeamish," Crook told him, " and what's
the sense in committing a murder if you don't get what you
came for. And we assume that X did."

" And forgot to lock the safe ? "

" I think perhaps he didn't have time."

" You mean, he heard me coming ? But—why didn't I see
him as I came up ? The stairs are pitch-black and I didn't dare
use a torch, but even so . . . I don't understand."

" Don't you ? " said Crook. " Suppose you were rifling a
safe and you heard someone on the stairs ? You wouldn't stay
to be caught and you wouldn't go down. How many other
rooms are there in the flat ? "

" I don't know. I . . . Good God, do you mean he was
still on the premises ? "

" It could be," said Crook. " It could be."

" Then he could have sworn to Burke's innocence, too, but
he didn't dare come forward because that would show he was
there even before I was."

" Sure it would," Crook agreed. " And now you've got
yourself nicely tied up he'd be more than a fool if he took any
action. He's seen what the police do when a man tells the truth."

" Two and two make four," murmured Kenneth. " You
can't blame the police."

" It's a waste of time," Crook grinned. " All the same two
and two can make ninety-six if you know how to go about it.
It's a pity," he added casually, " your girl chucked that stick
in the river."

" She meant it for the best," said Kenneth quickly.

Crook sighed. " I know. Women always do. A bad woman
don't achieve nearly so much harm as a good one when she puts
her back into things. Thank God," he added piously, " all
women think I'm the missing link and jump a hedge if they see
me coming. Now, if you and me are going to play ball you can't
keep anything back. Remember what Mark Twain said ?
' First get your evidence and then you can arrange it how you
please.' Is there anything you've left out ? "

" I don't think so," said Kenneth. " I'm pretty grateful to
you for taking on the case at all. It's not a very cheerful one."

" Well ! " Crook looked genuinely surprised. " What kudos
would there be for me if it was all plain sailing ? Besides, I'm

a snob, though you mightn't think so to look at me. I'm like the wife of the man who made his money in trade and isn't called on by the County. She won't stop at anything to score off the toffs, and I like to score off the police, and the tougher the assignment the higher the score. Just you remember that. And remember, too, that though for you and your girl this is an intensely personal affair, to me it's just another case. It'll make things easier for us all if you keep that in mind."

" I suppose the real difficulty will be that the chap who did the damage will keep out of the limelight," said Kenneth thoughtfully. " I don't see how you're ever going to identify him."

" I shan't, not so long as he stays in the shadow. But he won't. They never do. Virtue 'ud never get a chance if Vice had any common sense allied to it. Of course, at the moment the fellow's in clover. There's two ways I can deal with him. Lull him into a false security, as they say in the lesson-books, or else go snouting round and drive him into the open. You know how it is, if you know a thing well it's hard to believe that everyone else doesn't know it, too. It's like some chap with a scar on his face or a girl with a pimple on her chin. You or me, having our own chores to get on with, haven't got the time to notice these little things, but every time that chap or that girl passes a mirror the spot's got bigger. After a while they start apologising for it, and so they draw attention to it. When this fellow finds he's up against what the writing chaps call an organised opposition he'll start getting flustered. He'll think if he'd done this or that he'd have made himself a bit safer. Then he'll start doing things. That's when we'll drop on him."

Crook spoke the truth when he said that patience was his strong suit ; he said that it was the man who waited longest who laughed last and his capacity for patience would have satisfied St. Paul. He said that more men were hanged for precipitate action after a crime than for the crime itself ; and he believed that what was sauce for the goose was also sauce for the gander.

But if he was prepared to return to London and become involved in the affairs of other men while he waited for someone else to open the ball, his amateur colleagues were less cool-headed. Bess Carter waited five days and then rang up Mr. Burke.

" I wanted to know if you'd heard anything from Mr. Crook," she said.

" I was coming to-night to ask you," said Burke. " I don't suppose he'll bother about me till it's time to foot the bill. What's happened to date ? "

" He was going to see Ken and he said we weren't to interfere. All the same, I'm worried. I wondered if you could do anything."

" I have to go up to town on Ministry business in a day or two," said Burke. " I'll look in on him, if you like. But you know what these lawyers are. Take their time over things. Why, they take 18 months to clear up a will. . . . "

" I'm not interested in wills," said Bess desperately. " I can't help thinking of Ken, waiting and waiting. . . . "

" I'll write to Crook," said Burke.

When Crook got the letter he tossed it over to Bill Parsons.

" I was expecting that," he said. " These chaps are all the same. Put a seed in the earth in the morning and dig it up at night to see if it's begun to put out roots."

Burke appeared for his appointment looking a little sheepish. " I quite appreciate you've not had much time for developments," he said, " but naturally Miss Carter's anxious. You'll appreciate that."

" I'm not a bit surprised women suffer from indigestion," returned Crook frankly. " They never give themselves a chance. Sure I know she's worried, but that's her headache. She's put the thing in my hands and she should be content to leave it there."

" Then—you haven't any evidence ? " Burke ventured.

" The criminal ain't been so obliging to date."

" Suppose he doesn't oblige ? " Burke couldn't prevent himself putting that question.

" Then I'll have to manufacture it. It comes more expensive that way. That's why I like to give the chap plenty of rope. But don't make any mistake about it. The evidence 'ull be forthcoming."

Burke was looking at him as though he'd never seen anyone like him before.

" Do you suppose the judge will accept home-made evidence ? " he murmured.

" He won't have any choice," said Crook heartily. " We're all putting up with substitutes in this war, if we can't get the real thing."

" But suppose the jury detect something—spurious—about it."

" Ever sat on a jury ? " enquired Crook, affably. " No ? Why has Providence singled you out for such blessedness ? Well, if ever you do, you'll realise it's expectin' too much of twelve good men and true to know the difference between truth and the other thing. It's like these dishes the Ministry of Food are always tryin' to coax down our gullets—if you put on enough sauce or vinegar or whatever they recommend, it 'ud take an army of Colonel Llewellins to tell you what the original thing was."

" And you haven't any scruples ? " Burke matched candour with candour.

" Scruples ? I'm a mass of 'em. If you could see into my mind it 'ud be like looking at a drop of water under a microscope —all agog with foreign bodies. No, the difference between my conscience and the chap next door is that his is artistic and mine's professional. Most chaps really mean their reputation when they talk about their conscience—mustn't do anything to damage it. My clients come to me with reputations that are damaged anyway, and ask me to put 'em into circulation again. Sort of moral dry-cleaning. See ? "

If Mr. Burke didn't he was too wise to say so. " And what do you anticipate ? " he wanted to know.

" Trouble," said Mr. Crook laconically.

" And it doesn't bother you ? "

" If I was to bother every time a spot of trouble came my way I'd have died of a tired heart in my teens," retorted Mr. Crook ungrammatically.

" You don't think this chap may come for you, once he knows you're on the job ? "

" If he does," said Crook, " he'll be in very good company. Chaps have been coming for me, one way and another, since 1914, but I'm not a paralytic yet."

Burke sighed. It was difficult to know how to deal with such a nature.

" I know Miss Carter would want me to remind you that young Jardine's case depends on you."

" Like her cheek," said Crook in unemotional tones. " You go back and tell your lady friend that I never hankered for a safe life. You're dead a long time. Still, don't make any mistake about it. Sooner or later this chap's going to strike. I don't know where, I don't know when, I don't know what weapon he'll use. He might be waiting outside my office when I go back to-night ; he might be hidin' on the staircase outside my flat ; he might be on the platform waiting for a chance to push me on the live rail. But—and this is the important thing— wherever he is I'm ready for him."

" But," Burke had gone rather white, " you're not forgetting this chap hasn't got so much to lose. I mean, he's killed one man already. . . . "

" Who was unprepared, who was blinded by vanity, who

thought he was safe because no one would dare attack him.
Besides, a murderer nearly always sticks to the same method for
his crime. Look at Smith and his brides in the bath, look at
Landru, look at Palmer. . . . Take it from me, one corpse
generally follows another as night follows day, and you remember
what the P.M. said—' We're all in the front line now.' I'm
not the only enemy this chap's got. This girl's dragged me into
it, but if it wasn't for you—well, I'm not a philanthropist.
And Bess Carter wouldn't give a tuppenny damn for your life
or mine, so long as her young spark don't swing."

" Are you suggesting she's in danger ? " asked Burke, quickly.

" We're all in danger, same like St. Paul, standing in jeopardy
every hour. Well, if you were the murderer and you knew I
was on the trail, what would you do ? You might try and put
my light out, but you'd have a lot of trouble with the police if
you did. You'd be more likely to try and distract my attention
by makin' it look as though another of G.C.'s victims was
responsible. And the choice ain't so large as you might think.
It's like one of those sums they put on the blackboard when
you're a kid. If X equals Y what's the colour of the engine-
driver's hair ? "

" I suppose," observed Burke rather sarcastically, " I should
thank you for your candour."

But sarcasm was wasted on Crook, who waved a huge freckled
paw and said, " Pleasure, I assure you. Now, don't go putting
ideas into Miss Carter's mind."

Burke said that perhaps she'd thought of these possibilities
already, but Crook said in comfortable tones, " Not she. Women
don't have the logical mind. It's one of the things we have to
thank Providence for."

He nodded in what he thought was a reassuring manner, and
said, " I'll be seeing you, if we're lucky," and Burke got up to
go, feeling considerably less comfortable in his mind than on
his arrival.

" These chaps," said Crook patiently to Parsons, " never seem
to have learnt arithmetic. Of course he's in danger—he's in
terrific danger—and if he knew how great it was he'd be a darn
sight more grateful to me for warning him than he is."

Then a man came in who wanted Crook to show he couldn't
possibly have been involved in a notorious fur-stealing escapade,
since he wasn't officially in the same county on the night the
affair had taken place.

" You tell that to the police," said Crook. " The police ain't
jolly imaginative men like you and me. They depend on facts
and so far the facts support their view."

" I'm paying you to show that the facts do nothing of the sort," snapped his unreasonable client.

It was a tricky job and Crook had no more time to think of the murderer of James Chigwell. But all the time the murderer was thinking a lot about Mr. Arthur Crook.

CHAPTER SIX

THE MURDERER sat by the counter in the private bar and scowled at a tankard of beer. The unpredictable had happened, the thousand to one chance the wisest man couldn't have considered. Arthur Crook had undertaken young Jardine's defence.

The ordinary lawyer would not have presented much of a problem. He'd have done what he could for his client which, in the circumstances, would not have amounted to very much. There might even have been a defence of insanity, though it would have cut no ice with a jury unless they could prove some head injury during the young man's service with the R.A.F. and subsequent abnormal reactions. Quite soon the whole thing would have been over. But Crook was a horse of a very different colour. He would know that what was practically equivalent to a " Not Proven " verdict was very little use to a young man with most of his life before him. Crook would insist on finding someone to put in Jardine's place, and, other things being equal, the odds were he would find the real criminal. More, he would be exceedingly difficult to put off the scent. The obvious thing, reflected the murderer, lifting the tankard and getting no more pleasure out of its contents than if they had been sea-water, would be to obliterate Crook, but that presented almost insuperable difficulties.

To begin with, he would be quite aware of his own danger and therefore would be on his guard, and that augured no good to his adversary. Then, too, there was nothing obscure about Mr. Crook. Rupert Burke had been obscure, Kenneth Jardine had been obscure, Bess Carter to anyone who didn't know her was just another barmaid, but Crook was different. Anything happening to Crook would be news, and the man who put him out of the way would instantly find himself up against an army of tough dimensions and fibre. The police mightn't care for him but they had a healthy, if unexpressed respect for him. There'd be a hue and cry after his murderer, and it would be obvious that he'd only been killed because he was dangerous. Of course, the authorities might not realise at once that it was on account of the Chigwell case the he had been obliterated but a process of elimination would probably lead them to that conclusion in the long run, and once that had struck home they'd only got to go through their files in the maddeningly patient way the police do, and sooner or later they'd drop on their man. It wasn't likely there would be a wide choice. There might be a lot of people who wanted to see Chigwell out of the way, and a lot more who would find the world more comfortable without Crook in it, but not many who would want them both got rid of simultaneously.

No, murdering Crook was too dangerous. Besides, Crook wasn't the kind of person who gets murdered easily, and he'd be worse to have as your opposite number than the whole Police Force. So, reluctantly, X put aside the thought of sending Crook where he couldn't do any more harm, and considered other and more discreet solutions.

The trouble with Crook was that you could never be sure which way his mind would work; it wasn't likely that he had any foundation as yet for a case against any particular person, but he had a sublime disregard for the ramifications of British justice, which asserts that every man is innocent until he has been proved guilty. Crook would prefer to consider every man was guilty until he had proved his innocence. And now he would be waiting for the real murderer to give him a lead. Because that was Crook's gospel and he proclaimed it everywhere.

" So if I sit perfectly tight and do nothing I ought to be safe," the murderer argued. But sitting tight was an ordeal. He knew the same sense of desperation that Kenneth Jardine had experienced when he came back from the dead man's rooms, a desire to stand up and take action of some kind, but whereas Kenneth had wanted to go down and shout, " Chigwell's dead. I've seen him. No one need be afraid of him any more," the murderer wanted to distract attention from himself, and the only way of doing that was to build up a case against someone else. The difficulty was he couldn't really believe Crook would do nothing. He was like a burrowing beetle, he would work in the dark, and suddenly he would appear with a case that, however fantastic it might seem, would carry conviction in every sense of the word. It was essential, therefore, the murderer should take some contrary move. If Crook could be deflected and induced to follow up a false trail, all might yet be well. As for the police, he was convinced he had nothing to fear from them. They had got a man against whom they could build up a strong case with no apparent loopholes. True, the evidence was purely circumstantial, but that was true about most evidence in similar cases. It's not often a man is obliging enough to commit a murder in front of witnesses. The trouble with Crook was that he'd make loopholes if he needed them, with a gimlet or a hatpin or anything handy. He might already have got a plan of campaign and he was both unscrupulous and cunning and you'd never guess. X knew he was batting on an exceedingly sticky wicket, and couldn't be too careful if he didn't want to be bowled middle stump.

Mr. Rupert Burke took the first of the anonymous letters out of his letter-box twenty-four hours later. The envelope was a cheap white one of commercial shape, with his name and address sprawled across it in straggling capitals. Inside was a piece of white paper, ruled in blue with a rough edge at the top. The message read (in the same capitals as the address) :

YOU ARE WARNED TO KEEP YOUR NOSE OUT OF WHAT DOESN'T CONCERN YOU. YOUVE ESCAPED A NASTY DEATH HAVENT YOU SO WHY DO YOU TEMPT PROVIDENCE ? IF YOU GO ANY FURTHER YOULL BE SORRY.

Burke had crumpled up the envelope and tossed it into the waste-paper basket, but now he retrieved it and smoothed it out. He could just hear Crook say in his rather scornful voice, " Well, that's a hell of a lot of use for fingerprints, isn't it ? " The letter had come by post and he bent over the blurred post-mark. There wasn't a doubt it was a local letter ; the date and time of posting showed that, but you couldn't ascertain whether it had actually been posted in Pullcheston or in the larger market town of Whipley Cross. The envelope had been stamped carelessly.

He thought of ringing London but decided against it. He didn't know where Crook might be at this hour of the evening, and in any case he couldn't move without the document itself. He intended to send it to Crook. He was the professional, he might be able to make something of it. He decided to go down to " The Case Is Altered " and show it to Bess. It made an excuse anyway for seeing her. He could ask if she'd been similarly favoured. There was absolutely nothing in the ill-formed letters to identify the writer ; even Crook, he supposed, couldn't do much with that. Crook, of course, would chuckle and say it was just what he'd anticipated ; give a man a long enough rope and he'd hang himself. All the same, that need not be the universal view. Everyone knew that when a murder is committed any number of people living on the borderland of sanity and madness made confessions or sent accusations or offered evidence, spurious for the most part, either in good faith or because their tormented wits urged them to seek notoriety in this undesirable fashion. He brooded a long time over the slip of paper. Crook had said the danger might come from any direction, might be directed against any of the three of them. It might be wondered why he, Burke, should be selected. He wasn't doing the detecting.

"But I'm paying for it," said Burke aloud. Crook had said, "Keep that under your hat. We don't want to give the authorities a chance of suggesting that you and Jardine are in this together, and you'd be surprised at the things the police think of." He wondered if Crook had anticipated that the first dart would be flown against the man who'd already been accused of James Chigwell's murder.

"Not that he'd tell me," he confessed to himself frankly. "He wouldn't confide in the Archangel Gabriel. Anyway, I'll go round and see Bess."

He put on his raincoat, for there was damp in the evening air, and walked round to "The Case Is Altered." The man who had proved himself a champion dart-player was there again, and offered to take him on. Burke looked quickly round. Bess was engaged, and the civil servant in him warned him against ruining his welcome with the proprietor by trying to distract her from her legitimate work. After all, William Cotham didn't pay her to save young Jardine from the gallows, and Bess, who had earned her bread all her days and would probably continue to do so until she dropped, knew it. So Burke accepted the challenge and lost the game, and someone turned on the wireless, but it wasn't functioning properly.

"We'll have to get Bairstowe to overhaul it," said Cotham. "I wanted him to come in yesterday but he was on duty and to-day he had too much on hand. The fact is, he needs a permanent man at his shop if he's to keep going. That wife of his is no good. He told he's me not paying his way, and of course the landlord doesn't put down the rent."

Someone said what they paid wardens was a scandal compared with what chaps were getting in munitions and Cotham said that Bairstowe had made a little gold mine out of the shop in the old days.

Bess, overhearing the conversation, called out, "One of the boys 'ull mend it to-night, Bill. That'll save you the price of a War Savings Certificate."

"The last time one of the boys mended it it cost me a couple of certificates," returned Cotham rather sourly.

The darts champion played another game and was again the

victor. He offered a round of drinks and while these were being sampled Burke found his opportunity. He managed to segregate Bess for an instant.

" Look here," he said, " I wanted a word with you. I take it you haven't had any anonymous letters ? "

" About Ken ? Oh, I'm not worrying about them."

He looked staggered. " You mean, you have ? "

" There's always a lot of Nosey Parkers about without enough to do."

" But—do any of them connect you with the murder ? "

" Most of them," agreed Bess, composedly.

" Are any of them in this sort of writing ? " He dragged the letter out of his pocket.

" I don't remember," said Bess. " I didn't read them all."

" Did you show them to Crook ? "

" What on earth for ? He wouldn't have been interested."

" But—suppose the real murderer had written them ? "

Bess began to laugh ; she hadn't laughed on quite the same note since Ken's arrest, but to-night the sound was cheerful and unforced.

" You tell that to Mr. Crook," she said. " The last person likely to push himself forward is the murderer."

" And you tell that to Crook," retorted Burke, a little nettled, " and he'll assure you that the chap will do something damn' silly before he's through, and that's how he'll condemn himself. Bess, I wish you'd go away for a bit."

" I ? " She looked at him as though she thought he had taken leave of his senses. " I've got a job, haven't I ? "

" It's pretty obvious to me that the murderer's somewhere in the neighbourhood. He's already killed one man, and if Crook's right there'll be another murder or attempted murder before we're finished. I'd be happier if you were a hundred miles away."

" You don't have to bother about me," said Bess. " I'm used to looking after myself."

He groaned. " That's the trouble. You're too damned independent, Bess ; don't you ever think you'd like to give someone else a chance of doing things for you ? "

She said, " I've got to stay and see after Ken. Show me that letter again."

He put it on the table in front of her. " What's the sense of it ? " the girl inquired. " If you'd had it before you said you'd frank Ken it might have meant something. But now . . . "

" I suppose," said Burke slowly, " it's a suggestion that I should withdraw."

" Do you think Crook would drop out if you did ? "

" He'd be the first person to tell you he's not a philanthropist."

Bess thought for a further minute. " Do you suppose you're really in danger ? "

" Yes," said Burke frankly. " I do. You see, supposing I were—eliminated. . . . "

" Do you think Crook would really give up the case ? " repeated Bess. He saw that the prospect of his possible elimination didn't move her in the slightest.

" Look at it this way," he said. " The police are very Judaistic in their views. An eye for an eye, a tooth for a tooth, a corpse for a corpse. They've got James Chigwell, and they've no intention of his going to hell unaccompanied. They've got to have someone else. I don't suppose they much mind who he is. I don't mean they want to get an innocent man but they're as anxious that their choice shall be proved guilty as Crook is that he shall be proved innocent. Bess, I believe there's a lot more in this than I realised at first. Crook says criminals get caught because they've no intelligence. I believe this one's got an outsize intelligence." He shivered.

" Cold ? " asked Bess.

" Someone walking over my grave perhaps." You didn't need to have any sort of intelligence to realise she'd much rather it was your grave then Ken's. " This chap means business," he added abruptly. He saw the long road winding into dangerous places stretching from the very spot where he stood. He thought —since self-preservation's the first and instinctive law—I'd have been better to have stayed out of this. But the next minute he knew he couldn't have stayed out. Bess had made that impossible. He was still thinking this when there was a sound behind him, and he turned quickly.

" What was that ? "

Bess looked surprised. " Nothing. Only the darts chap going out. I hope he doesn't come too often. He buys a round every time he wins and as he never loses we're getting short of beer. I must be getting back or I'll be queueing up at the Labour Exchange in the morning."

" One thing." He put his hand on the arm of the bright red coat she always wore in the bar, " If you should get any more anonymous letters you'll let me see them ? "

Bess looked a little embarrassed. " I don't know if I could promise that, Mr. Burke, honestly I don't. You see, some of them are a bit queer. I mean, the people that wrote them are having a bad time or something—women, I guess. It isn't as if they mean anything either."

He saw that she hadn't any fear at all, not for herself, that was.

All her fear was for Kenneth Jardine. A surge of anger moved in him. It seemed to him he was making no headway at all.

When Crook got Rupert Burke's letter he said, " So it's begun. Well, it's to be expected. All the same, I'd have looked for something a bit more subtle. And yet—I don't know."

He looked at the mutilated sheet of paper thoughtfully. " The chap has some sense," he said. " You're never going to trace a thing like this. Know what this is ? It's a bit of a bill. It might have come from a newspaper-shop or a butcher or an antique dealer—oh, anywhere. Ordinary notepaper can often be traced. The chap must have bought it somewhere. But this is another pair of shoes." He brooded, his big stubborn chin in his big freckled fist.

" Fingerprints ? " murmured Bill. " I suppose not."

" What a hope ! " said Crook. " It was handled by the chap who originally made out the bill, it's been handled by Burke, who probably slept with it under his pillow, it's been shown to the girl—he says so. No, I'm still going to play poker, wait till the right hand turns up. There'll be more of these if I don't move. You see."

But before any more letters arrived Crook came down to Pullcheston, sampled the beer and passed favourable judgment, played darts with the professional and beat him, and then sitting snugly with Burke in a corner of the bar he asked if there had been any more letters.

" Not yet," said Burke. " I'd have let you know if there had."

" That's what I thought."

" I'm always on the look-out," Burke continued. " By the way, I suppose you haven't been honoured."

" He won't waste his small ammo. on me," Crook assured him. " Not if he's the man I think he is."

Bairstowe and Clarke came and sat alongside, and Burke thought they were looking interested, so he suggested they might shift into Cotham's private room. " He won't object," he added.

But Crook said that in his experience far fewer crimes took place in bars than in private rooms, which often had an inconvenient number of doors and windows and he knew the lie of the land of the bar but he didn't of the rest of the house, and anyway there was generally safety in a crowd. " Besides," he added, " it's nice and noisy here. He'll appreciate that. Why, I swear you could make a public confession of murder in a bar and no one 'ud hear you."

Burke looked astounded. " Do you mean you think that he . . . ? "

49

"I mean I think you and me can have a nice confidential chat here in much more privacy than we'd have in Mr. Cotham's parlour. Parlours have key-holes—see." He stopped to give the beer some attention and continued, " By the way, since you're paying the piper, I'd better tell you I'm trying to get Aubrey Bruce for the defence."

"Bruce? He's the chap that got Denniston off, isn't he?"

"And a lot of others. Mind you, he's not cheap, but the best quality never is." Come to that, he wasn't very cheap himself.

"Tell me something," said Burke suddenly. "Do you think Jardine has a chance?"

There weren't many people who could claim to have caught Crook off his guard but in that minute Burke added himself to their number.

"A chance?" said the lawyer, when he was once more able to speak. "Why, he's got me, hasn't he?"

Burke stuck doggedly to his guns. " I appreciate that, but all the same, it's going to break Bess Carter if things go wrong, though what use that chap'll ever be to her . . ."

"I have a reputation, too," Crook assured him.

"Have you ever thought," asked Burke, eyeing his man warily, "that perhaps he did do it?"

"Teach your grandmother!" said Crook rudely. "Of course I've thought so. And for all I know he did. But Truth—and they'll find this written on my heart when I die—truth is what you can make the other fellow believe—in this case, twelve of them. And since we're on the point and you raised it, d'you really give a row of beans whether he did it or not? Or, come to that, whether he swings or not, so long as you please the girl?"

The difficult colour came into Burke's face. " Suppose Bruce won't take this on?"

"Then he'll break his own record. I've sent him some nice left-handed cases before, and he's never let me down on one of them. Y'see," he waxed confidential, " Counsel goes on what his client tells him, and his client tells him what he's been coached by his lawyer. Oh, Bruce'll take this on all right. It 'ud ruin my faith in human nature if he refused."

"I wish to God it were all over," said Burke. He looked up and caught Bess's glance; her gay face had hardened, her merry eyes were sombre. The other fellows mightn't notice much change, but he could see how the suspense was telling on her. She looked her age now and " she'll never see thirty again," reflected Burke. He could see the thoughts moving through her mind as you watch goldfish moving under water. Get Kenneth off, never mind about right or wrong, never mind if he's innocent or guilty—just get him off the rope. Heaven help justice when women get it into their hands, he reflected. They'd knead facts into whatever mixture suited them, just as they kneaded flour and fat into dough.

"You can bet the murderer's thinking that," said Crook in his comfortable way. "Don't you worry. Only—if you should get any more of these letters, let me see 'em right away. And the same goes for the young lady."

Then he ordered a last pint for the road and slammed his appalling brown billycock over his beetling red brows and rolled out. He hadn't said much when you came to think of it, and Burke was blessed if he could see what the chap had done to earn the money he was clearly going to demand. But the sense of power he left everywhere was stupendous. Burke thought of that phrase "masterly inactivity." Surely even a criminal might shake in his shoes confronted by that vast imperturbable self-assurance. As for the possibility that his life also was in pawn, that didn't seem to bother him.

Burke went back soon afterwards but there wasn't any letter in the box to-night. Mrs. McKay, who had noticed his eagerness when the postman called, thought, "Owes money, I suppose." His typist, whose head he bit off for making no more than the average number of mistakes in a specification and who was Soviet-minded anyway, thought, "Wait till after the war. Shan't have any more bosses then." His secretary, who arrived about half an hour late, was told tartly she'd better get her boy-friend to buy her a watch and when she'd got it learn to read it. "Ten isn't the same as nine-thirty," he told her.

"Must be in love," said the secretary, a composed young woman who wouldn't have been put out of countenance if the Minister himself had hauled her over the coals.

The typist sniffed. In the Soviet Union they didn't allow love to assume those ridiculous proportions.

Burke was on the *qui vive* all the time. He went down to see Bess whenever he could, but he came back more jumpy than ever. Because Bess had never been able to spell patience, and it seemed to him she'd be capable of any folly now that would help young Jardine. He asked if she had had any more letters and she said "No," and he said nor had he, but the murderer might be planning something more subtle next time. All the week following Crook's visit he thought about anonymous letters, but in fact the next one came not to him but to Mr. Aubrey Bruce, K.C.

CHAPTER SEVEN

IT WAS obvious that the murderer wasn't leaving any stone unturned. Various people obstructed his path, the path to liberty, and he tackled them all in turn. Bruce's letter arrived one morning and it was as terse as Burke's had been.

A WELL-WISHER ADVISES YOU TO LEAVE THE CHIGWELL CASE ALONE. ONE MAN IS DEAD AND ANOTHER'S GOING TO DIE. IT WOULD BE A PITY TO BE THE THIRD.

It wasn't, of course, the first letter of its kind that the little red-headed Scotsman had received. All men living more or less in the public eye are bound to attract a certain amount of attention. Bruce hadn't had the number of attempts on his life that Crook had, but his days hadn't been altogether uneventful. When the letter arrived he rang up Crook and suggested an appointment. He made no statement and Crook asked no questions, but when he saw the letter he said, " It's not the same kind of paper but it's our man all right. You know, he's not so intelligent as I imagined. Neither you nor Burke is going to drop out of this—that must be obvious to an outsider—so these threats are so much hot air."

" Most threats are," said Bruce composedly. He was five foot six to Crook's five foot seven, and nearly as red as his companion. But you'd have had to go to Cruft's to find a greater contrast. " And besides, if we both dropped out it wouldn't make any difference in the long run, not to the case, I mean. You'd hang the Prime Minister sooner than see your man swing."

But Crook, lowering another pint, said gravely they must hope it wouldn't come to that. Then, still looking grave, he added, " You might mind your p's and q's all the same. This chap means business, if he is going about it in an old-fashioned sort of way. He's got the wind up and if that's when they show their hand it's also when they become dangerous. So far as I'm concerned I'd have an army of corpses laid out on the shining sands before I'd let a hair of young Jardine's head be hurt, but it 'ud be damned annoying for me if anything did happen to you."

" You seriously think it might ? " asked Bruce, and you could hear he wasn't funning.

" It's possible," said Crook.

" Of course, these chaps have no natural sense," reflected young Jardine's counsel-to-be. " Any attempt at violence now, with Jardine behind bars, weighs down the scales in his favour, since he clearly can't be sending these letters."

" And the only other person likely to be sending them is the murderer. By the way, have you any idea . . . ? "

" If I were a jane, which God forbid," said Crook, " I'd say I had intuitions, As it is, I have hunches."

" Which means you've got something up your sleeve besides your arm."

" I've always got something extra up my sleeve," agreed Crook, meaning the ace that wasn't in the original pack.

But he spoke seriously enough, because no one knew better than he that there was only one ace and everything depended on its being played at the right moment—and for all his slapdash manner he could be cautious enough in a crisis.

And after all, Burke didn't have to wait long for his second warning. Two days after Bruce had received his illiterate scrawl Burke set off on a round of inspection. The Ministry of Goods and Chattels wanted him to undertake investigations at a factory where complaints were being received from certain of the workers about the management. It made a change from the factories where complaints were being made by the management about the workers. It was at this stage of the war of first importance that industrial affairs should go smoothly. The press was putting out cautionary advertisements. The Second Front, it said, and showed pictures of munition factories in full blast. Since this particular factory had been erected, for security reasons, in a comparatively un-get-atable part of the country, Burke was making the journey by car ; his mission accomplished, he was to report to the authorities in London, and he booked a room at the Stuart Hotel, Southampton Street, for the night. It was latish when he arrived, and he found on the table a number of letters that had been forwarded by Mrs. McKay, letters that had arrived during the two days his tour had occupied. On the top of the pile was a letter in a used and patched-up envelope, addressed MR. RUPERT BURKE in large straggling capital letters running crookedly across the paper. Mrs. McKay's careful handwriting had readdressed the letter, and he wondered what she had made of such a missive or if she didn't give it a second thought. She'd been caretaking for five-and-twenty years, she had once told him, so probably she was past any kind of interest or surprise. Practically everything, every kind of situation in which a tenant could be involved, had come her way already. He wondered whether those sprawling letters would reveal anything to an expert. Then he ripped open the envelope.

YOU REMEMBER SILENCE IS GOLDEN MR. NOSEY BURKE (the letter ran). KEEP THAT BIG MOUTH SHUT UNLESS YOU WANT IT SHUT FOR YOU.

It didn't seem likely that a message like that was going to help Crook much. Probably a sane murderer wouldn't have sent it—and Crook was right when he said the wise ones lay low and said nothing. But were murderers ever sane ? Wouldn't the fact of being one of that dreadful army be so imprinted on a man's consciousness that he'd cease to think of himself as a normal being ? " Don't you believe it," Crook had said, " your murderer's just the same as you or me. Looks the same, wants the same things, lives very much the same life."

Burke looked down again at the bit of greyish-blue pasteboard lying on the table. Crook said, " Bring me everything," but what was Crook or anyone else going to make out of that ? What would he imagine the murderer was driving at ? For the message was pointless enough. It threw no light on the situation —or would it, for Crook, illumine some hitherto dark corner ?

With a sudden gesture of impatience Burke picked up the telephone. But Crook had left his office, and he had to leaf through the directory to find out his Earl's Court number. Even then he tried three times before he got connected.

" I've got another exhibit for you," he announced baldly when at last he got through.

" Sporty boy-ee," said Crook approvingly. " Come up and see me sometime." Burke pointed out that he had to go back the next morning but that didn't disconcert Crook, who carolled that the night was still young. So Burke found a taxi, because he wasn't supposed to use Government petrol for what the authorities, with a mistaken sense of humour, would have called joy-riding and drove over to Earl's Court, where Crook had a large hideous roomy flat on the top floor.

" I've brought everything this time," said Burke.

Crook shot him a quick glance. He looked more haggard than he had done.

" Getting you down ? " asked Crook sympathetically. " Have some beer ? "

He offered beer as evangelists offer the Kingdom of Heaven as a panacea for all ills. Burke produced the envelope and Crook took it without any of the care Burke had anticipated.

" If you're thinking of fingerprints, this wouldn't be any more use than a sick headache. Too many people handled it, see ? The chap who wrote it, the woman who sent it on, you ... "

" The postman who brought it," added Burke.

" Well, I don't know about that," murmured Crook. " Did you look at it carefully ? "

Burke leaned forward. " What do you mean ? "

" It's got a stamp on it, I know, but there's only one postmark, and that Pullcheston. But if it had been delivered in Pullcheston by post and then sent on by your Abigail, as you might expect, it ought to have been stamped twice. But it's only got last night's postmark."

Burke sat thinking for a minute. When he lifted his head, his face looked puzzled.

" I don't think I understand."

" If that letter came from your house, but has only been once through the post, what does that add up to ? "

This time Burke gave him the right answer. " You mean, it was left by hand ? That's a new stamp, though."

" So it is," agreed Crook.

" That means it was left by someone who knew I'd be away." He sounded a little doubtful and he looked at Crook for confirmation.

" It could be," acknowledged Crook carefully.

" Which shows it must be a local man. Well, that's what I suspected."

" It's what we both knew," amended Crook. " Chigwell was killed after nine o'clock at night. Pullcheston's a small place, the bus service stops hours before, there weren't likely to be many trains running and if there were, a traveller would be very noticeable, so unless he came by car or motor-cycle he'd have to be within walking-distance. The pity is the snow covered the road-tracks, so we can't be certain there wasn't a car. But the warden said he saw no one, and he'd be certain to have remembered a car because, except for members of H.M. Government, they're getting as rare as behemoths."

" That narrows the field a bit," murmured Burke.

Crook shrugged. " There are lodging-houses and pubs, there's one honest to God hotel, there's a cinema where a chap could skulk and come out and do his stuff before the end of the big picture and who's to know he didn't stay for the close-up ? And of course there are private houses. It was different," added Crook, warming to his subject, " in the old days, when the nobs had a butler and a lady'smaid and a variety of other possible servants below stairs. They could watch and snoop and report progress ; what novelists and playwrights do without 'em I don't know. When I was a lad the lady'smaid always feathered her nest by threatening to tell her mistress's husband just where the lady had spent last night."

" Suppose," asked Burke, " she had spent it in her own bed ? "

" They never did, not when I was a young man," said Crook. " Well, hell, there wouldn't have been any story. Have a heart."

" I wonder if anyone saw him delivering the letter," brooded Mr. Burke.

" How many flats are there in your block ? "

" About forty."

" Well, he's less of a criminal than I take him for if he's going to let anyone see him push an envelope through any particular flap."

" I wish we could get a trailer on him," said Burke, walking restlessly up and down the room. Crook drew his attention to his refilled glass. " I don't know why you should be so anxious," he said. " If the chap's out for your blood it might be better for you not to meet."

" Tell me something," said Burke. " Do you think that girl's in any danger ? "

" I wouldn't bother too much about her," said Crook. " She's about as defenceless as a rattlesnake."

But Burke wasn't satisfied. " I've always hated the dark," he said, " I hated it as a kid, and I hate it still. And that's where I am now—in the dark. I don't know what's happening, I don't know how I stand, or how long I'll stand there. . . . "

" Cheer up," admonished Crook. " No one's got much sense of security these days, what with air raids and Army manœuvres. Besides, the police would tell you that chaps who send threats they daren't sign aren't the really dangerous fellows in the long run."

" They're quite dangerous enough for me," said Burke with unconcealed bitterness. " I suppose you agree with the police, though."

" Now don't say things like that," Crook besought him. " It wouldn't do me any good with my customers if it got round that I agreed with the police. It's just because me and the police are like the sun and moon, each with their separate paths, that we don't clash. By the way, you're in good company. Bruce has had one of these, too."

" Bruce ? " Burke looked incredulous. " But surely the murderer wouldn't be such a fool as to take a shot at him ? "

" Very considerate of him to warn us," said Crook.

" He seems to be keeping abreast of the times," Burke offered.

" That's the way I like it," said Crook heartily. " I don't like these chaps that stay a hundred yards behind. You never know with them when you won't get a knife in your back."

Burke smiled crookedly. " That's known as looking on the bright side, I take it."

" Be your age," advised Crook pleasantly. " One of these days he'll get so darn sure of himself he'll shoot ahead of me, and then I can do the knifin'—see ? "

" All the same," said Burke doggedly, " I don't quite see where he thinks he's getting with all these notes."

" I'll tell you," Crook answered him. " Right up to the foot of the gallows. And when he gets there he'll find me waiting for him."

" But—I can't see—they don't say anything definite. Just vague threats."

" He don't say anything definite because if he does he's bound to give himself away."

" He might do that without meaning to, so why take the risk ? "

" It's like a flea," Crook explained. " No one dies of a flea-bite, but it's damned irritating and it takes your mind off your work."

" But eventually it's the flea that gets scotched, whereas if it kept quiet you wouldn't know it was there."

" And it would die of starvation. Don't worry, this flea's going to die too. You know, if fleas had any intelligence along of their other qualifications they might be a real menace. By the way, did you hear they'd found the stick ? "

" The stick ? Oh, you mean the one that Jardine took with him."

Crook grinned. " I thought for a minute you were going to say the one that killed Chigwell. No, they ain't found that one yet."

" Does that help ? " enquired Burke.

" Not us. I dare say the police are pleased, though they won't be able to prove much after all this time. Now we've got to sort the real weapon."

" Is that a stick, too ? "

" If Chigwell had any public spirit it 'ud be one of his own. But murderers never help you that way. Oh, it might be a poker, of course, though there weren't any coal fires in the flat and a poker's an awkward sort of thing to go carrying around. You can't say it's on account of your rheumatism."

Burke was still considering the question of the stick. " The water will have washed away all fingerprints," he suggested.

" It will. Not that there ought to have been any."

" But if he held it. . . . "

" I didn't think there was a chap living who didn't put on

57

gloves when he set out to commit murder. The Armchair Detective's taught 'em that if he's taught 'em nothing else."

" Well, if he had any sense it won't be in his possession now," murmured Burke.

But Crooke said you could never tell, and if the chap had any sense he wouldn't be writing these letters.

Burke had a further appointment with a Ministry official early the following morning, and then he motored back to Pullcheston. When he reached his flat the telephone was ringing furiously. He unshipped it and said " Hullo ! " and Bess's voice, low and breathless, exclaimed, " Mr. Burke. Thank Heaven you're back. I must see you. I believe I've found something."

" That's more than Crook or I have done. By the way, you saw they'd found young Jardine's stick ? "

Bess swept that aside. " That's not important. But I believe I'm on to the real weapon."

" Good God ! "

" Oh, I don't know, of course. But I want to hear what Mr. Crook says. Listen. Did you see in the paper about that kiddie who fell into the E.W.S. tank at the foot of The Crescent the day before yesterday ? Everyone's been talking about it, and how dangerous it is not to cover these tanks or put them underground or something, and how they've always said so, only most of them have said it to themselves up to now. Oh, yes, drowned, poor little mite. Well, what chance has a kid of four in a tank that size ? The coroner had a lot to say about the authorities putting tanks in unsafe places and more about mothers who didn't keep an eye on their brats, but then he doesn't have to find safe places for tanks and he isn't a mother either, so he doesn't understand that even mothers only have two eyes and two hands. Anyway, she had hysterics in court, poor thing, and said the little soul was wearing a gold bangle and it was missing now, and it must be in the tank. The police tried to shut things up, but the coroner said it was high time the tank was emptied and cleaned out anyway—and there they're right. It 'ud poison any fishes that tried to swim there—so they cleaned it out to-day—and what do you think they found ? "

" Not another body ? " exclaimed Burke. " Oh, no, I remember, you said . . . "

" A hammer."

" A hammer," repeated Burke. " But—what an anti-climax."

" No, no. Don't you see ? It may be most awfully important. Because Mr. Crook's looking for something that could have killed Mr. Chigwell, and a hammer's just the thing."

" It would have to be a whopping big one," said Burke doubtfully.

" It is. It weighs about half a hundredweight."

" What do the police think ? Or haven't you told them ? "

" What's the good of me telling the police anything ? They've got Ken's stick and they're satisfied. Besides," added Bess in her reckless feminine way, " they'd probably just put it away somewhere and forget all about it. They don't want their case upset now."

" Is there anything special about the hammer ? I mean, it's going to be a bit difficult to link up a hammer that's been chucked into a water-tank with a murder. It might have been there for ages. . . . " He wasn't going to be too encouraging. Girls like Bess got such ideas into their heads and by this time she'd probably got the whole thing worked out in her mind, and if she was proved wrong she'd go absolutely haywire.

" It might, only who's going to throw away a hammer in perfectly good condition in these days, when you can't get new ones. This isn't the sixpenny sort. This wouldn't cost nothing before the war. What I thought," continued Bess, warming to her subject, " is that if we could find out who it belonged to— and then check up to find out if he'd ever had anything to do with Chigwell. . . . "

" My God, you're the best of the lot now," exclaimed Burke. He thought that if Jardine was found guilty she was quite capable of swiping the judge who condemned him with the hammer that weighed half a hundredweight. " Of course, the chap wouldn't imagine anyone would empty the tank just at this particular moment. It would seem safe enough. Of course, mind you, you've got no evidence yet. . . . "

" Mr. Crook hasn't seen it yet," said Bess tersely.

Burke couldn't help thinking how Crook would appreciate that. " Who's got the hammer, by the way ? " he asked.

" I have. It didn't belong to anyone special and nobody seemed to want it so I said Bill Cotham wanted something of the sort for breaking coal and nobody thought it mattered, so they let me buy it."

" And you've got it at the pub ? "

" Yes."

" Have you shown it to anyone ? Bess, for God's sake, be careful."

" But . . . "

" No, listen. You may be in more danger than you know. Who knows you've got it ? "

Bess sounded vague. " Well, all the people who were there,

I suppose, when I bought it. There were a good many standing about. Well, you know how it is. They'd never seen a tank emptied and there's not much going on. And then they got all worked up about the kiddie's bracelet. . . . "

But Burke wasn't interested in the kiddie's bracelet. " Who ? " he repeated. " Don't you see, if it's a local man, as we're pretty sure it is, and he happened to be in the crowd and saw you buy the hammer. . . . Oh Lord, Bess, I almost wish you hadn't thought of it."

" Don't be silly," said Bess, more crustily than he'd ever heard her speak. " It might mean a chance for Ken."

" I know he's valuable," said Burke, " but damn it ! you're valuable, too." A damned sight more valuable than young Jardine, come to that. If he'd had to reply on oath he'd have admitted he didn't give a row of pins for young Jardine. He said again, " Well, for the Lord's sake, don't go waving that hammer about, and stick to your story of having bought it for Cotham." It passed through his mind that between them she and Crook could gaol the Archangel Gabriel ; he remembered how the lawyer had told him that though he wouldn't undertake to manufacture a pack of cards, put one on the table and he'd guarantee a Grand Slam without a single picture in his hand. Hypnotism or something, I suppose, thought Burke.

Bess's voice said urgently, " Are you still there ? " and he said, " Of course. Look, I'm coming over. I've got a feeling you could do with someone around."

" No, don't come here," said Bess. " I mean, if there really is any danger this is where they'll come looking for it—the hammer, I mean. And if I were to come to you—no, let's meet somewhere outside, somewhere where no one would dream of looking for either of us."

He said gloomily, " It's getting infernally dark. Mist—or fog."

" Oh, that isn't anything," said Bess in her easy way. " That comes up from the river, but it doesn't last. Look, I've thought of a place. There's a kind of teashop about half a mile along the Halton Road. It's called ' The Lady Anne.' You know the sort of thing—home-made cakes that don't rise and everyone in cretonne overalls. Well, none of the boys would go there. I'll meet you there at half-past four. I could bring the hammer with me done up in a corset box. Then if anyone was looking for it they could come here and see what sort of a welcome Bill gave them. How about that ? "

He said doubtfully, " I still think it might be better for me to come over," but she said, " No. If you're right they'll be watching this place, and it isn't going to help for your body to be found in a ditch. As it might be," she added thoughtfully. Thoughtfully, but not pitifully. If anything happened to him her first reaction would be " How's this going to affect Ken ? " Rupert Burke was useful as a colleague, but as a man she hardly knew he was born.

" Have it your own way," said Burke, admitting that there were points to her scheme. " The Lady Anne " was right off their normal beat. Why, even the notorious Bess probably wouldn't be recognised there. " For Heaven's sake, put on some stout shoes. We don't want to have you dying of pneumonia."

But he knew she wouldn't—put on stout shoes, he meant.

Bess had rung off. Burke thought about telephoning Crook, then decided to wait. Crook was an enterprising fellow—granted. Give him a chance and he'd not only make bricks without straw, he'd make 'em so damned well you wouldn't know there wasn't any straw in them. All the same, it was a tallish order giving even a chap like that an anonymous hammer and asking him to conjure up a murderer from it. Still, Burke wouldn't put it past him. He and Bess together could make the whole War Cabinet look pretty silly, he shouldn't wonder.

It was now a little after half-past two. There were two hours before he had to meet Bess at the arty-crafty teashop—half-past four, she'd said—and he supposed he might spend part of them trying to co-ordinate his conclusions for his report. He got out a typewriter and some paper and began to jot down some notes. But they were disconnected, scrappy. He didn't care a damn whether he turned in this report or not. It wasn't going to make any real difference to the war. Like all his countrymen he knew England would muddle through to victory, whatever went on in factories. At three o'clock he pushed the machine away and went to stare out of the window. The mist was rolling up. A good thing, Bess would say. Not so much chance of being followed or identified, but it would be good for a man with violent intentions, too. The telephone rang and he jumped for it, but it wasn't Bess, it was his office suggesting that he might come in and deliver his report *verbatim*. He stalled them somehow, giving them a lot of information over the 'phone. They rang off reluctantly and he found himself thinking that the four-ten bus that Bess meant to take—because though it was a bare half-mile along the Halton road it was five miles to Bess's shoes—was bound to be even later than usual. They'd be lucky if it got her to " The Lady Anne " by five. He wandered about, unable to settle to anything. The fog was getting thicker all the time. At about a quarter to four he went down to the hall and looked up and down the street. It wasn't quite so dense from below, but it wasn't the sort of afternoon anyone would go out for pleasure. Or at least only a woman. He knew the indomitable Mrs. McKay had set out as usual with her basket on her arm. She was more like a machine than a human being. Weather didn't affect her, and it wouldn't affect Bess—Bess, who'd run headlong into any danger if by so doing she could help Ken Jardine. He came back to his flat and picked up the telephone. It was almost four ; she mightn't have left " The Case Is Altered " yet, allowing for the fact that the bus was bound to be late.

Cotham answered him. " This is Burke here. Do you know if Bess has gone out yet ? "

Cotham seemed to stop a minute as though he weren't sure. Then he said, " Yes. She went a minute or two ago. I told her it was suicide. . . . "

" Damn ! " said Burke. " In this fog ! "

" Bess doesn't bother about fogs," said Cotham. He didn't ask if there was a message, he didn't seem to care why Burke had telephoned, and since there really wasn't anything to say Burke rang off.

" At least," he said aloud, " I could have picked her up in the car." It wasn't garaged yet, but was standing by the kerb a few doors along. " Come to that," he decided, " I could take it now. That bus won't come till four-thirty." She could show him the hammer in the privacy of the car, and if anyone they knew came by they would be as safe as if they wore an invisible cloak apiece. He snatched up his raincoat and came into the small hall. At the same instant his front door bell rang loudly.

He opened it at once, but whatever he might have thought it wasn't Bess standing outside, but Mrs. McKay, forbiddingly robed in a weatherproof cape, with one of last year's disused birds'-nests on her straight iron-grey hair. She had an envelope in her hand.

" I found this on the mat just now," she said, holding it out with her usual ungraciousness.

" For me ? " He didn't take the envelope at once.

" Says so outside. That's as far as I've read. Fellow who brought it was a cripple, I suppose. And it's a wonder I'm not the same the way some folks ride their bicycles in a fog. A warden, too. Nearly had the legs off me. And then an old man pushing a barrow and talking to himself. ' Maybe you think I'm some of your rotten old salvage, too,' I said to him." Her tone held a note of piercing irony.

" Thank you for bringing up the letter," said Burke, wishing she'd go away.

" I thought it might be important," said Mrs. McKay, not budging.

Burke looked at the envelope. He'd never had a letter in that handwriting before. It looked like the writing of someone who had only just learnt to hold a pen, the downstrokes thick and backward-sloping, the crosses of the T's flying affectedly across the paper. He said vaguely, " You didn't happen to see who left it, I suppose," and she said, " If I had, he'd have brought it up himself."

She saw he wasn't going to open it while she waited, so she took herself off with a sniff, and Burke went back into the flat. Inside the envelope was a bit of ragged paper with a message scrawled on it, which said :

" Too foggy for ' The Lady Anne.' Wait for me at home.—B. C."

He frowned, and the bit of paper shook in his hand. Is it all right ? he thought. Why didn't she telephone ? That 'ud be the obvious thing to do, especially for Bess. He remembered that the line had been occupied for a while, but it wasn't really a satisfactory explanation. He still felt uneasy. Automatically he switched on the wireless ; it made him feel less alone. Some hot rhythm blared into the room, and though he didn't really like that sort of music he left it on. It was better than the silence. He looked at his hands and saw they were shaking, which was absurd. Everything was all right. He looked at his watch again. It was now four-ten. Anyone walking from " The Case Is Altered " to his block of flats should be here during the next few minutes. Allow a little longer because of the fog. He went restlessly into the other room. The wireless followed him, shouting triumphantly :

" Maybe I'm wrong again
Trusting in you."

CHAPTER EIGHT.

AT FIVE O'CLOCK Bess Carter hadn't turned up at Burke's flat. At five-past five Burke was ringing " The Case Is Altered," and getting Bill Cotham, who seemed more put out than ever.

" Who is it ? "

" This is Burke. About Bess . . . "

" Oh, my God ! What's happened to Bess ? "

" That's what I want to know. I was expecting her here, but. . . . "

" Well, I suppose she's changed her mind."

" I don't think that's very probable, not in the circumstances."

" Then perhaps she's on her way."

" According to you she left more than an hour ago. Even Bess, who isn't a champion racer, couldn't take more than about twenty minutes to get here." .

" Then she must have run into someone on the way. You know what Bess is."

" She'd have telephoned, if so. I tell you, this wasn't just a date. It was important."

Cotham laughed in an uncomplimentary sort of way. " Lots of men have thought that. Bess isn't a one-man girl, you know."

The receiver shook in Burke's hand. " I'm damned worried," he said.

" To hear you talk anyone would think the girl had been murdered."

" Murdered ! " He repeated the word softly. " Look here, did she leave alone ? "

" I'm afraid I wasn't watching," said Cotham grimly.

" And even if she left alone, that doesn't mean someone didn't join her at the end of the road. Good God, what a fool ! I oughtn't to have let her stir alone. I should have come and collected her. Suppose someone was waiting, deliberately, to offer her a lift or . . . " But Cotham had rung off. When he realised that, Burke hung up, too.

The situation, however, was still fraught with tension. He couldn't think of anything but Bess. At six o'clock he was walking desperately up and down the floor of his sitting-room telling himself angrily that at this stage in the proceedings he couldn't afford to give way to nerves. The wireless was playing but he wasn't listening to the news ; he didn't at that moment care if the long-promised invasion had begun. He pulled himself together to listen at the end, in case there was a police message, though, of course, there wouldn't be. He was crazy to expect . . . There was a police message, after all, and for a moment his heart stood still. But it wasn't anything to do with Bess. It concerned an old woman who'd been run down in Birmingham by a non-stop vehicle forty-eight hours before. When the news was over he left the wireless running. He thought of ringing Cotham again, but hesitated. The fellow would think he was mad. By six-thirty, however, he'd decided he didn't much care what Cotham thought. He called the inn again, but, as he'd

anticipated, they had no news. After dinner he went down to
" The Case Is Altered." He couldn't stand this solitude, and
there was the chance he might hear something. The place
didn't seem the same without Bess. It was as though the lights
had fused or something. He bought some beer and watched
the fellows coming in, all eager for a sight of Bess, their faces
falling ludicrously when they discovered there was no one there
but Annie. Annie—a girl by courtesy—was a big lumpish
creature of over forty, with black frizzy hair and a heavily
facetious manner.

" Bess not here ? " said someone.

" Under the counter," said Annie.

" Gone off with the Colonel," suggested one of the habituees.

" Couldn't blame the Colonel if she had," said another.
" To see his wife is to fly headlong to a monastery."

Then the door swung open again and some other young fellow
came in.

" Hullo, what's happened to Bess ? "

Barring the Prime Minister, thought Burke, they'd be more
concerned at anything happening to Bess than at the annihilation
of the whole War Cabinet.

No one who came in had seen her—or at least no one would
admit to it.

The murderer was in the bar that night. He knew that a
wise man doesn't draw attention to himself, stays at home in
the dark, but the advice was more than he could accept. Because
the man in the dark can't tell what's happening, can't hear,
can't watch. The enemy may be making straight for him, they
may have learnt something—and men whose lives are forfeit
can't afford to be ignorant or take chances. He's got to put on
his mask and persuade people it's his real face ; he's got to go
here, there and everywhere, always listening, intelligent,
receptive, playing his part, never betraying himself, never
relaxing his constant vigilance. . . . Perhaps murder takes
more courage than most people understand.

X leaned on the counter, staring into the mirror behind
Annie's frizzy head. You could see the door swinging open,
notice who came in, getting an instant's warning if that should
prove necessary. There was always the chance Crook would
walk in, and though Crook couldn't know the truth he had odd
ways of ferreting it out. He saw the young men in uniform,
the older civilians, Rupert Burke leaning against the counter
with a tankard in his hand, his eyes moody. The usual gaiety
was missing to-night. No one (bar himself) knew that anything

might be wrong, but it was enough that Bess wasn't there. They didn't stay as long as usual.

The champion dart-player took on Bairstowe and then Rupert Burke and then some of the lads, but everyone seemed a shade below their usual form. Burke got hold of Cotham before he left and said in a bullying sort of voice, because of the fear in his heart, " Look here, have you had a message from Bess ? "

" No," said Cotham, " I haven't. But I'm not worrying. Bess has got as many lives as a cat, and like a cat, she always alights on her feet."

" Even a cat won't pull it off the tenth time," Burke reminded him. " Besides, people don't act out of their character and letting people down isn't one of Bess's characteristics."

" What do you want me to do ? Ring up the police ? "

" I wonder if it might be worth while trying the hospitals."

Cotham looked exasperated, but he controlled himself.

" Look here, you're sure you haven't made a mistake ? You didn't get the message wrong ? Perhaps she didn't say she was coming to you, she suggested meeting somewhere else."

(But Cotham must have known, just as Burke did, that in that case she'd have been back at " The Case Is Altered " by now.)

" But, dammit, it wasn't a message, it was in writing," said Burke. " Look here."

He took the envelope and the bit of paper out of his pocket and handed them across.

Cotham took them impatiently. Then his face changed. " Holy smoke ! " he said. " There is something in this after all. That's not Bess Carter's writing and never was ! "

There was a minute's silence. Then Burke said, " I knew it was all wrong. I tried to pretend there was some good reason why she shouldn't telephone, but I knew inside me it didn't add up. Besides, Bess doesn't write. She told me once she hardly knew which end of a pen to put in the ink. As for that," he looked bitterly at the slip of paper, " even the police are going to have their work cut out discovering who wrote that effusion."

" How did it come to you ? " asked Cotham and Burke said it had been found on the mat.

Bairstowe was eyeing them curiously. Burke thought of what Mrs. McKay had said and exclaimed, " I suppose you weren't my way this afternoon ? "

Bairstowe looked surprised. " Why, no. I had to go over to Halton to get some spares."

" By the bus ? " asked Burke, but Bairstowe looked at him sideways and said No, he'd gone by car. He was careful with

petrol—he got a small allowance partly because he did civil
defence duties and partly because he supplied radio service to
an Air Force camp over at Barkley. " You can't bring batteries
back on the bus," he added. Cotham nodded absently. His
sullen look had gone. Now he was thoughtful and anxious.

" What is this about Bess ? " Bairstowe asked, and Burke said,
" Well, she isn't here to-night, and having regard to the fog
and the fact that she never is away. the idea of a road accident
came into our minds."

" The bar seems odd without Bess in it," said Bairstowe.

Other people seemed to think so, too. It was strange, when
you reflected on her probable past, her unexalted present and
her problematical future—for she was one of those people that
all Sir William Beveridge's subtlety wouldn't be able to help—
to reflect how much influence she had. She wasn't rich or young
—but she was cosy, she was warm. . . . The bar thinned out
before Annie said " Time, gentlemen, please," and no one
seemed disposed to linger. The fog had cleared but it was a
damp drizzly night, and no one who cared two straws for Bess
liked the notion that she might be lying out somewhere, hurt
maybe—even betrayed. Because her kind has plenty of sense
for everyone else, but not very much for herself.

Burke had suggested telephoning the hospitals, but Cotham
had demurred. " There's always the chance there's a rational
explanation," he said.

" Oh, yes ? " murmured Burke. " And the note ? "

" I admit I don't like the note," Cotham acknowledged.
" And yet there may be quite a simple answer even to that.
Suppose—Bess seems frank enough but she's a mysterious girl
in some ways—suppose she wanted you to stay in that flat and
left the note herself ? "

Burke glared. " I never heard such a damfool suggestion."

" And suppose she comes back this evening and finds we've
rounded up the police ? think of the fools we're going to look.
Even if they were prepared to take the matter seriously," he
added. " After all, girls like Bess do take French leave
occasionally. It's like the ladies that lose dogs. In less than a
couple of hours they're reporting the loss to the Police Station—
but a dog has to be lost longer than that for the police to get
interested. And—I don't admittedly know a lot about the law—
but I'd say a girl like Bess has to be away from her job more
than a few hours before the police 'ull start makin' enquiries."

" I suppose," hazarded Burke, " that if it were an accident
she'd have an address on her. You'd be notified."

" If it were within a five-mile radius it wouldn't matter if

67

she had an address on her or not, I should hear. Everyone knows Bess."

"My point exactly," exclaimed Burke. "Everyone knows her."

Cotham looked as though he were at the end of his tether. He exclaimed with some violence. "Well, for God's sake, what do you want me to do?"

Burke hesitated. "I suppose I'm being unreasonable," he acknowledged. "I admit the chance of accident. I even admit the thousand-to-one chance that she's double-crossing me, but neither of those explanations seems to me nearly so probable as that she's the victim of foul play."

"Well, wait till the morning," Cotham urged.

"The morning may be too late," said Burke.

"You're letting this get on top of you," Cotham warned him. "Why on earth should anyone want to put Bess's light out?"

Burke hesitated again. Then he said, in a sort of rush, "As a matter of fact, she believes she's stumbled on something that may point to the real murderer of James Chigwell."

Cotham made an impatient sound. "Oh, keep that for the women," he said. "Look here, Mr. Burke, you and I and most other people know perfectly well who killed Chigwell, and that was Kenneth Jardine. Mind you, I don't say he hadn't got his reasons and that they weren't good ones, but the fact remains that you can't do that kind of thing in this country and get away with it. Besides, I knew Jardine. You didn't. He was one of those neurotic, highly-strung chaps that do suddenly pitch themselves under trains or put a knife in some other fellow's back. And if you ask me, Bess thinks the same as the rest of us. What is this clue she's found or imagines she's found?"

"Oh, some alternative sort of weapon," mumbled Burke. "I grant you it's not logical, but when you're as desperate as she is. . . ."

"Just what I said," pronounced Cotham. "She's clutching at straws and it's no good. If you ask me, she did send that note and she had her reasons, though it's no use asking me what they are. No man understands how a woman's mind works. But she'd got some crazy notion in her head and she meant to put it to the test, and she didn't take you into her confidence because she knew you'd think it crazy. . . ."

"And so she sent that note?" Burke shook his head. "I don't know what happened, but I'll swear that wasn't the way of it. Why ring me up and tell me about the hammer. . . ."

Cotham's head came up with a jerk. "What hammer?"

"Oh, she'd found a hammer and she thought it might be connected with the crime."

Cotham looked incredulous. " She must have got more to go on than that."

" I don't think so. As you say, she clutched at straws. . . . "

" Did she pick out a hammer because it was the only handy weapon ? Why not a poker ? Or was it feminine intuition as usual ? "

Burke said desperately, " How the devil do I know? I don't know anything but what she told me on the 'phone and that was damn all. But I do know Bess wasn't the kind to make a fool of a man who was trying to help her. And you can say what you please, but I'll never believe she wrote that note, and I wish to God I knew who did."

He thought seriously about going to the police, but there was a lot in what Cotham said. It might be disastrous in the end. He could imagine the derision on their faces—though subsequent events might wipe that look off. He broke out fiercely, " If anything happens to her and we might have stopped it . . . "

Cotham glanced at his watch. " This is all a bit melodramatic, if you'll forgive me saying so," he observed. " But if Bess had been side-tracked, as you seem to imagine, the odds are it's too late by a long chalk for us to do anything now. She'd be back if she'd meant to come back—and could. And, for your consolation, Bess is pretty good at looking out for herself."

" In the ordinary way—I agree. But this isn't ordinary. She's not thinking of herself. It's this young fellow, and she'll take risks for him she wouldn't take for another living creature. I know."

" You think she's been lured away ? That's not so easy."

" If it was someone who said he could help Jardine—oh, you're right. We can speculate till the cows come home, but we don't get any further. Only—do me this favour—if Bess does turn up, let me know."

" It matters a lot to you, doesn't it ? " suggested Cotham, looking at him curiously.

Burke replied, with truth, " More than anything in the whole world, since you're kind enough to be interested. More than my whole life." He'd never guessed at the beginning he was going to feel like this, that she was going to make all this difference. . . .

He went back but he couldn't sleep. He put on the wireless and heard someone reading a short story, one of those experiments, in horror the B.B.C. love to put on last thing at night to ensure pleasant dreams. It was the story of a murder for which an innocent man was hanged, and he winced—it was too near the bone. There was nothing to hear, of course, nothing of importance to him, that is, but he kept the wireless playing till the last National Anthem sounded. He couldn't get Bess out of his mind, Bess in her little short red coat swinging out of " The Case Is Altered," Bess not guessing what treachery awaited her, Bess who now—" Oh, hell ! " he muttered. He put out a blind hand and fumbled with the knob of the radio.

Burke was not the only sleepless man in the neighbourhood that night. At " The Case Is Altered " William Cotham sat up late, also thinking about Bess. He hadn't sent for the police ; he'd thought a good deal and decided it was best to wait. He used to say grimly there was never any sense heading for trouble. It came at you fast enough. If they found out anything about Bess they'd be on the spot all right. He thought about Rupert Burke, wondered if he knew anything, suspected anything. There was one thing—he wouldn't let the grass grow under his feet, and he'd have the co-operation of half the place if he wanted it. It was odd to think that a man like James Chigwell could create all this havoc just by dying.

The murderer crouched in his room behind heavy black-out curtains and fought off the horror that threatened him. He'd heard about the Russian advance and an American attack in the Far East, a British bombing raid and the resignation of a Cabinet Minister. Great things were pending, you didn't know where you were from day to day. Any minute the authorities might take your home or your job, the country was fighting for safety, but the man who fought couldn't spell the word. But he didn't care. He didn't care about anything except what might happen to him. He knew that if anyone learned the truth he mightn't have to wait for a trial. He'd be lynched as like as not. Four and a half years of war had released a lot of reticences ; the old system was dying hard and the new system was in the first savage steps of evolution. He thought of the eager fierce young faces of Bess's admirers, the fellows in uniform crowding round the bar ; he thought it would go hard with any chap who got into their hands. He moved impatiently as the sirens went, but though the guns started up at once he didn't worry about them. He was much more afraid of the police than of the German bombers. Already they might be on the job—you couldn't tell. He didn't specify even to himself what job he had in mind. There was only one job that mattered. It wasn't likely, of course, but you had to guard against every contingency, and he'd got to know right away what was happening. He'd got to keep step by step with them somehow, he didn't know how. He could telephone, of course, but they'd ask why he was so anxious when other people were prepared to wait. Wait ! He sat huddled in his chair, his linked hands swinging between his knees, thinking, thinking. What chiefly impressed itself on his consciousness was the fact that he wouldn't dare rest now. When he struck down James Chigwell he'd thought, " I'm getting out of my cage, and I'll never go' back." He hadn't known he was simply walking into a larger prison, that no one deed stands alone, but there is a series of incidents leading up to it, and a string of consequences to follow, and if you're not to pay for the first step, probably with your life, you've got to go on down the road you've chosen, even though most likely it leads to the endless dark.

He got up at last, shivering. No sense sitting up any longer. There'd be no more news till morning, and there was no reason to suppose there'd be any then. Only, when Bess didn't come back, surely someone would make a move. He'd got to be on the spot, know what the move was, be ready to counteract it if it seemed dangerous for him. He'd got to wait and watch, wait and watch. It was difficult, but if he slipped up now he was lost. He thought of some lines he'd read years ago :

" Could'st thou not watch with me one hour ? Behold
Dawn skims the sea with flying feet of gold,
With flying feet that graze the gradual sea,
Could'st thou not watch with me ? "

The words went round and round in his head. He mixed himself a strong whisky and soda and went desperately to bed. But waking or sleeping the same nightmares pursued him.

The next morning when Burke came down to breakfast there was still no news about Bess. He felt shy about ringing up Cotham, the fellow would think him daft. But he had a heavy day before him at the Ministry. If they tried to get him there, the odds were they'd find the line blocked. So just before he left he snatched down the telephone and rang the inn.

" Be your age," snapped Cotham irritably. " She wouldn't be back before nine."

" How long," enquired Burke, " do you intend to wait ? "

" If she's not back this evening—say by five o'clqck—I'll try the hospitals," promised Cotham.

" If she were there they'd have got on to you already," Burke urged.

" You can't be sure. They keep changing personnel. Besides, though Bess is important enough to a good many people, I daresay a hospital matron mightn't think much of her. They're

71

impersonal, women like that. They have to be. To them an accident's just a case. . . . "

" Why do you take the trouble to say all this ? " Burke enquired. " You know perfectly well you don't expect to find her in a hospital."

" I know nothing of the sort," returned Cotham. " I know nothing about the affair, except that Bess won't thank anyone who pushes his nose into her concerns. Look here," his voice softened a little, " you won't do anything rash, will you ? I mean, if she is all right, think of the fools we'd look—and the kind of fool we'd make her look."

" Oh, I daresay what you said last night was true, it won't make any difference by this time." He hung up. There was nothing to be gained by this aimless interchange of views. He was glad he had a heavy day in front of him. It gave him less time to think about Bess.

By midday, however, the work had folded up. A scheme he'd been nursing for months was casually disposed of by a visiting official, who said the Head Office didn't think it practicable, had other plans. He was so much dismayed that he could only stare for a minute before he broke into a fierce defence of his adroitness. But the official only smiled and said you had to leave it to the experts, and then he got back into his car, that was marked Priority, and sailed off, leaving Burke feeling like a cat without a tail. Because everything was so flat it occurred to him he might telephone Crook. He went back to his own place for the purpose, and was lucky enough to get connected at once.

" These amateurs ! " ejaculated Crook. " Always think they can put one over on the pro. Why the devil didn't she get in touch with me ? "

" I was going to wait till I'd heard her story. I didn't guess—"

" That it might suit someone's book that she shouldn't repeat it ? You know, this is my cup of tea and I'm damned if I like drinking out of a cup that's gone the rounds before it's my turn. I'm not fussy, but I do draw the line somewhere. What did she think she had anyhow ? "

Burke told him about the hammer. " I know there's no logic behind her argument," he wound up, but Crook surprised him by saying, " It ain't logic that solves murders. If it were no murderer would ever escape the little covered shed. Y'know, that girl didn't give me the impression she was a fool, and if she has been decoyed away it's because X couldn't afford to let her make her story public. What we've got to do is find out who she met after leaving the pub."

" Cotham says she left at four and left alone . . . "

" Except for the little hammer. Interesting to know where that is now. If I had my guess I'd say back in the tank where they found it. It's always wisest to hide a thing where someone's looked already. You remember that when your turn comes."

" Do you think something's happened ? " demanded Burke. " I mean . . . "

" I know damn well what you mean and—yes, I do."

" Then oughtn't I to get in touch with the police ? "

" That's her employer's job. After all, if she was anywhere where she could make contact she'd have done it by now."

" Unless she thought it might make things dangerous for me. There's always that chance. . . . "

He'd known it was a pretty low card to play, but he hadn't realised how low till he heard Crook's roar at the other end of the line.

" Come right off it," Crook advised him. " I ain't a married man myself, but I know something about that kind. You just get it into your head that all she cares about is this chap they've got in chokey. If getting you hamstrung would fetch him out, she wouldn't hesitate. If she hasn't contacted you it's for one of two reasons : (A) Someone's prevented her, or (B) She's playing a lone hand and she knows if she lets anyone else in on it they'll take her cards away from her. You pays your money and you takes your choice, but if you ask my opinion there ain't much choice. You know, I'd be inclined to wake up the police if I were the girl's employer, but, of course, that's only point of view."

But Cotham said doggedly he was going to wait till five. Burke wondered how he'd face another night of uncertainty like the last. But, as it turned out, he didn't have to wait till morning for news, because a man who hadn't previously figured in the case found Bess late that afternoon.

CHAPTER NINE

I

IT WAS ONE of the rules of Mr. Allen Wilkinson Stout, the Independent Member for the Parliamentary Division of Malvoisin in the County of Kent that constituents should address their appeals or criticisms to him at the House of Commons. Only so, said he firmly, could they be sure of receiving a reply. For he held that only a fool (and no one but his viperish mother had ever dared call him a fool to his face) kept a dog and barked himself, and he employed an inhumanly competent secretary to deal with his correspondence and tell him which letters he ought to answer personally and, so far as possible, what he ought to say. Correspondence, he held, should form a very small part of the activities of a Member of Parliament and since women liked writing letters and men very seldom did (except the long-sighted and ambitious who had a view to subsequent publication), it was a reasonable division of labour to expect Miss Bennett to tackle what he called the donkey-work, while he set about the infinitely more important business of saving the country for Independence.

In theory he disregarded letters sent to his address at Bramham Manor, and indeed these were not many, since most of his constituents were a good deal more afraid of the terrifying Lady Catherine than of an anonymous secretary, and were convinced that she would open and quite probably destroy any letter in a female handwriting. Moreover, if Mr. Stout had reason to suppose that a letter came from a constituent, he would dump it in a basket marked " Miss Bennett " and take it up to London at the beginning of the following week when he returned for the sittings. Now and again, however, people got past his guard by being unsporting enough to have handwriting resembling that of one of his friends, and twenty-four hours after Bess's disappearance from " The Case Is Altered "—that is, on a Saturday morning, one such letter reached him. He opened it, thinking it was from his cousin, Laurie, who'd married an American just before the war and was the only woman, Mr. Stout sometimes said, he might have married himself if only she'd had the sense to wait—" Until I died, I suppose," suggested Lady Catherine with her usual asperity, " and you found that, after all, there's something to be said for having a woman about the place." But he was deceived, because it came, in fact, from a woman who had pestered him pretty often before (only Miss Bennett had always dealt with her letters so he hadn't recognised the handwriting) to find her a suitable cottage for herself and her two-year-old son. Her husband was in the Navy and she said she must keep a home going for him to come back to on leave. Cottages in Malvoisin, like cottages all over the country, were in very short supply and when they did fall vacant were either snapped up by farmers trying to house agricultural labourers or else were reserved by the Ministry of Health for people evacuated from bombed areas. Mr. Stout, like an obliging and conscientious Member, had (through Sarah Bennett) taken up the case with the Ministry of Health (who said there were no cottages available for private residence, and suggested that Mrs. Ewell spend the rest of the war with her parents, who had plenty of room for her), with the local authority, who said much the same thing and Mrs. Ewell herself, who said that she couldn't possibly accept that solution, because her mother's pre-war outlook would have a deleterious effect on Sonny Boy's development. She was at present housed in a condemned cottage whose sole water-supply was a well that threw up slugs, frogs and an occasional decomposed mouse. She, therefore, walked half a mile to the nearest uncontaminated source of supply, carrying a pail, and she pointed out that she could hardly do this all the year round. She had no one with whom to leave the child—he was too young to walk uphill, and she couldn't manage a push-car and a pail. And was this how the country treated the wives of the men who . . . At this juncture Mr. Stout skipped considerably, because that was what they all said, and when you'd heard it once you'd heard it once too often. It appeared, however, that she had now discovered a cottage that neither the Ministry of Health nor the local authorities wanted, though doubtless now that she was asking for it they would find it was ideal for their purposes. Still, it had been blitzed and one wall practically removed, but she was convinced that a little patching would make it weather-proof, and if the Ministry of Works made a fuss about that, how could you expect men to want to go on fighting. . . . Mr. Stout skipped again. She added that it stood back from the road and that was important because Sonny Boy was so forward for his age, and so inquisitive she was sure he'd be an inventor one of these days, and would run out whenever he heard anything pass, which augured well—didn't Mr. Stout think so ?—for his future.

"Up among the angels," thought the unsympathetic Mr. Stout, wondering why Providence had made women so fussy. Suppose there was an occasional mouse in the water ? You only had to boil it, and if Sonny Boy jibbed at such trifles it was a poor look-out for the country if he was destined for its future Prime Minister.

"If these mothers knew what they themselves drink in bars and smoke in what they call cigarettes, they wouldn't make all this heavy weather about water-supplies," he said. But he had found that women who were accustomed to a town life had very little sense of proportion.

He wasn't quite sure which cottage she meant. She said it was called "The Cottage" and was on the Pikle road. There were two or three who might fit that description, dotted in fields that had received a bomb or so from a fast-departing Junkers some months earlier, and for the most part it hadn't been thought worth while to repair them. As Lady Catherine Stout said, " Well, they're really not much more picturesque now than they were before, and what about the Council for the Preservation of Rural England ? "

Sighing deeply, the Member for Malvoisin swung on a big black hat to match his big black handlebar moustache and his jet-black hair (and at the moment the black scowl that rested like another hat on his eyebrows) and went out. It was a golden afternoon with a wind like silk and no trace of yesterday's fog, and he thought of all the fools who prefer a town existence and are lucky to get one Saturday morning off in four and spend it in Oxford Street or the pictures. His cow, in obedience to the laws of nature and in defiance of the Minister of Agriculture, was about to calve, and he rather thought he had the income tax authorities by the short hairs. He wouldn't see his secretary till Tuesday and no one was coming for the week-end. Altogether it was ungrateful to complain of Mrs. Ewell as a crumpled rose-leaf in his silken bed.

The cottage stood, as Mrs. Ewell had informed him, some way from the road, and he knew, from six years' Parliamentary experience, that even if the Minister of Works would sanction the necessary repairs she wouldn't have been there three months before she found she was too far from a bus stop for her convenience or the child's legs. Still, she was quite a long way from Bramham Manor, too, and there wasn't a bus within a couple of miles of him. He climbed a stile and went down one of the old roads that the Romans made. He thought of the centuries that had passed since that road was first laid, and of the workmanship that had been displayed in the making. They'd brought their chariots and contemporary vehicular traffic along here, for it had been a military road then. The little cottage, when at length he reached it, had a lopsided appearance. The bomb, that had come down in the field close by, had taken off the greater part of one wall, and it looked like a child's doll's-house with the door open. There were still pictures hanging on nails, and a green china vase stood on a cottage mantelpiece. He looked at it thoughtfully. It was no use trying to persuade anyone as knowledgeable as the Minister of Works that he could do the necessary repairs over the week-end, though it was a testimony to the sturdy labourers who'd built it that it hadn't collapsed altogether under the force of the explosion. He remembered what they said about those London houses that came down like packs of cards.

" A Jerry built 'em and now a Jerry's destroyed 'em."

76

He tried the front door, but that had been jammed by blast, so he went round to the back. It was amazing to see that there were, even now, rags of curtains hanging at the windows. Obviously the raid had taken place during the darkness, because those rags were still undrawn. It was odd that in more than two years they hadn't been pulled back. The back door opened without much trouble and he stepped straight into the kitchen. It was a little place, two rooms above and two below, and the kitchen ran straight into the living-room. It would be the same with the bedrooms; there wouldn't be a door between them, but something like a hole in the wall. He went through into the living-room; the furniture had been taken away, what remained of it, but there was a built-in ingle nook and a calendar with a picture of red and yellow roses in a blue bowl still hung on a nail.

Someone was sitting on the ingle-nook with her back to him. He was so surprised that for a minute he stood stock still. Then it occurred to him that it might be Mrs. Ewell herself, anticipating just this contingency. Still, there wasn't any child and there wasn't any push-chair and the local Moral Welfare Secretary had complained to him sternly that the cottage was used for immoral purposes, and for all he knew it was. If so, he'd said, there was all the more reason why he shouldn't frequent the place. The woman, who didn't move when he came in, wore a bright red coat and had a blue scarf round her neck and one of those red silk shrimping-net affairs that women wore nowadays instead of hats, over her blonde hair.

He said tentatively, " I beg your pardon," but she didn't move, and he supposed she'd gone to sleep, though it seemed an odd place to choose. The shoes she wore were emblematical of a house-and-town environment, and so was the red coat. Women in this part of the country wore sensible woollen coats in drab colours, and low-heeled shoes suitable for walking; they didn't look like an advertisement or the cover of one of the women's magazines. Still, the general effect was rather attractive —bright gold hair, bright red coat—he supposed his Moral Welfare Secretary was right, and she was waiting for some one or resting after someone had gone, and he wondered what a Member of Parliament was supposed to do about that.

He took a farther step and still she didn't move, and he came still farther into the room, so that he could see her face. And after that the picture ceased to be attractive in any way, because any beauty she might have possessed had been choked out of her by the blue scarf round her throat. It was no wonder she hadn't heard him come in; she'd never hear anyone come in again. He stood staring stupidly at her, wishing this had happened in London when he could have summoned Miss Bennett, who, he was sure, would deal with the situation far more efficiently than himself, and he noticed in a vague sort of way that one of the red buttons, shaped like dolphins, was missing from her coat.

He didn't do any of the obvious things that anyone who read detective stories or went to the films would have done. He didn't methodically open her handbag—bright red, too, and defiantly shiny—and look for her identity card. He didn't remind himself that he mustn't leave any finger-prints or obscure any footmarks. He just stood gowking, as his mother would have said, thinking that, though you read about things like this in the papers and though lots of people, though he wasn't one, ask for no better recreation than a good detective yarn, you never think of them as realities, not the way you think of burst boilers or cows dying when they drop their calves. He knew, because he'd fought in the first great war, the one they'd called Armageddon, that men never really believe in their own deaths ; men will fall all round them, but they'll be safe. Every time he'd gone back to France he'd walked round Bramham the night before thinking, " The last time, perhaps," but in his bones he'd been convinced he must return. And this girl, coming here presumably for pleasure—because people (though again he wasn't one of them) admired long finger-nails painted London Rust and artificial waves in brilliantly gold hair —couldn't have dreamed it was going to end like this. All the same, he'd have expected to find her in a dance-hall, not a blitzed cottage.

His next thought was a purely political one. Lord, he muttered, she's probably a constituent. He wasn't sure what you were expected to do for dead constituents. If they'd fallen in war, of course, you looked after the interests of their dependants, if you were asked to do so, and fought mighty battles with the appropriate Departments to see that they got the highest of what the arrogant Mr. Stout considered the miserly pensions given to widows and orphans. But this, he reflected uncomfortably, was murder. There couldn't be the smallest question of suicide here, and the motive, he supposed, wasn't far to seek. He felt a spasm of impatience, with which Mr. Crook would have been in sympathy, that he, a busy man much concerned with post-war plans for agriculture and agricultural housing (he didn't mind about people in towns ; they could die like flies for him), should now be involved in what were bound to be most unsavoury proceedings for a woman who, if she was old enough to be going about at all, was surely old enough to take care of herself. He wasn't one of these chivalrous men who want to protect women ; he said the average male had his work cut out protecting himself, and all his sympathy now was for the poor devil—some chap from the camp, most likely— who'd eventually be run in for this. It was asking for trouble meeting in this sort of place. Any local girl knew its reputation. Naturally the man would think—or at least Mr. Stout assumed he would. Personally he'd have fled a mile through an air-raid to avoid five minutes alone with Bess.

After some time he plunged out of the cottage and made for the nearest A.A. 'phone. There was one quite near, but he found he'd forgotten his key so he had to go back to Bramham Manor, a tramp of two miles. His mother was telephoning to the butcher—the fact that it was five o'clock on Saturday afternoon made no difference to her—and he hung about so obviously that she asked what was wrong. He said tersely, " Murder. I want the police."

" Oh, dear ! " said Lady Catherine. " You do get yourself involved in queer cases, Allen. I hope your constituents won't mind. Who is it ? "

Mr. Stout repressed the obvious reply and said it was a woman. He didn't know who it was, she wasn't on his visiting-list.

" If she was," said Lady Catherine, " she wouldn't be a woman." And relinquished the telephone.

2

One of the nameless hussies who had replaced the pre-war staff at the Manor overheard Allen telephoning, and having sharp ears and no scruples she scampered down to the kitchen to spread the glorious news that Mr. Allen had found a corpse.

" Lor'. He never put it there," said Hussy No. 2.

" Not likely. Why, if you was to give him a pencil he couldn't draw a picture of a woman."

" I bet you I know who it is. That girl from ' The Case Is Altered.' Where'd he find her, May ? "

" In a cottage, he says."

" Wonder what she was doing there," speculated Hussy No. 1.

" You couldn't guess, of course," giggled Hussy No. 2.

" Wonder what he was doing there," put in a third voice.

Hussy No. 1 sighed. " That's the best of being a Member of Parliament. You can be as nosey as you like, and no one can ask what you think you're doing and why don't you mind your own business, because anything that happens can be your business, if you choose. Like a clergyman, only worse, because at least you can say you're chapel and put the chain on the door."

Long before the police arrived at the cottage the news had started to spread. Hussy No. 1 saw to that. By the time the authorities were interviewing William Cotham all the locals knew that Mr. Stout had found a girl with her throat cut and blood all over everything, and some of them knew that he'd found the knife it had been done with. On the whole, as usually happens, the police knew less than anyone.

Burke heard about the finding of the body from William Cotham. He was working late that Saturday afternoon, and his secretary had gone so he was taking his own calls. As soon as he heard the landlord's voice, he knew what the news was going to be.

" They've found her," said Cotham abruptly.

" Bess ? " No sense beating about the bush, pretending not to know what it was all about, when this was what you'd been expecting. Besides, ' they ' couldn't be anything but the police.

" Yes. You were right, it seems. Might have been wiser to ring up the police from the start. But you can't ever be sure. . . . They seem to think so, anyhow."

" I suppose I was expecting this," Burke heard himself say. " When she didn't come back. . . . "

" I didn't really believe it. Matter of fact, I thought she might have gone to London to see that chap. You can't imagine a thing like this happening to Bess."

But Burke said in a dull unemotional voice. " Oh, somehow you couldn't imagine her dying quietly in bed. Go on. Tell me anything else there is. Who found her ? "

" Last person you'd have expected. Member for the Division. Went to look at the cottage for some reason. . . . "

" Cottage ? " Burke's voice sharpened. " What cottage ? "

" That empty cottage on the Pikle road, the one that got blitzed. There's been talk about pulling it down or repairing for a long time now."

" But what in heaven's name was Bess doing at a place like that ? "

" I suppose that's what the police will have to find out. By the way, they'll be wanting to see you."

" I suppose so, though I don't see how I can help much. How—how was it ? Another blunt instrument ? "

" Strangled with her own scarf. I've seen her. Had to identify her. They found her card in her bag and came to me at once." There was a movement of impatience that you could easily detect even over the telephone. " They want to know about her family. So far as I know she hadn't got one. Did she ever say anything to you ? "

" Nothing. Cotham ! "

" Well ? "

" Do they think—the police—that it would have made any difference if we'd put them on the scent when she first disappeared ? "

" I don't know what they think. They didn't tell me. But I should say not. If she'd been alive at six o'clock she'd have been at ' The Case Is Altered.' "

" I still don't understand what took her there. Why, it's nowhere near our rendezvous."

" They found a note in her bag changing the place."

There was a moment's deathly silence after that. Then Burke whispered, " My God ! He thought of everything, this chap. He even arranged to commit a murder in a fog."

" Well," Cotham spoke after a short pause, " just thought I'd let you know."

" Yes. I'd better get along to the police unless they're coming here. I'll call the Station." He was silent for so long that Cotham said, " Are you still there ? " and he replied in an odd dazed voice, " I was trying to see what it added up to. Do they know who sent the note ? "

" It was signed R. B.," said Cotham. " That's all I know."

He rang off and Burke sat for a time, thinking, not ringing up the police, wondering where this was going to end. If you're a temporary Civil Servant and you've been arrested once for murder, and then get yourself involved in a second, you can hardly blame the Government, that has the fair name of the Civil Service to guard, if they find you're redundant. And there wasn't any hope that this thing could be hushed up. He wondered if the police would show him the note. Most likely, in view of the initials. He tried to think of all the things they banked on in detective stories—ink, paper, idiosyncrasies of handwriting—only, of course, it wouldn't be a normal handwriting —could experts tell who'd written a thing if the letters were printed, for instance ? He didn't know. One didn't know any of the important things in life. He took up the telephone and rang the station, but before he got through the police had arrived.

They weren't, he thought, particularly sympathetic. He supposed it would be too much to expect. They'd found a perfectly good murderer to swing for the Chigwell crime, and it wasn't their fault, their manner implied, if a girl who had nothing to do with it officially chose to butt in and become a second victim. Not that they would even admit Bess's death had anything to do with Chigwell or the arrest of Kenneth Jardine. But they did insinuate that they didn't expect Members of Parliament and Civil Servants to get involved in this kind of sordid affair.

As he had anticipated, they showed him the note that had been taken out of Bess's handbag. "Go straight to Finlay's Cottage on the Pikle Road," it read. "Coming four-thirty. All explanations then," and it was signed "R. B."

"It's what I assumed as soon as I heard of it," said Burke, dully. "She must have let out about her plans to someone, and he faked the two notes." He produced the one Mrs. McKay had brought up to his front door. "It's reasonable to suppose the same person wrote both," he suggested.

"Reasonable, but not proven," authority agreed. Marlowe wasn't there to-day, though he'd come back on the case when they understood it was mixed up with Chigwell's death. There couldn't be much doubt really, because the ink was similar in both notes and so was the paper, though it was going to take the police all they knew to show just where that paper came from. It was the sort you buy in cheap pads practically everywhere. X could easily get hold of one without attracting attention.

Burke asked, "Was this left at 'The Case Is Altered'? Yes, I suppose it must have been, just as mine was left on me. Then it must have been left before four o'clock, because that's when she went out. And mine was left at about the same time. What took this chap to the cottage?"

"He says he was going to see if it was fit for a woman to live in."

Burke heard his own voice say on an hysterical note, "Anyway it was fit for one to die in." And then stopped, aghast.

The policeman said, "Why was she meeting you?" and he began to explain about the hammer. The man looked less sympathetic than ever, but that again was only what you'd expect.

"Do I have to see her?" asked Burke quickly, and the man said there wasn't any necessity. She'd been identified. He had to explain his own movements that afternoon, and he told them about the note and Mrs. McKay and how he'd got anxious when Bess didn't turn up, but hadn't liked to get in touch with the police.

"That's the trouble," said the man sombrely. "We don't get the information till it's too late, and then we're blamed for not preventing crime. It doesn't make sense."

Burke asked the question he felt he had to ask. "Would it

have made any difference ? I mean, do they know when . . . ? "
But the other said that was medical evidence that would be given
at the inquest. It would be held on Monday and he had to be
present. He quite saw that, but he saw, too, that a lot of people
were going to blame him for not doing something active when
things began to go wrong. He said, " I'm a fool. I had a feeling
this wasn't straightforward. That note—it wasn't like Bess.
Who on earth could she have told ? " Then he stopped. " Do
you see what this means ? She must have told the murderer,
without knowing what she was doing. Then if we can find out
who she saw that afternoon . . . "

The policeman said, " There's been enough amateurs mucking
about as it is. You let the police get on with their job."

" Even the police make mistakes," suggested Burke with
tremendous irony, and saw the other fellow wince. You couldn't
blame the authorities for thinking that Rupert Burke had
murdered Chigwell, but it did call for a certain delicacy of
handling.

" I wondered at the time why she sent a note," Burke continued, " but of course she didn't. She didn't know anything
about it. She'd have telephoned, but I suppose the chap who
wrote it didn't dare telephone because his voice would have
given him away."

They seemed to keep him an unconscionable time asking
questions, but they let him go at last, and he rang up Crook,
wondering if the police were tapping his telephone wires.

" It's what I told you," said Crook. " Give X enough rope
and he'll hang himself."

Burke said in a furious voice, " So that's all you think. The
girl's been killed. . . . "

" One murder follows another as night follows day," said
Crook, reasonably. " Hold everything. I'm coming down."

While he waited Burke wondered if the police would try and
pin this murder on him, too. The police didn't have to prove
motive, he'd been told. But in view of Mrs. McKay's evidence
and Bill Cotham's, provided Bill remembered what time he
telephoned . . . he put his hand to his head. He had meant
to say something about the hammer. The policeman hadn't
asked any questions. That must mean they hadn't found the
hammer. And even if they did find it, what could they do ?
You couldn't prove anything. Bess had said, " It's a queer
place to put a hammer. You'd only hide it there if you didn't
want anyone to find it," and that was logical enough, more
logical, really, than he'd have expected Bess to be, and the
most farsighted murderer could hardly have foreseen that a

little girl would get herself drowned in the one emergency water tank where he'd hidden his weapon. And even if he could have foreseen that, he couldn't imagine that Bess would jump to the conclusion she had. And even then—it was like the House That Jack Built—what proof could anyone bring that the hammer had been used ? He followed that argument up to its logical conclusion. If Bess started out with the hammer and if Bess was later found murdered and the hammer was missing, it was safe for anyone (except perhaps the police) to assume that the hammer was the point at issue. And if X was so anxious to conceal the hammer again any logical person would be justified in assuming that the hammer stood for something dangerous.

"And because she argued like that, Bess has lost her life," he said aloud. "What's Crook going to make of that ?"

CHAPTER TEN

CROOK said, "It's what I've been telling you all along. This chap's a fool. He won't let sleeping dogs lie. If he'd let her produce her hammer and tell her story, how much harm was that going to do him ? Unless you could trace the hammer to him, and even so you'd have your work cut out to prove it was used in the Chigwell case. But he lost his head, the way murderers mostly do."

"Another point's occurred to me," said Burke abruptly. "How did Bess get to the cottage ? The bus doesn't go within a couple of miles, and I don't see Bess walking half that distance."

"Nor do I," agreed Crook heartily. "I'd say she drove."

"You mean—by car ?"

"Well, she didn't go by bicycle or they'd have found the bicycle. Anyway, she hadn't got a bicycle. I enquired."

"There can't have been many cars out in a fog like that," suggested Burke. "It was all right later in the evening, but it was thick enough between five and six."

"And even so we can't exactly advertise for details of the cars that were out," agreed Crook. "I suppose a jane like that 'ud take a lift from a gorilla if he offered one."

"No caution at all," returned Burke. "Mind you, anyone who knew her—and a good many people did—would offer Bess a lift." He paused. "I suppose that couldn't be the explanation, that she went with some stranger. . . ."

"Who put the note in her bag ?"

"No. I didn't mean that. I meant that he might have given her a lift, and then. . . ."

" You've been reading fairy-tales," Crook told him frankly.
" That girl could look after herself, if anyone could. Besides,
there were none of the disarranged details so beloved of the
Sunday press, nothing but the button missing, and that might
have just fallen off."

" Bess always looked as though she'd come out of a band-
box," said Burke quickly. " It's not like her to go out minus a
button."

" Then perhaps she gave it to the chap for a keepsake. Anyway, it wasn't torn off. There are loose threads."

" The whole case is loose threads," said Burke, beginning to
lost patience. " If only I could put my finger on the thing that's
wrong. I think it's the rendezvous. I mean, if I wanted a
place where I could talk quietly I wouldn't go so far afield."

" If you wanted to murder a woman on the quiet you could
hardly do better," Crook assured him. " Two miles from a bus,
well off the high-road, solitary. And if anyone should see a man
and a girl going that way they'd be likely to be delicate about
it and not look too close or ask too many questions. Oh, he had
his head screwed on all right, this murderer of ours, only he's
like too many of these chaps, will overload the bus and then he's
surprised it breaks down."

" The police didn't find the hammer at the cottage," said
Burke. " They don't like the laity asking questions, but they
did admit that. Doesn't that seem significant ? "

" Too damned significant," said Crook. " It means one of
two things—either the hammer is important or X wants us to
think it is. Might be interesting to learn who knew she had
the hammer—besides you."

" I gather a good many people saw the tank being drained.
You know how it is, anything at all out of the ordinary makes
people stop, and there have been so many pictures in the papers
of things found there, well, it increases curiosity."

" Besides, they might have found another body or a part of
one. Hope springs eternal—you know."

" Do you think," enquired Burke a little diffidently, " the
hammer really was used ? "

" It could be," said Crook. " It could be. Anybody certain
the girl took the hammer ? No, don't tell me she said she was
goin' to. Because what the soldier said ain't evidence."

" I suppose Cotham would know what tools he had on the
premises," suggested Burke. " If there's an extra hammer—
besides, it would be in Bess's room. Only, if you're asking me,
I'd say she took it with her."

" So should I," agreed Crook. " Well, we can ask a few

questions. Trouble is half the time you can't believe the answers."

The police went on methodically with their enquiries. They got into touch with Cotham and checked up on Burke's telephone calls. Cotham said he remembered the first one, because Bess had just gone out, and the second, he thought, was about five. He couldn't actually place the third, but he'd been able to hear the sound of a dance band on Burke's wireless—and there was a dance band on shortly after six. That fixed it pretty closely. He didn't remember hearing the wireless at five, but he was ready to swear to the time. The policeman went on to see Mrs. McKay. He'd put a man on the spot to see that Burke didn't come back and prime her. Of course he could telephone, but as soon as the man saw the housekeeper he hadn't many apprehensions on that score. He'd as soon have tried to melt a rock as get her to tell a fancy story. Mrs. McKay, as he had anticipated, bore out the main points of Burke's story. She had found the letter on her way back from shopping, and it had been striking four when she got into her room. She had gone out just after three and the letter hadn't been on the mat then. She had taken it straight up to Mr. Burke, and he had looked at it and put it in his pocket.

" You didn't see him open it ? "

Mrs. McKay took umbrage. " I'm not interested in other people's letters," she said.

" You're going to be the only woman in a ten-mile radius who isn't when this breaks," the man assured her.

He gathered that she didn't sympathise with Bess. " Girls like that can't expect to die decently in their beds," she said. " Mr. Burke, he was wild about her. She did that to all kinds of men. That young chap they've taken for the murder—I wouldn't be surprised to know she knew more there than she'd say."

" I take it you're prepared to substantiate that," said the policeman, and she said coldly she was never one to gossip. She added that she couldn't abide women that weren't content to be what Nature made them, but no one was contented these days to look themselves. She said that she didn't remember what programme was on Mr. Burke's wireless (this in reply to another question) but it was noisy, all wireless programmes were. He was a terror for the wireless, just as if there wasn't enough noise in the world anyhow.

On the whole the authorities didn't get much satisfaction out of her.

" Of course, we're hampered by the fact that we can only

work on the evidence," said Marlow later in the day. "Crook has the advantage of us there."

Like a good many men in his position, he didn't pretend to like Crook but he had to admire his results. A man who could create a glorified mountain out of a molehill half the world wouldn't even notice, could be trusted to make a three-part fairy-tale out of a murdered girl, a missing hammer and two forged notes.

Crook at that moment was feeling far from sanguine. He'd have told you that though his conscience mightn't be that of the average man in the street, it was capable of giving him hell just the same. He wasn't fool enough to hold himself responsible for what had happened to Bess—he'd warned her to come straight to him if there were any developments. What this girl should have done was to have kept her mouth shut and come speeding to him like an arrow winging towards its target. It wasn't safe when you were playing with murder to assume anyone could be trusted. He wondered who had seen her buy the hammer. He got in touch with Bairstowe at the inn that night, and asked him if he knew anything, and Bairstowe said he'd congratulated her on picking up a hammer for nothing, practically. She'd said Cotham wanted it, but Cotham said he didn't know what they were talking about. Bess hadn't mentioned a hammer to him. Anyway he had all the hammers he needed.

The man who called himself Clarke and was the darts expert joined them and said he understood the young lady had been found. He said it in an undertone and added that it was a bad break for the landlord. Crook said that was the kind of world it was and offered to take him on at darts. He mightn't look much with his tubby figure and his thick red thatched eyebrows, his little red-brown eyes and his enormous red-brown suit, but you had to admit that he threw a pretty dart. Clarke said thoughtfully, "If you're as good at detecting as you are at darts the murderer ought to be shaking in his shoes."

"Heard of me, have you?" said Crook. "That's nice."

Clarke said, "You'd be difficult to forget," and Crook grinned. If you wanted people to look for you you had to stand out from the ruck, he told him, and personally he always suspected men who were afraid of being conspicuous; it showed they had something to hide. All the same, he didn't feel jovial. He was wondering whether this case was going to end without a third murder being committed. There was danger everywhere. He thought he'd better keep a close eye on Burke. A man with two murders to his credit isn't going to hesitate if a third will save his life for him. And there was no doubt about it, Burke was important. Crook couldn't afford to lose him. Losing Bess was bad enough in all conscience. It occurred to him as he neared his destination to wonder if anyone had told young Jardine, and if so what his reaction would be.

But the next sensation wasn't provided by Crook or Burke, as it happened. It came via someone hitherto unconnected with the case and it achieved publicity through that indefatigable parliamentarian, Mr. Allen Wilkinson Stout.

CHAPTER ELEVEN

FOLLOWING his grim discovery in the derelict cottage, Fate, who clearly had never intended Mr. Stout for obscurity, showered attentions upon him in the shape of interviews (police, press and constituents), and correspondence (constituents pointing out that they hadn't sent him to Westminster to get involved in scandals with barmaids, and busybodies offering him advice, to say nothing of anonymous letters of every description) and an occasional telegram or telephone for makeweight. Mr. Stout was furious. He said he wasn't a business man and he wasn't an actor, and he could get all the advertisement he wanted by means of a few well-chosen words in the Chamber at any time.

" I'm surprised at you, Allen," said his mother, quite inaccurately, for no one could surprise her. Her son used to think that if she'd been given an overseas command the whole history of the war might have been altered. " A man who enters the political ring should be prepared for anything."

" Oh, I know murder's just a word in a printed book to you," retorted her son hotly, " but then you didn't find the body."

" If you were a film star instead of a Member of Parliament you'd be hopping with delight at all this publicity," Lady Catherine reminded him.

" I've already received a number of more or less unveiled suggestions that I'm in some way implicated—those who hide know where to find kind of thing—and Miss Armitage has told me to my face that if I'd had the cottage closed down as she suggested, in the interests of morality, a thing like this couldn't have happened."

" A face like hers could never further the interests of morality," said Lady Catherine, thus disposing of Miss Armitage. " And personally I wouldn't give a snap of the fingers for a murderer who abandoned his plans simply because a particular site was closed to him. A man of any ambition would instantly find another."

" I wish you'd tell Miss Armitage that. She regards me as an accessory before the fact, as it is."

" If you are going to let a little thing like that upset you you shouldn't have gone into Parliament," said his mother, more coldly than before. " You might point out to her, too, that if you'd pulled the cottage down brick by brick with your own hands it wouldn't have prevented the locals making love, which is why she wanted you to take action. If she'd ever tried going to the bad herself she'd appreciate so obvious a fact."

Mr. Stout felt like a Victorian spinster enclosed in a walled field with a determined cow. Not that Lady Catherine was remotely like a cow ; she was one of those deceptively fragile women who used to be described as eggshell, but she was as tough as a 1000 lb. bomb and quite as ruthless.

He picked up his pen and said in a desperate sort of voice that he'd got to write to the Minister of Health about spinsters' pensions.

" What about them ? " enquired Lady Catherine.

" They're asking for them at fifty-five," explained her son, " and I think they have a case. After all, poor girls, it's not their fault. They probably did their best."

" It might even be their good fortune," suggested Lady Catherine. Mr. Stout shut up like a daisy at closing time. His mother was always having that effect on him.

" Anyway, they have my sympathy," he said rather desperately.

" If you really mean that you should stand at Whipley Cross-roads with a label round your neck. There'd be at least one spinster less within the half-hour."

" It's not a Member's job to find husbands for his con-stituents," said a defeated Mr. Stout.

" It would get you a lot of women's votes at the next election if you did. Good Heavens, what's this coming up the drive ? "

It might have been St. George complete with the dragon from the tone of her voice, but Mr. Stout was so driven he'd have welcomed the dragon unaccompanied as an alternative to the terrible Lady Catherine.

" Probably a representative of ENSA," said his mother. " No one else would dare come calling in a top-hat."

" A top-hat ? " repeated the dazed Mr. Stout.

" Now, Allen, mind, not more than half a guinea," she told him. " I know you'll have to give something because of the war and the shows for Our Boys, but if you do anything con-spicuous you'll jeopardise the Nonconformist vote. They think of entertainment in terms of Tea and Table-Games."

Mr. Stout stood up and looked over her shoulder. The most extraordinary little figure was certainly advancing towards him. From the curly-brimmed top-hat to the tips of the polished pointed boots he looked like something out of a Christmas supplement. Mr. Stout had only to close his eyes to see sprigs on a satin waistcoat, and when he opened them again there were the yellow gloves, the silk handkerchief of fierce design and the cane with the clouded amber handle.

" He's much more likely to be collecting for the ' Salute the Soldier ' campaign," announced Mr. Stout, but his mother had the last word as usual. Even at Waterloo, she said, they weren't equipped like that. Then a maid came in and said a Mr. Posselthwaite was asking if he could see the Member. Mr. Stout began to ask what was Mr. Posselthwaite's business, but he didn't get far, for the little figure suddenly bounded into the room, saying with some indignation, " That is not the message I requested you to deliver. I believe I am addressing Mr. Stout ? "

" Yes," agreed the Member, wondering if he looked as dazed as he felt. Constituents were supposed to come at stated times and by appointment with his agent, not march up the drive as though he kept a shop and they'd bounced in to buy. He looked round for his mother, but she had disappeared like Nellie Wallace in a pantomime.

" I have the honour to be one of your constituents," continued the apparition, taking off his hat (thus proving he was human and not a marionette as Mr. Stout had for a moment imagined) and laying it with the cane and gloves on a chair, " I have always voted as a conservative, no matter who the personal Member might be. My father taught me that a bad conservative was better than a good radical, since conservatism has its roots in the history of our country, whereas radicalism is . . . "

" Tell me how I can help you," interrupted Mr. Stout, wondering if the little fellow had escaped from somewhere and, if so, how soon they'd find him. He rather hoped they wouldn't track him here. A corpse and a cuckoo in one week were more than even the reputation of a Member of Parliament could stand.

" I believe I am correct in saying that I have the right to claim your attention," the little man continued.

" Certainly," acknowledged Mr. Stout in a voice that suggested he wasn't altogether sure about that.

" That," agreed his visitor, " is how I read our bargain. We send you to Parliament and in return you are available to redress our—grievances."

" Well," murmured Mr. Stout cautiously, " naturally I do

my best. Very glad of the opportunity," he added, remembering his parliamentary manners. He offered his visitor a chair. The little man—Mr. Stout put him down at about 70—sat down and touched his fine white moustache. Sympathetically Mr. Stout smoothed his.

"This is the first time I have ever approached my parliamentary representative in a personal capacity," said Mr. Posselthwaite. "But I have a right to claim that justice shall be done to me as an individual and representative of the thousands of voters in your constituency."

Mr. Stout suppressed a sigh. Another lunatic, probably a man with a persecution mania. There were several of them at the House, tackling one Member after another with a laudable lack of prejudice.

"You must tell me," he began, and Mr. Posselthwaite interjected, "That, my dear sir, is why I am here. I have not come to ask for pecuniary assistance or to suggest that you alter the laws of the country to benefit me as an individual. I am not, I hope, a grasping person ; all I require is the freedom of my two rooms, such services as my landlady is prepared to give me, and a little paper and ink."

"You—er—write ? " murmured Mr. Stout intelligently.

"I am at present engaged on a work to be entitled ' The Evolution of Manners in Anglo-Saxon Britain.' But that is not why I am here to-day. As I say, I do not wish to make any extravagant claims. I am not of those who complain of the action of the Chancellor of the Exchequer in taking half my income for his own purposes. On the contrary, I congratulate myself that I am permitted to retain half my income for my own use. But—and this is the crux of the situation—none of these advantages will continue to benefit me unless I retain the necessary liberty to enjoy them."

It was just what Mr. Stout had supposed. He was cuckoo, and either his relatives, clearly more intelligent than himself, were trying to put him under restraint, or else he'd managed to give his keeper the slip. A normal person would never have thought of approaching a Member of Parliament in this contingency.

"You mean, someone is trying to deprive you of your liberty ? " It was a delicate way of saying that he supposed someone was trying to shut the little fellow up.

"Believe me, Mr. Stout, there is a plot on foot to rob me of my life." He leaned back as he spoke and folded his arms across his chest.

Mr. Stout said, displaying the enterprise for which he was

notorious at Westminster, " Well, that's a matter for the police, you know."

Mr. Posselthwaite's eyebrows bristled. " On the contrary, I have every right to demand protection from my Member. I expect you to take the necessary steps to secure my safety. That is not, I believe, an unreasonable demand."

It was perfectly obvious he didn't think it was.

" Suppose you open up a little," suggested Mr. Stout. " Who's trying to murder you ? "

" That," said Mr. Posselthwaite, " is what I wish you to ascertain. I have not the smallest notion why my existence should be offensive to anyone. I find it hard to believe that I possess anything that can be of value to a living soul ; my means are exceedingly small, there is no one living who has, as we say vulgarly, expectations from me, I have no goods of any particular value—and yet it is not only my life but my goods also that are threatened by this—ruffian or ruffians, whoever they may be."

In spite of himself Mr. Stout began to feel interested. At least it made a change from the innumerable constituents who wanted sons and husbands home on compassionate leave at a time when the authorities wouldn't sanction such requests for the purpose of keeping a business going. " Do you mean someone's broken into your house—and assaulted you ? " he enquired.

" When I was out recently—the fellow is clearly a coward who dare not meet me face to face—a man called and enquired for me, having, doubtless, assured himself that I was not at home. He represented himself as being a relative of mine, which is absurd, since at my age a man must not be surprised to find himself without living relatives. He even produced a letter, so my landlady assures me, purporting to be signed by me, in which I invited him to call at that particular hour and to wait until my return, should I chance to be out."

" Didn't she notice it wasn't your handwriting ? " asked Mr. Stout.

" Mrs. Lewis is an excellent cook, within the limited range permitted by the Ministry of Food, but she cooks by instinct rather than by intelligence. The notion of comparing the handwriting would not occur to her. I speak with certainty since I raised the point myself. I may say she was inclined to take umbrage."

" Could she describe him ? " asked Mr. Stout, wondering if these questions put him in the wrong with the police. A Member of Parliament isn't allowed to intervene in matters that are the concern of the Local Authority.

" She just said he was a man wearing a coat with a turned-up collar and a hat pulled down over his face. She is an excellent woman in many ways, but a trifle wall-eyed, and the hall in that house is very dark."

" So she let him go up ? "

" She did. It was most remiss of her and I told her so, but she is like so many ladies. They may see both sides of a case, but your side is always the wrong one."

" Was anything missing ? " enquired Mr. Stout.

" So far as I am aware—nothing. And my possessions are so few I find it difficult to believe I should not notice any loss."

" The chap wasn't there when you got back ? Didn't wait, I mean ? "

" I thought," observed Mr. Posselthwaite in a pained voice, " that I had made it clear the visit was not a casual one. Whoever it was had informed himself that I should be spending that afternoon at the Domesday Hall. I assist the local Home Guard Office with their records on Tuesday afternoons and I am never back till about six o'clock."

" Surely your landlady would have known that ? " suggested Mr. Stout, feeling he was doing rather well for a layman.

" It was about five when this person made his impudent appearance, and according to the forged letter I intended to return earlier than usual. Naturally, this was not, in fact, the case, and at about twenty minutes past five the man, whoever he was, came down the stairs and called out from the hall that he was unable to wait, that he had left a note."

" And had he ? " asked Mr. Stout simply.

" Oh no," replied Mr. Posselthwaite in a patient tone. " That was intended to deceive Mrs. Lewis. She assures me that she hurried from the kitchen—although hurrying is a euphuism where she is concerned—but she was too late to see him. She heard the front door close and by the time she had reached it the visitor had disappeared. It was a damp night and she says she never saw his face clearly."

" How very mysterious ! " murmured Mr. Stout, now thoroughly intrigued and not caring whether he was poaching on the police's preserves or not. " Were there any other incidents ? "

" The following day I found myself standing in a very crowded bus going into Halton. As you are aware, there is some dissatisfaction locally at the withdrawal by the Company of a number of vehicles. Those that remain are always unpleasantly overcrowded, and when I realised that another passenger had his hand in my pocket I naturally assumed it to be an accident.

But in the light of subsequent developments I am less certain. On my alighting from the bus I contrived in some way to lose my footing. Some fellow whose face I could not see assisted me to my feet, but I am certain that in so doing he contrived to examine the contents of my pocket."

"That," reflected Mr. Stout, losing interest a little, "sounds highly improbable." But he didn't say so. For all his smallness of stature and apparent fragility, he thought Mr. Posselthwaite had probably been a tiger in a previous incarnation.

"Next," continued the visitor inexorably, "came the attempt on my life." He paused. "I must add that I have absolutely no proof of what I tell you, but then it is unusual for men to attempt murder in the presence of witnesses. I was taking my usual constitutional down the Pikle, which is normally deserted since the building of the by-pass, when I was aware of a motor vehicle coming up very fast behind me. I instinctively drew near the wall, for so many unusual types of vehicle are seen among us now that one must be prepared for all eventualities, and the path there is not very wide. Looking over my shoulder, however, I saw that it was a small dark car bearing down upon me, driven by a man who had apparently taken leave of his senses."

"Scorching?" suggested Mr. Stout, beaming with intelligence.

"If that is the appropriate word," agreed Mr. Posselthwaite. "He must have seen me, in spite of the fact that he wore a hat pulled low over his forehead, but he came so close that he almost grazed my knuckles, and even so I had drawn quite close to the wall. I admit that I was angry at the discourtesy. There was no excuse for it. There was plenty of room in the lane for myself and a car of far greater dimensions. He went past at this tremendous pace—scorching, I think you said is the word —and was shortly out of sight. I proceeded at my normal rate (And if, thought Mr. Stout, you're no quicker on your feet than you are with your tongue he was probably at Timbuktu before you reached the cross-roads) and presently I was aware of a car coming from the opposite direction—that is, coming directly at me. I am naturally aware of the rule of the road— face oncoming traffic, and the traffic that comes up behind you is responsible for your safety."

"I've never thought that a very consoling idea," murmured Mr. Stout, "if they don't accept their responsibility, that is."

But the little figure had a true British disregard for such considerations. "It seemed to me that this car was proceeding at practically the same pace as the first, and I began to wonder if this might be some civilian exercise—by which I mean a military exercise in which the participants wear civilian dress—and I was perhaps unwittingly trespassing on ground that had been reserved, so to speak, from the public. This car also seemed to be travelling in a most reckless fashion, and I drew near the edge of the ditch to prevent myself being seriously splashed. To my horror, just as the vehicle drew almost abreast, the driver swerved and it was only by the greatest agility that I avoided a fatal collision."

He stood up to illustrate what had actually happened. Mr. Stout was surprised to realise that for all he looked as though he'd been picked out of a museum his use of the word agility had not been misplaced. There was a remarkable suppleness about his movements, and his hand-grip, as Mr. Stout later discovered, was that of a man twenty years his junior.

" Nippy on your pins," commented Mr. Stout admiringly. " Mr.—er—that is, Captain . . . " (He never could remember people's titles, and for some reason the little man with his finicky band-box air suggested the army.)

" No," said Mr. Posselthwaite in rather sharp tones, and Mr. Stout thought he coloured, though whether with pride at being mistaken for an army man or with embarrassment at the inevitable denial the other couldn't be sure. " As a matter of fact I was—er—connected with the entertainment world."

" Of course," thought Mr. Stout. " That's what he really reminded me of—a colonel—or perhaps a major—on the stage." And aloud he said heartily, " My mother suggested ENSA when she saw you coming up the drive."

Mr. Posselthwaite looked really distressed now. The Member thought he was probably one of those old-time ham actors who play little character parts in touring companies. That would account for the impression he made of having been about a good deal—South Africa, probably, Australia—and all the minor towns in Britain, minor from the entertainment point of view, that is—like Oldham, Bolton, Wolverhampton, Wigan. . . . He wondered what the little chap lived on now. Being in Parliament made you think a lot about ways and means, because constituents were perpetually drawing your attention to their financial difficulties. A little legacy perhaps—or a grant from some theatrical charity—or even a pension from relatives who didn't particularly want to know him. Mr. Stout, who'd have made an admirable novelist if he'd been able to spell or understand the foundations of grammar—decided he looked like a man with a story. But then if Mr. Posselthwaite had said he'd trained seals Mr. Stout would at once have looked for that kind of

95

resemblance, and found it, for he was a tenacious creature and his experience had increased his natural gifts.

"Now," continued Mr. Stout briskly, "you are quite sure you are not—er—exaggerating a somewhat odd coincidence?"

The little figure stiffened; the old elegant face was rigid with distaste.

"I fear we cannot hope for a speedy end to hostilities if those who represent us at Westminster wilfully close their eyes to realities," he said.

Mr. Stout blinked. For a moment he had fancied himself back in the Chamber. Weakly he gave in.

"Do you mean to tell me it was the same car?" he asked.

"I am convinced it was the same car. Mind you, I admit I was unable to see the driver's face. . . . "

"And of course you didn't notice the number?"

"The number?" Stout thought it probable the old fellow had never realised that cars carry numbers. Rip Van Winkle was his middle name. Probably he'd never spoken on the telephone or owned a wireless.

"In plain words, Mr. Stout, that driver deliberately attempted to run me down." Then, as Stout continued silent, he enquired in offended tones, "May I ask, sir, if you consider me a fool? or inebriated?"

"It sounds like something off the films to me," confessed his parliamentary representative.

The old face opposite his twisted in an expression of disdain. "One of the mistakes that *young* men are so fond of making is to suppose that film stories are original. Why, take the word of a man who has seen a good deal of the world in his time, there is nothing shown on a screen that has not its facsimile in real life."

"You win," said Mr. Stout. "By the way, when did this happen?"

"Yesterday afternoon. I should have called yesterday at about six o'clock, but I was a little disturbed by the occurrence and decided to sleep on it. However, I am convinced that there is a definite plot against me, though for what reason I cannot imagine, and I feel I must claim the protection I have a right to demand from my parliamentary representative."

Mr. Stout thought if he used that expression again he'd go womanish on him and scream. He wished, too, that Miss Bennett was there to advise him. If you were a Member of Parliament things kept happening to you all the time, not, as appeared to be the case with old jossers like this one, just now and again. A couple of murder attempts in one afternoon was tough—

granted. But look at the age of the old boy—and this kind of thing couldn't have happened to him often or he'd either be dead or hardened to it.

" Well, actually the people for you to approach, as I said before, are the police," he said.

" The police exist to detect crime when it has been committed," said Mr. Posselthwaite. " That is certainly more profitable from their point of view than preventing it. Doubtless it would delight the local constable to run my murderer to earth, but you appreciate that it would be of little service to me. No, I am here to ask your advice."

" As to why these attempts are being made ? My dear sir, how can I possibly guess ? It sounds to me like the work of a homicidal maniac."

The little man drew himself up. " Are you seriously suggesting the Home Office would grant a licence to a lunatic to drive a car ? And if you are making such a suggestion I would point out that a question in the House would not come amiss."

Mr. Stout was too broken to protest. Anyway, it was no more ridiculous than a good many other questions that get put to long-suffering Ministers three days out of six.

" Well, if you can't suggest anything better," he observed, but in his own heart he wasn't sure that the maniac was necessarily the man in the car.

" And even allowing you are right," continued Mr. Posselthwaite, who clearly had a one-track mind. " How does that explain the mysterious visit to my room ? "

Mr. Stout had to admit he'd forgotten about that. " Quite true," he said, making a swift recovery. " Then clearly you've got something somebody else wants. And it's no use asking me what that is," he added quickly, " because I couldn't possibly know."

" Nothing out of the ordinary has happened recently that could account for such mysterious conduct," Mr. Posselthwaite assured him. " I follow a very simple regimen, a short constitutional after breakfast, an occasional trip by bus to execute one or two small commissions. I play such part as my years and abilities admit in the national effort. I attend divine service on Sundays. . . . "

" In a minute," thought Mr. Stout, " he'll be telling me what temperature he has his bath." And aloud he added, " Nothing stands out in your memory ? "

" Nothing," said his visitor firmly. He drew the fiercely-designed silk handkerchief from his pocket and something tinkled to the ground. Mr. Stout stooped politely to retrieve it. But instead of handing it back to his companion he remained in a curved attitude, gowking at what he had picked up.

It was a scarlet button shaped like a dolphin and when he saw that, Mr. Stout knew why Mr. Posselthwaite was being followed, and he knew, too, that he hadn't exaggerated the danger in which he stood.

CHAPTER TWELVE

THERE was a long pause.

" I beg your pardon ! " said Mr. Posselthwaite at last, and his Member came back to life.

" There's your answer," he said, slamming the button on the table. " Why on earth didn't you tell me you'd got that ? "

" Do you suggest that that offers any explanation . . . ? "

" Of course," said Mr. Stout. " How did you get hold of it ? "

The old gentleman bent his noble hawk-like nose over the gaudy trifle. " Ah dear ! For the moment, I had forgotten. As a matter of fact, I had been hoping for an opportunity to return it, but I fear it is unlikely. . . . "

" It's not only unlikely, it's absolutely out of the question," said Mr. Stout bluntly.

" If I could meet the lady again—she at all events would recognise me. . . . "

" You won't, not this side of the cemetery. Look here, this is what I'm trying to say. That button is an important clue in a murder mystery. It's no wonder someone wants to relieve you of it. That's why your room's been ransacked and some chap's been trying to run you down."

" Murder ? " The old gentleman sat very still. " But—I had no notion. . . . "

" Good Heavens, man ! " exclaimed Mr. Stout, exasperated at last. " Don't you ever see the papers ? "

" I subscribe to *The Times*—naturally," returned Mr. Posselthwaite, " though I fear it is not the paper it was in my father's day. But really, sir, I fail to see. . . . "

" Never heard of *The News of the World*, I suppose ? " suggested Mr. Stout.

" That is—er—a Sunday organ, I understand. I do not read newspapers on Sundays. I remember so well the days of our great Queen, days that I fear have gone beyond recall. In those days . . . "

" I was going to say that if you did read *The News of the World* you'd understand why this button's so important. The police are anxious to trace the movements of the girl who wore the coat from which this button was—was detached." As so often in the House, he found he'd got tied up and couldn't end his sentence gracefully. " Now, if you can remember the circumstances in which you found the button and can give that information to the police, they may be able to follow up and find out who killed the girl."

" Murder ! " said Mr. Posselthwaite for the second time, not having, apparently, taken it in at first.

" Yes," said Mr. Stout patiently, " Murder. And the police don't know who did it."

Mr. Posselthwaite looked horrified. " You are surely not suggesting, sir, that I . . . "

" Of course not." These old bustards were all chock-full of vanity. Why, Bess could have wrung his skinny neck with one hand. " But—where did you find that button ? "

" I discovered it in the road just after the lady left me. It must have fallen off her coat unperceived by us. . . . "

" And where were you ? " Mr. Stout felt like a child trying to steer its engine away from the kerb.

" I was waiting for the bus to Pheasant Green. It was that very foggy afternoon, and I had to go over on business—important business. I had serious doubts as to my wisdom in attempting the journey in such weather, but I had made the appointment and these fogs are frequently merely local, and I had no means of warning my host that I could not keep the appointment. The lady—whose name I did not know and whom I had not previously met—was also waiting. We—er—got into conversation."

Trust Bess, thought Stout, surprised that he should know so much about a girl he, too, had never met—not living, that is. She'd talk to a wig on a bed-knob sooner than nothing.

" She asked me if I thought the bus would run in such weather, and when I said I devoutly hoped so she observed that we seemed to be the only two optimists in the neighbourhood. She volunteered the information that she was meeting a friend at a tea-shop, and she hoped the fog wouldn't put him off."

He stopped. " Yes—go on," said Mr. Stout in goaded tones.

" I remember now, though I do not think I paid much attention to the fact at the time, that she seemed a little—perturbed. I naturally asked no questions. It was not for me to betray any vulgar curiosity, but—I have always been interested in my fellow-creatures. I thought she was afraid that her companion—her would-be companion—might make the fog an excuse for not putting in an appearance."

" She didn't happen to mention who her companion was,"
said Mr. Stout, but even he knew the answer to that one.

" No, no. We did not become so—er—intimate as that.
I noticed, however, that she was twisting the button round and
round while she spoke."

" Didn't she wear anything over the red coat on an afternoon
like that ? " demanded Mr. Stout, incredulously.

" She had a white mackintosh over her shoulders, but it was
not fastened in any way. I remember, too, she wore a scarf of
some bright colour, though the fog dulled it somewhat. However,
this was shortly after four and it was not until about six that
the fog became almost impenetrable. The bus back," added
Mr. Posselthwaite, " was an hour behind time, and the driver
observed to me that it was suicide driving at all."

" Would you know the lady again ? " asked Mr. Stout, and
then reflected that that was a foolish question. Because the
Bess he had found in the cottage bore little resemblance to the
girl who had talked so anxiously to Mr. Posselthwaite, and
anyway it was too late to do any identification this side of
Judgment Day.

" I can assure you she was no one I had met before and I
cannot pretend that I saw her very clearly. One cannot precisely
stare at a lady. . . . "

It wasn't any good. Though it was a safe bet he'd never seen
Bess before. You wouldn't find him in a bar, and if you did
he'd hardly recognise a barmaid from a block of wood.

" The odd thing is," his visitor continued, " that she seemed
to know who I was. Now that is very surprising, for I am not
a man who, as they say, gets about a great deal, and certainly
not in circles that young ladies frequent. She asked me, I
remember, if I didn't lodge with Mrs. Lewis, and she even told
me some quite gratuitous facts about Mrs. Lewis's husband,
who, it appears, did not treat her well. Indeed, if it is not
ungallant to say so, she was like Tennyson's brook."

" And if you'd given her half a chance she'd probably have
told you your personal history or mine, and she'd have got quite
half of it right. Did she make the journey with you ? " But
she couldn't have done, or why had the old gentleman still got
the button ?

" As a matter of fact she had left me before the bus arrived."

" Couldn't wait, eh ? Or got a lift ? "

" Some friend of hers came past in a car and appeared to
recognise her. He called her by her name and she went across
and said, ' I was beginning to think I should be there when they
rang the bells for the Armistice.' "

" The devil she did ! " ejaculated Mr. Stout softly. " And you've had all this information for days, and the police yearning for it like the hart for the water-brooks. . . . You seem to attract cars, don't you ? I mean . . . " He stopped abruptly, feeling that was one of the things that might have been more happily put.

Mr. Posselthwaite was very much on his dignity. " I hardly see how I was supposed to recognise that. A lady exchanges a word with me at a bus stop, a friend driving a car comes past and offers her a lift, and she accepts. Really, Mr. Member, it is unreasonable to suggest that I should instantly approach the police. Why, they would consider me unbalanced."

" Not instantly," said Mr. Stout. " Approach the police, I mean. Only when the news got round that a girl had been found strangled. Of course, I understand you didn't appreciate it was the same girl, but all the same it's a rare piece of luck for the police."

Mr. Posselthwaite, however, refused to be mollified. " I fear that any information I can give the police will be of little assistance. It is, for instance, only surmise that this is the lady who has been—has been ill-used. . . . "

" Not forgetting the button, are you ? " said Mr. Stout. " I mean, there won't be so many buttons like that going round the place, and even if there's more than one set the police can find out if any of them are missing."

Reluctantly his visitor yielded the point. " Nevertheless," he added, " it is hardly for me to intervene in a police case without invitation."

Mr. Stout, suppressing the ungallant supposition that all his voters were zanies and, as such, entirely ignorant of the law, said very politely that where murder was in question every citizen was automatically on the side of the police (who represented the people) and was therefore bound to give any relevant information. In fact, he added for Mr. Posselthwaite's benefit, any citizen had the right to arrest a criminal.

" Indeed ! " said Mr. Posselthwaite. " Now I had supposed that to be the prerogative of the authorities."

" I take it," said Mr. Stout without any hope at all, " you wouldn't recognise the man again."

" You are perhaps forgetting that there was a fog that afternoon and that the car was on the far side of the road."

" That's odd," said Mr. Stout. " It ought to have been on your side."

" It was coming in the opposite direction," said the old man, stiffly.

"Not going towards Pheasant Green at all? That's illuminating." But of course the body had been found in a cottage nowhere near Pheasant Green. He began to think Mr. Posselthwaite wasn't the only muddled thinker in the Division. Resolutely—for years of experience with constituents had given him perseverance—he ploughed on.

"You wouldn't know the voice again, either?"

"I should hesitate most strongly to involve a man in a serious charge on the strength of a few words overheard in a fog," Mr. Posselthwaite rebuked him. Mr. Stout thought probably the police would agree with him there.

"And the same perhaps applies to the car? You wouldn't know that again."

"It was a smallish car, as cars go, and dark. But then doubtless any car would have appeared dark in such weather."

"It didn't seem the same to you as the car that tried to run you down?"

That tickled the old man's imagination. "Really—my dear sir—of course it is impossible to say with any certainty, but I could state that it was not unlike it."

"I'm afraid that won't help the police much. Now one more thing—and I should like to thank you for the very substantial help you are giving us in this matter—can you remember if the lady said anything?"

"I cannot remember her precise words, which were indicative of satisfaction at not having to wait any longer."

"She didn't call the driver anything? Not John? or Archibald? or William?"

But Mr. Posselthwaite said he feared he had no answer to that one. Mr. Stout didn't say anything. He hadn't really had any hopes. One other thought occurred to him, however.

"Did she say good-bye to you?"

His visitor looked startled. "I—think not. But really there was no reason why she should."

"I only ask because it's possible the driver didn't realise you were there. It might make a lot of difference."

"As a matter of fact as the car drew up I drew back. It is quite possible he was not aware of my presence."

"All the same," reflected Mr. Stout, "he must have known about you, afterwards. Which means she must have said something."

It was obvious that Mr. Posselthwaite did not follow him. "Otherwise why is this chap trying to run you down? Obviously he wants the button. He couldn't know you had the button if Miss Carter hadn't said something to him."

" But," the little old gentleman was completely bewildered, " Miss Carter cannot have known I had the button."

" She could put two and two together as well as most people. Once she was in the car she may have noticed the button was missing. According to reports she was fussy about things like that, never went out without a button on her coat. ' Bother,' she might say, ' I've lost a button, and I know I had it a minute ago because I was playing about with it while I talked to '— did she know your name ? "

" I really have no notion."

" Well, anyway, she might say she was talking to someone, and he'd ask who it was, and if she told him where you lived that would probably help him to identify you. I mean . . . " He hesitated, searching for a polite way of saying there couldn't be two like him in the world let alone a Parliamentary Division.

" If he recognised his danger surely he would have—postponed—his violent action," offered the visitor.

" Perhaps he couldn't afford to postpone it. By the way, do you remember if she was carrying anything ? "

But Mr. Posselthwaite was quite unable to help him here.

" At all events, X suspected you had the button, and once you realised its value and went to the police he stood in considerable danger, more danger than he would in any case," he wound up in his rather involved fashion.

" But if he was not aware that I had the button . . . ? "

" He wasn't taking any chances, and there was always the possibility that you might be able to identify him or the car."

" But even supposing he had regained possession of the button," Mr. Posselthwaite clung obstinately to his argument, " what was there to prevent my going to the police, when I realised its significance ? "

" It wouldn't have been the same thing," said Mr. Stout. " The police have to have proof, and unless you had the button they couldn't swear (a) that it was the one they were looking for, or (b)—now don't get annoyed—that you'd ever had it anyhow. If you'd had nearly as much to do with the police as I have," wound up Mr. Stout earnestly, " you'll know they won't recognise the alphabet unless you've crossed the ' T ' and dotted the ' I.' And they'll tell you that half a score of people have given them stories about the button. It's a sort of phobia, a seeking for the limelight—psychopathic," he added, hoping he'd got the right word.

The little figure beside him made a gesture of distaste. " We were more—controlled, in my youth," he said. " We left medical matters to the medical profession, and our minds to our Maker."

Even the ready Mr. Stout couldn't find any answer to that. He saw that to Mr. Posselthwaite's simple intelligence all these scientific phrases were merely grandiloquent ways of saying there were a lot of liars on the market.

" Well," he said, trying to sound as assured as was suitable for a Member of Parliament, " the next thing to do is to get in touch with the police and hand over the button. I shouldn't waste any time if I were you."

" Dear me ! " said Mr. Posselthwaite. " I had hoped that by coming to you I might avoid that necessity."

" Now that you realise where the button came from you would be an accessory after the fact if you didn't make such a statement," Mr. Stout pointed out, " and what's more," he added, the truth striking forcibly home, " I should be an accessory, too."

" I suppose it would not be sufficient for you to make the report," suggested Mr. Posselthwaite.

Mr. Stout said, in more parliamentary language, that it jolly well wouldn't. He was prepared to do a lot for his constituents, sometimes nearly as much as they expected of him, but even he drew the line somewhere. Mr. Posselthwaite reluctantly rose to his feet, took up the curly-brimmed hat, fitted it carefully over his large forehead, drew on his gloves, slipped the button back into his pocket, took up the cane, and said, " I have to thank you for listening to me so courteously," just as though any other Member of Parliament would have greeted him with a bucket of water or a sack of flour on the edge of the door. He went out and Mr. Stout saw him walking gravely, with a slightly jaunty air, down the drive. He wondered if at the police-station they'd take him seriously ; he looked so ridiculously as though he'd stepped off the musical comedy stage in " The Naughty Nineties."

He hadn't been gone more than half an hour when Lady Catherine swept into her son's library.

" I hope you were firm, Allen," she said. " I know how these people talk you round."

" For once," said Allen politely, " you were wrong. He didn't want money."

" I suppose he's invented something that will sweep what's left of the Luftwaffe out of the sky ? or is it the Japanese fleet ? "

" As a matter of fact he had some evidence in the Carter case."

Lady Catherine looked nonplussed for a second, but only for a second.

" You like your melodramas highly-coloured, I will say that for you, Allen. What did he want you to do ? "

" Take his place in the road of the murderer," returned Mr. Stout.

" Oh," said his indomitable mother, " and are you doing it ? "

" I am not," said Mr. Stout. " Without wishing to appear conceited, I feel I'm more useful to my electors living than dead."

But Lady Catherine only replied that she'd be looking at a violet a long time before she thought of him.

" And what had he got to tell you anyhow ? " she enquired.

Mr. Stout explained. His mother stared at him. " And—what did you say you told him ? "

" To go to the police."

" You didn't think of sending him in your car, with a suitable escort ? "

" An escort ? "

" Do sort yourself, Allen," she advised him pungently. " You've got a man who's already, so we suppose, committed two murders. It isn't his fault he hasn't committed three. In fact, by this time he very well may have done. He's been caught bending as it is by allowing his man to come here, but I don't suppose it would occur to the average elector that anyone would approach a Member for personal protection. As a matter of fact, it's a very pretty compliment to you."

Mr. Stout disclaimed personal responsibility. " Give the credit where it belongs, to our Parliamentary institutions," he said. And then, suddenly waking up, he added, " Good Lord, you don't think X will make another attempt ? "

" Ring up the station and ask if he's arrived," suggested Lady Catherine. " Your little man, I mean."

But at the station they didn't know anything about Mr. Posselthwaite.

" Of course, he may not have gone straight away," said Mr. Stout. " He was a bit shaken, he may have gone home, decided to write. . . . "

Lady Catherine decided it was time to put an end to all this woffle. " Have you got his address ? "

" Yes. Somewhere." With the helplessness of a man accustomed to rely entirely on a secretary, Mr. Stout fiddled with the bits of paper on his desk.

" You'd better ring up and make sure he's there," insisted the intrepid Lady Catherine.

" I shouldn't think he'd be on the telephone," murmured Allen. And though he looked in the directory he couldn't find him.

" Then you'd better go round."

He was surprised by her insistence. She nearly stamped her foot at him.

" You're so used to that Circumlocution Office of yours at Westminster you don't realise that professional criminals move like greased lightning," she said.

" You mean, you really think he's in danger ? "

" I mean, I really do. And it won't do you any good in the House to be mixed up in a bunch of murders. You know what electors are. They'll say this sort of thing doesn't happen in other constituencies, and seeing that you found the girl and sent the little fellow to the police—well, they'll start putting two and two together. . . . "

" I know," said Allen bitterly. He'd had some experience of his electorate's mathematical abilities before to-day. " All right. I wonder if it would be justifiable to take the car."

" If you had an aeroplane I'd say take that," said Lady Catherine, from which he gathered that she really was in earnest.

He got out the car and drove off to Mowbray Crescent. No. 21 was tall and narrow and dignified, and in every way suited to Mr. Posselthwaite. Mrs. Lewis was fat and forbidding and wall-eyed. She wasn't in the least impressed when Mr. Stout disclosed his identity. She said Mr. Posselthwaite wasn't in. Mr. Stout suggested he might wait.

" You'll wait outside," said Mrs. Lewis grimly. " I've had trouble already allowing a gentleman up to his room."

" Do you remember what he looked like ? the gentleman who came, I mean ? "

" He looked like a gentleman," returned Mrs. Lewis. " Otherwise, of course, I wouldn't have let him up."

" Was he fair ? " asked Mr. Stout desperately.

" He might have been," said Mrs. Lewis.

" Or dark ? "

" Well, either's possible," said Mrs. Lewis.

" You couldn't see ? " suggested Mr. Stout.

" He wore a hat," pointed out Mrs. Lewis.

" Didn't he take it off, then ? "

" No," said Mrs. Lewis.

" I thought you said he was a gentleman," said Mr. Stout.

Mrs. Lewis said, meaningly, " Well, I must say I hope I know a gentleman when I see one," from which Mr. Stout accurately deduced that she didn't consider she was seeing one now.

Feeling he was cutting a pretty poor figure, he went back to the car and waited. He waited a long time, but Mr. Posselthwaite didn't come. Then he thought perhaps he'd lost the way to the police station, but had arrived by this time, so he tooled along to the nearest telephone box which wasn't, as it happened, very near, and rang again. The police this time were decidedly short with him. It was easy to find excuses for them. They were being badgered to death about this new murder, and were inclined to say that if Bess Carter had come to them instead of pinning her faith on amateurs she might still be pulling beer handles behind the bar of " The Case Is Altered." Mr. Stout found their attitude illogical. Here was he giving them advance information about a murder that (he hoped) hadn't been committed yet, and he was meeting with no encouragement at all. He tried to explain about the button, but he couldn't have done it very well, because the policeman said they weren't a junk store and rang off. Mr. Stout reminded himself that he was a member of a great democratic institution which meant he had some rights as well as the local authorities, and decided to go down in person. First of all, he braved the dragon at No. 21 once more. This time Mrs. Lewis didn't exactly threaten to call the police and summon him for molestation, but he felt pretty sure that if there was a General Election in the near future he wouldn't get her vote. However, he told her with cheerful savagery that she'd better have her bonnet ready as she might have to join him at the police station any minute, and having thoroughly upset her digestion for the day, he breezed back into the car and disappeared.

When he had told his story to the police they changed their attitude, and practically told him that if any harm should have befallen Mr. Posselthwaite he couldn't be absolved from responsibility.

" He's probably all right," said Mr. Stout, but without any conviction. " Stopped to have a quick one, I daresay."

It occurred to him that if he'd been one of these quick thinkers he'd have stopped for one himself en route.

" Well ? " said Lady Catherine on his return.

He shook his head. It wasn't well at all. And it continued to get worse. Because by nine o'clock that night they still hadn't located Mr. Posselthwaite.

CHAPTER THIRTEEN

MEANWHILE the innocent Mr. Posselthwaite, misliking his errand with all his heart, had walked staunchly down the drive and out of the gate and turned his footsteps towards the police station. For some reason best known to themselves, exclusive people like M.P.s don't live near municipal authorities and it was quite a step to the station. It never occurred to Mr. Posselthwaite, however, that Mr. Stout might have offered him the car or even suggested coming with him. He knew that in a war petrol costs lives, and the fact that his own life might be in jeopardy in no way militated against his patriotism. He was, like a true Briton, mainly concerned with the fact that during the coming interview he was almost certain to be made to look a fool. He even wondered whether the police would suspect him of shielding the murderer, though logic was opposed to so absurd a supposition. As he went he tried to remember the whole scene more clearly but, being naturally upright, he had to admit he wouldn't have recognised Bess if he had met her the next morning. Certainly he had heard the man's voice calling her name, but it was ridiculous to imagine that a man could be identified on a criminal charge by such a detail. The fellow had worn a dark hat and that was as much as Mr. Posselthwaite had been able to see. Whether he were dark or fair, tall or short, stout or lean, he had no notion.

" It is unfortunate," reflected the simple-minded Mr. Posselthwaite (they'd called him Fossil as a joke even at school), " that I am so unfamiliar with motor-cars. Otherwise I might have been in a position to render greater assistance."

He had not proceeded very far on the long road to the station when he heard the purr of a car coming up behind him and then slowing down. " Lift ? " said a voice.

Mr. Posselthwaite looked round. " It is exceedingly kind of you," he said, " but I fear that rapidity of motion is never very pleasant to me. And the day is fine. . . . "

" You mean you're afraid I'll tip you out," said the driver, who wore a dark hat pulled over his eyes. " Well, that's all right. You couldn't go more than a snail's pace in this little bus."

Mr. Posselthwaite hesitated.

" Far to go ? " enquired the other.

" Only as far as the station—the police station, that is."

The other whistled. " It's a goodish step. Getting on for a couple of miles."

" Really ? Mr. Stout gave me the impression that it was a matter of a few minutes."

" Mr Stout ? You mean, the Member ? "

" Yes. I had been to see him for some advice. . . . "

" And his advice was to go to the police."

" Yes. To tell them about the button. . . . "

" Then you must be Mr. Posselthwaite."

" That is my name certainly. But. . . . "

" Mr. Stout's just rung the station about you. He seemed a bit anxious."

" And you have come to meet me, in consequence ? But how kind, how very kind ! "

" Don't want to run any unnecessary risks," said the driver, " and Mr. Stout seemed to think . . . "

" He believes that I have information that may be invaluable to the police. Naturally, if that is the case, I shall be only too happy to render all possible assistance."

" Quite so," said the driver, and swung open the passenger door. When he leaned forward Mr. Posselthwaite could see him more clearly. He had a big dark moustache and a curious puckered scar on one cheek, and horn-rimmed glasses. When Mr. Posselthwaite was seated beside him they looked like part of a repertory company going down to a dress rehearsal. The driver, who said his name was Stacey, plunged his hand into his pocket and drew out a bit of pasteboard.

" Plain-clothes police," he said. " My warrant."

" Oh, ah—yes. Most interesting," agreed Mr. Posselthwaite. " I must say it was very thoughtful of Mr. Stout. I thought at first he was a little—er—sceptical."

" Well, we can't afford to lose you," said the man who called himself Stacey. " You may be our chief witness yet."

" I am afraid," said Mr. Posselthwaite deprecatingly, " that my evidence is not likely to be very helpful. I did not know the young lady, nor should I recognise her companion."

" Still, you might have noticed the car."

" I fear that to me one car is very like another. But perhaps the police would know which of the unfortunate young lady's friends owned a car."

" According to our records, she was probably on good terms with most of the locals and any of them may have owned cars."

" So unfortunate that I can't be of more assistance," murmured Mr. Posselthwaite in apologetic tones.

His companion swung the car round a corner with such verve that the little man was almost thrown out of his seat ; he cannoned against the driver, and pulled himself away, muttering confusedly. " Sorry, sorry," said Stacey. " That's not really a good sample of my driving. I can go the same rate as a funeral hearse when I try."

" I must confess I had no notion of the button's significance," said Mr. Posselthwaite, gallantly keeping the conversational ball rolling, and feeling more frightened than he had ever done in his life. " It was sheer good fortune that I didn't give it to Mrs. Lewis in case—ladies like these trifles."

"She'd have known what it was all right," said Stacey. "Look here, how much do you remember? I mean, now you come to think it over. Up till now it hasn't seemed important, but when you appreciate that it may be going to bring a man to justice. . . ."

"I could consult my diary, of course," said Mr. Posselthwaite.

"Your diary?"

"An old-fashioned habit of my younger days," said the old gentleman. "Naturally, living so quietly I have very little to record, but in my travelling days" (for Mr. Stout was right; he'd done a lot of travelling in his time) "it used to amuse me to set down the little adventures and happenings. . . . Now a man of my age living in seclusion has nothing much to write about, but the little daily encounters—I was always interested in my fellow-beings. . . . And, of course," he added, "it is also helpful where budgeting is concerned."

"I'm afraid I'm one of the fellows that can't keep accounts," confessed Stacey, swinging the car, but more gently this time, round another corner.

Mr. Posselthwaite said nothing; to have put his thoughts into words would have been impolite, but his whole attitude was expressive of the conviction that life had changed and certainly not for the better since he was a young man.

"By the way, you've brought the button with you?" his companion said.

Mr. Posselthwaite plunged his hand into his pocket. "Why, certainly." He frowned and put his other hand into the other pocket. "Dear me! This is most peculiar. I could have sworn . . ." He sat more erect and began a systematic search of his pockets.

"Perhaps you left it with Mr. Stout," suggested Stacey.

"I had it on the table there, I know. But I was quite sure I had taken it up. All the same, it seems to be missing. Perhaps it would be as well to drive back and make enquiries."

"We can telephone from the station," returned Stacey briefly. "You're quite sure it's not there?"

He slowed down the car and Mr. Posselthwaite emptied his pockets, one by one. They looked on the floor of the car and in the rug, but there was no trace of it.

"I can see an A.A. telephone box just ahead," suggested Mr. Posselthwaite. "Perhaps you could get in touch with Mr. Stout and enquire whether I did, in fact, leave the button in his possession."

"Oh, there's no hurry," Stacey assured him. "We can do it when we get there."

" It is very fortunate for me that you did overtake me,"
observed the old gentleman. " This is certainly the longest
mile and a half I have ever travelled. In fact," he looked out
of the window and there was a puzzled expression on his face,
" it would appear from a cursory glance that we are travelling
steadily away from any sign of human habitation."

" We're going to the main station," said Stacey casually.
" The Super's there. It'll save time, and this is important.
Murder. . . . "

" Oh, is that the answer ? " asked Mr. Posselthwaite, and he
smiled for the first time. " Do you know it has just occurred
to me that if this were a film instead of real life you would not
be a member of the police force at all."

" What's that ? " demanded Stacey.

" You would, instead, be the murderer, who had deceived me
by a simple ruse, and would now be driving me to my own death.
I do not make a habit of attending the cinema," he added,
" but once or twice I have visited the Odeon at Pheasant
Green, and I have always been struck by the—the tidiness of
life on the films. For instance, as I say, were this fiction instead
of fact, you would now be driving me to ruin. But since you
would be the villain of the piece, and since the British are a
law-abiding people, you would not be allowed to succeed.
At the eleventh hour the hero would drive up and deliver me,
justice would be satisfied . . . "

" And a good time be had by all," finished Stacey.

" Except, of course, the murderer," Mr. Posselthwaite
reminded him. " Mr. Stacey, would you be kind enough to
tell me something ? "

" What is it ? "

" Is—you will smile, I know, but—pardon an old man's
fancies—is there the remotest possibility that life and the films
do ever coincide ? "

He felt the car rock an instant. Then Stacey said coolly,
" What's that you're asking ? "

" I'm asking if you are by any chance the murderer of Miss
Carter. Was it you who drove up in the fog and collected her
from the bus stop ? Are you quite sure Mr. Stout telephoned
to you to say I was en route for the police station ? "

" Look here," said Stacey, slowing the car down a little, " are
you serious ? "

" If the facts are as I suspect the situation is a very serious
one," the old gentleman replied. " I should imagine that by
this time the murderer must be feeling decidedly uncomfortable.
Each time he commits a fresh crime he lays a new trail leading

to himself. I greatly fear, however," he added, " that where the true life story breaks down is in the conclusion. I have several times looked over my shoulder, but I fear that no car is following us."

" And no car will," agreed Stacey as coolly as ever. " Make your mind easy on that score. Oh, you're clever, Mr. Posselthwaite, but you know what they say about the man who laughs last. It's always a mistake to go pushing your nose into things that don't concern you."

" Our Member, who should be an authority on the subject, assures me that murder is the concern of every member of the community," said the old man in his serious way. " Would it be indiscreet to ask what you intend to do ? "

" You will know very little about it," his companion assured him. He put his foot on the accelerator, and the car gathered momentum and tore ahead along the empty road. Mr. Posselthwaite by this time was quite sure that life isn't like the films, and that no rescuer was going to appear on the horizon and put a summary end to Mr. Stacey's plans.

" If I may say so," suggested Mr. Posselthwaite, " you made one mistake. You drove up from behind me, saying you had had a message from Mr. Stout. But if that had been the case and if you had been the person you claimed to be you would have come from the other direction, and you certainly, even driving at your present pace, could not have reached the spot in the time. I worked that out," he added gently, " en route."

" I hope it makes you happy," said Stacey. He glanced over his shoulder. There was no one in sight. They were now in a very desolate part of the country. On the left the road sloped steeply downwards, a rough stony decline dotted with shrubs and young trees.

" Is this the place ? " murmured Mr. Posselthwaite, looking out of the windows and perceiving the possibilities such a site offered to a murderer.

" That's right. You can get out now, and remember you've no one but yourself to thank. The odds are you won't be found for weeks ; no one climbs up and down that sort of precipice for fun. And by the time they do find you it'll be too late for you to do any harm."

Mr. Posselthwaite got out gingerly and stood on the very edge of the road. Any passer-by could have told you the little fellow hadn't got a chance. He'd go down like a bundle of old clothes. Stacey came round the side of the car. The old gentleman moved quickly, wavered, put out his arms. But a mouse might as easily have put up a fight against an elephant. The murderer barely touched him ; he staggered, his feet slid, he was over the side, going down and down, like a bouncing ball, though Stacey watching him, black hate in his heart. Well, darkness was coming on now and it couldn't come too fast for him. Even if his luck gave out and someone found the body while it was still recognisable there was nothing to show it wasn't sheer accident. There had been one or two local demands for a fence to be put up here, but timber was in short supply and not many people came this way, and wood was needed for the war effort, and so nothing was done. He stood there for a moment, breathing heavily. One thing, he thought, when I hide things they aren't easily found. There was the white mackintosh that the girl had pushed off her shoulders in the car and he'd found— afterwards. The police weren't going to find that for a month of Sundays. Weighted with stones it was at the bottom of a quarry in another spot as lonely as this one. He pulled a handkerchief out of his pocket to wipe his face. There was something in his pocket besides the handkerchief, something smooth and hard and cold. He took that out too and let it lie in the palm of his hand. Slowly his fingers closed over it.

It was a bright red button shaped like a dolphin.

CHAPTER FOURTEEN

THE USUAL CROWD at " The Case Is Altered " that night was increased by Mr. Stout, who didn't usually go so far afield. When he was released from the rough handling of the police, it occurred to him that he could do worse than get in touch with Mr. Crook, and this he accordingly did, sensibly looking for him where he was most likely to be found. Mr. Crook was the centre of a little group that included Burke, Bairstowe and Cotham himself. Mr. Stout joined them. The story of the disappearance of Mr. Posselthwaite had spread in the way in which gossip always does spread in the country. The native tribes who send out their news by way of tom-toms have nothing on villagers.

" I feel responsible," said Mr. Stout. " Of course, I should have suggested going with him."

" You might only have had two corpses instead of one," rejoined Crook in his sensible way. " A chap as desperate as this chap's bound to be isn't going to draw the line at an extra body."

" But if there had been two of us," reflected Mr. Stout, thinking that though the missing man was a bit small for fighting

113

he might at all events have come in useful for telephoning the police, assuming that the murderous assault they were all convinced had taken place had been tactfully located near a telephone, "We might have outed the fellow."

"You might be wearin' the whole armour of righteousness," said Mr. Crook earnestly, " but that wouldn't help you if you came up against a gun. And anyway," he added, " it may be through this last attempt that we'll nail our man."

Burke said restlessly, " I can't help feeling the police are being damned incompetent about this. We've got two murders for certain and one possibility, and what have they done ? "

" They've arrested a man for the first murder, they're makin' enquiries into the second, and the third one hasn't eventuated yet."

Burke looked sullen. He didn't actually say, " And what the hell have you done for your spending-money, beyond letting Bess get herself murdered ? " but he looked it.

" They haven't even found the hammer," he went on in dissatisfied tones.

" If they can't find a noticeable thing like a body they're not very likely to find a hammer," returned Crook sensibly.

" But this one weighed half a hundredweight—Bess said so."

" Even hammers that size can be hidden," Crook assured him. " There are about a couple of thousand places where it might be, includin' the water tank, as I told you, and unless they find it in some compromising place how they're going to show it's got anythin' to do with Chigwell's murder beats me."

" It obviously has got something to do with it," Burke insisted, " or why has it disappeared again. If it's in the tank . . . "

" If you can get the local authorities to empty the tank again within the week you ought to be in Parliament yourself," said Mr. Stout unexpectedly.

" That could be the way X will argue," approved Crook.

" All the same, this Posselthwaite business bothers me," Stout continued. " There doesn't seem any sense in it."

" Not from your point of view, perhaps, but a hell of a lot from the murderer's. After all, he had something to say."

" Nothing that could have convicted a man."

" It's wonderful what he might have remembered by the time enough people had asked if he wasn't sure it was a red car or that the girl had called the driver Jim. X wasn't taking any chances."

The telephone rang and Cotham went to answer it. He was looking drawn and haggard and had taken remarkably little part in the conversation.

"He's off his feed," suggested Bairstowe and Burke said, "Well, wouldn't you be in his shoes?"

Cotham came back, saying that it was for Crook, and when the lawyer had rolled off the other three men thought they might as well have a hand of darts. Mr. Stout showed himself a pretty pitcher and Burke found an instant to mutter to Bairstowe, standing very close, "What do you make of him?"

Bairstowe said, "He's all right, isn't he?"

"Got the wind up, if you ask me," said Burke.

"Not surprising if he has," said Bairstowe. "He's the last person to see this chap, Posselthwaite, before he disappears into the blue. He found Bess's body. . . ."

"Good Lord!" said Burke. "You don't think . . . But that's absurd."

Then it was his turn, but he wasn't playing up to his usual standard to-night. He said it had been a filthy day; he'd had to go over to Parkford—trouble in the factory there for the second time in three months.

"Beats me," said Bairstowe, "how these chaps can keep threatening to down tools if they don't get more money, when you think of the fellows out in the front line, getting about half nothing a day."

Mr. Stout unexpectedly took up the challenge. "Less surprising than that the man in the street expects 'em to sweat their guts out for a penny less than they can make the authorities pay them," he said inelegantly. "I've lived here all my life, and I tell you that for years before the war, these chaps—or the majority of 'em—were on short time and will be the same again if we don't watch out."

Someone observed audibly that there really was no need to buy the *Daily Worker* when this chap was about, and Bairstowe said, "I thought Sir William Beveridge . . ."

Burke called hurriedly for more beer and Stout said, "I'd be sorry to have to live on what I'd get under that scheme and so would you. It's a minimum allowance." Then he stopped. He'd got into the habit of catching fire whenever anyone mentioned social security, having strong feelings on the matter, as all his colleagues in the House were only too well aware. The conversation then became violently political, and there might have been yet another murder but for the timely reappearance of Mr. Crook, who came back whistling fit to beat the band.

"Well," he said, "the ball's begun to roll again. We shall get our man yet."

The three dart players turned to him expectantly. Cotham pricked up his ears. Mr. Stout said, "Was that the police?"

and his manner implied that if so, they might as a matter of courtesy have asked for him who represented Government in the neighbourhood rather than for Mr. Crook, who was merely an inspired amateur.

"Oh, no," said Mr. Crook, pretending to look shocked. "That's practically *lese-majeste*. No, as a matter of fact, that was Mr. Albert Posselthwaite. In short, chaps, the game's in the bag."

There was a moment of dumbfounded silence. Then Mr. Stout said : "My God !" but he said it so reverently that no one could have taken offence. And he added, "Where is he ?"

"Oh, he's not speaking from the Other Side," Mr. Crook assured them hurriedly. "He's very much alive, and it's goin' to be my duty and my delight to see he stays that way."

Mr. Stout forgot all about social security. "Where is he ? They may be after him again, if they know."

"I though we were agreed there was only one man in on this," offered Crook mildly.

"One too many," opined Mr. Stout. "And while we sit here. . . .".

"So long as we're all here, he's safe," said Mr. Crook deliberately.

They all turned to stare at him, like feeding cattle all turning the same way.

"Because so long as we're *all* here," wound up Mr. Crook impressively, "the murderer can't move."

Burke was the first to put the implication into words. "Do you mean he's one of us ?"

"I'll eat my hat if he isn't," said Crook, simply.

There was an uncomfortable pause. Each man's eyes slid round to his neighbour ; attention became rigid, imagination stiffened, reading guilt into the movement of a hand, the tensing of the muscle of a jaw.

Cotham said harshly, "Do you know who he is ?" and Crook said, "Well, I'd bet a year's pay I do, but that won't be good enough for the police. They'll expect proof."

"And how do they get it ?" asked Mr. Stout testily.

"They depend on the poor bloody man in the street," said Crook with simple oratorical effect. "Half the murders that are committed get found out, where they are found out, because someone pops into the picture when he isn't expected. It's no good blaming the murderer, because it's not his fault. He couldn't foresee the particular development that ruins him. Rouse, for example, couldn't know that he was going to be seen by two young chaps coming back from a dance at two a.m.,

116

but that was the first bit of ill-luck that guided him to the little covered shed. Pat Mahon couldn't guess that his wife was going to pick up the cloak-room ticket he'd dropped and give it to an ex-policeman. And that isn't all. It's because the people concerned in a murder aren't what the murderer suspects. You know what the poet says—things are not what they seem— and I don't mean that for the beer, Mr. Cotham, though I don't doubt the manufacturers have passed on the penny on the pint to the consumer. For instance, no one seeing me ever thinks I'm a lawyer, and no one seeing Mr. Posselthwaite would guess he was once an acrobat."

" A what ? " The question burst from Burke and Stout simultaneously.

" An acrobat. That's why he wasn't killed when he pitched over the edge of the precipice."

" He told me he was connected with the stage," muttered Mr. Stout in a dazed voice. " I didn't dream . . . "

" How did he come to fall over a precipice ? " asked Burke.

" It's quite a story. He was followed from Bramham Manor by our old friend, the villain, who seems to have leaned pretty heavily on the make-up box. He was a bold, bad, black-mustachioed chap, laughing ' Ha-ha,' like the war-horse when he heard the trumpets, and he told Mr. Posselthwaite a cock-and-bull story that wouldn't have deceived a district visitor, and lured the old boy into his car."

" I suppose I'm dense," said Burke, " but frankly I'm all at sea. If Posselthwaite (what a name !) saw through the fairy-tale, why did he get into the car ? "

" For one thing, he'd only have been slogged and then run over if he'd refused, and for another he'd got the spirit that's made the boy scouts great. He conceived the idea that he'd trick the villain and have the murder avenged. Oh, he was a game little cock, there's no doubt about that. He told me he kept wondering what the fellow intended to do with him, and he meant to even up the score somehow, whichever way things went."

" Sort of haunt him ? " asked a bewildered Mr. Stout.

Crook looked thoughtfully at them all. They were alike tense, grave, keyed up for any development, but a recording angel might have been hard put to it to choose the criminal.

" He left a clue, a clue that's going to go a long way towards solvin' the case. That clue was the red button. When he realised he was for it he began to lay his plans and when the car took a sharp corner he saw his chance, and he slid the button into the driver's pocket. Then when the driver asked him had he got it he made a great show of turnin' his pockets out but it wasn't there ; and they looked in the car and it wasn't there. . . . "

" Do you mean," exploded Stout, " it's there still ? "

" That's what we're goin' to find out," said Crook. He spoke calmly enough, but there was a jut to his jaw that might have discouraged the whole German army.

" What happened after that ? " asked Cotham sharply.

" The villain explained to him that he was going to die of a broken neck—if he was lucky—and Mr. Posselthwaite decided he'd rather die in bed. He had to watch for his chance but you have to hand it to the little fellow—he is nippy on his pins."

" That's what I told him," exclaimed Mr. Stout involuntarily.

" He was a practised acrobat and he knew the art of falling. And if you ask me he's something above the average if he managed to get down that slope without breakin' his spine. He says he hadn't time to bother about that, all he wanted to do was get on to the police and tell 'em all he knew. And then I suppose he thought he might have a word with a perishing amateur first, and tackled me."

" He didn't happen to mention my name, I suppose ? " asked the discomfited Mr. Stout.

" I said I knew you'd be relieved."

" Kind of you ! " Mr. Stout still sounded a bit disgruntled.

" You can't blame X for thinkin' that was a through ticket to Kingdom Come for the little chap," Crook continued. " Even if he wasn't killed outright he'd be so badly mauled he wouldn't be able to move, and you don't get hikers in these parts nowadays. Come to that, he was speakin' from his bed, I understand."

" He's back here ? " said Bairstowe.

" With an armed guard," Crook grinned.

" But, look here," Mr. Stout laboriously followed the point to its starting-place, like a patient but untrained dog after a not very satisfactory scent, " he can tell us who the murderer is."

" He said he was a chap called Stacey."

" Stacey." Cotham looked up sharply. " That's a new one on me."

" He might be a teetotaller," said Mr. Stout without humour.

" Or it could even be that Stacey wasn't his real name," contributed Mr. Crook. " Anyhow, he said he had a great black moustache . . . " everyone looked at Mr. Stout, " and wore glasses and had a disfigurement on his cheek. That chap was wasted as an acrobat. He'd do better at Scotland Yard."

Burke said impatiently, " And where do we go from here ?

Seems to me whenever we do get on to a path we find it's a blind alley."

" That's all right," said Crook in his easy way. " Just batter through. My head," and he grinned again, " well, I'd back it against a wall of steel bricks."

And so, thought Mr. Stout, would he.

" How about the button ? " asked Burke.

" I'm comin' to that. Now if Posselthwaite put it into the chap's pocket this evening the odds are . . . "

" It'll be there still."

" It's worth trying." He turned to Cotham. " Any objection to our borrowin' your private room for a few minutes. No need to give a free show in the bar. It ain't as though we were taking the hat round."

Cotham said, " Do you mean you think it's going to be in that pocket still ? "

" Figure it out for yourself," said Crook. " Suppose while we were talking I'd slipped—say—a suspender buckle into your pocket. What are the odds you wouldn't find it till you turned your pocket out at night."

" That's so." Cotham spoke slowly. " Then your idea is we all turn out our pockets. . . . "

" We are five," said Crook. " That means four of us against the man with the red hand."

Cotham was looking a bit white about the gills. Murder isn't a healthy thing anywhere, in spite of what the circulating libraries tell you, but it's fatal in a public-house, and he didn't like the tension that was thickening round him like a fog. He didn't know how much some of the regulars had taken in, but he thought he could feel eyes burning his coat as he turned and led the way to his private room.

Mr. Stout said, " Have you any idea yourself where the button might be ? " They were all in the room now, eyeing one another warily like dogs, aware that in a moment there's going to be a devil of a hullabaloo, but not quite sure which of them is going to start. If this had been a play it would have been Mr. Crook's great moment. All the limes trained on him, everyone rigid and intent.

" I could make a guess," said Crook softly, " If you were to ask me, I'd say it was in Mr. Bairstowe's pocket."

Bairstowe went whiter than you'd have thought it possible for any man to go. He opened his mouth to speak, but no words came. Burke took a quick step forward, but Stout caught him by the arm. " He's right," said Crook. " Murdering the chap isn't going to help you."

119

" You're mad," said Bairstowe.

It was a feeble retort, and even he recognised it.

Cotham said, " All right. Prove it. Turn out your pockets."

Bairstowe sent a hunted glance round the room. " If—if it is there," he said, " it'll have been planted on me."

" You'll have to think of something better than that," Cotham warned him, roughly.

Still the warden hesitated. Crook took a lunging step forward and before anyone realised what he was doing had his leg of mutton fists inside the other man's pockets. A moment later he stepped back.

" No deception, ladies and gentlemen," he said, and opened his hand.

In it lay a bright red button shaped like a dolphin.

CHAPTER FIFTEEN

FOR A MINUTE there was silence, and following the silence complete pandemonium. Burke shouted, Bairstowe exclaimed, Stout said, " First ENSA and then Maskelyne and Devant " as if to indicate that even six years in Westminster hadn't prepared him for this. " It's a bloody frame-up," cried Bairstowe, and Burke said, " All right. But you'll get your chance of proving that in a court of law. That is, if you're lucky."

His meaning was unmistakable, and Stout said in authoritative tones, " Constitutional methods," while Crook added explanatorily, " Queensberry—which means you mustn't bite."

Cotham shoved his hands into his pockets, as if he were afraid if he didn't put them somewhere safe they'd be found round Bairstowe's throat and said, " I knew it would be fatal on licensed premises. All the same . . . "

" All the same, we can finish the discussion somewhere else," offered Crook obligingly. " Over at Mr. Bairstowe's shop, for instance."

" Why do you want to go there ? " demanded Bairstowe, glaring.

" Well, there's still the matter of the hammer."

" You think you're going to find that ? "

" I suppose if we do," taunted Burke, " you'll say that was planted, too."

" It could be," said Bairstowe ; " you chaps all know I keep a key under the mat for my regular customers, in case they want to call in for an accumulator when the shop's shut or I'm on duty. Anybody could have slipped in and planted it."

"Well, you'll be able to tell that to the police, too," said Crook. "The accused always gets the benefit of the doubt, you know."

Burke's expression changed for a moment to one of scepticism. He'd been there before, that look said. You couldn't tell him much and it was pretty obvious he didn't give a toss for Bairstowe's chances. It was Cotham who asked the question that was in everybody's mind.

"What put you on to Bairstowe ? I never thought . . . "

"It's a bit obvious to anyone who knows his onions," returned Crook, regaining some of his normal cock-a-hoop manner. He'd been definitely below his usual form that evening ; you might almost think he was sorry for Bairstowe. "You see, from the start there was one thing hardly anyone appears to have noticed, and that was that we had not one, but two men with the intials R. B., both admittedly on the premises that night."

"My God ! " exclaimed Burke. "The fools we are ! Naturally everyone thought the letters stood for Rupert Burke. . . . "

"Whereas they were equally applicable to Roy Bairstowe," wound up Cotham.

"As a matter of fact, once you'd noticed the similarity it was fairly easy to build up a case," Crook continued, never taking his eyes off the warden. "You see, on his own admission Mr. Bairstowe saw Chigwell alive at nine o'clock that night and we haven't found anyone who will admit to seeing him later—not until Kenneth Jardine let himself into the flat and found him dead. Now Jardine says he didn't arrive till 9.30, and the evidence bears that out, by which time it was all over bar the shouting. And really it's a bit tough to blame him, as the authorities do, for not giving them a hail right away. After all, he hadn't had much experience of the law, and he hadn't got an altogether clear conscience."

"What about the fellow Chigwell was expecting at nine o'clock ? " asked Bairstowe, and his voice wasn't quite steady.

"Well," Crook's level gaze held his, " speaking purely professionally, that's an uncorroborated statement."

"You mean, you've only my word for it ? And since Chigwell's dead you can't hope for any confirmation ? Still, you've only got Jardine's word that he was dead when he arrived."

"Jardine's my client," said Crook simply.

"How about the entry in Chigwell's diary—R. B., nine o'clock. Are you trying to make out that it referred to me ? "

"It could be," murmured Crook.

"God!" said Bairstowe, "whoever fixed this has been clever. All the same, you're not going to pin this on me. Chigwell meant nothing to me. I just went up to warn him about his black-out as I might anyone else. And you're not going to be able to show he had anything on me. Ask the police. They searched the safe, didn't they?"

"Well, there wouldn't be much sense murdering him and leaving the evidence where the police could find it," said Cotham in a grim voice.

"That's not evidence," exclaimed Bairstowe.

"We ain't the police," Crook repeated. "We don't have to find the evidence. We're just puttin' up a case—any case—to get my client released."

"And it's nothing to you if an innocent man swings?"

"Go on!" said Burke, and his voice was deadly in its savagery. "Anything more?"

"Well, there are the anonymous letters," offered Crook. "Most of you haven't seen those. And most of them might have been written by anyone. Cheap paper, cheap ink, nothing in the writing itself to help you. But the first letter was on a half-sheet of ruled paper, a small half-sheet, and a special kind of ruled paper. I haven't got it by me, but I can tell you what it was. It was half a bill-head. Well, a man who repairs wireless has that kind of paper on the premises. . . . "

"So does any other kind of shopkeeper," broke in Bairstowe. "If you think you can prove anything from that you're nuts. Why, anyone here could have produced a bit of paper like that. It might even be a part of one of my bills," he added wildly. "Everyone hereabouts who runs a wireless comes to me for repairs. There's no one else, not since the war. . . . "

"I'm only just setting down the facts," said Crook with that disarming gentleness that was more alarming than any tigerish display from such a man. "Then there's the fact that the second letter was left by hand. That makes it certain it was a local man, which we'd suspected in any case. Then came the third bit of evidence, the note found in the dead girl's bag. That, if I may say so, was a mistake and a bad one. The note Mrs. McKay brought up to you," he nodded at Burke, "was good. It fulfilled its purpose; but anyone who knew Bess Carter would know she wouldn't accept hers. To begin with, it spoke of a rendezvous miles from the one she'd proposed, and she couldn't walk more than a hundred yards on her heels. If she had agreed to go to the cottage—but then the evidence proves that she hadn't."

"How do you make that out?" asked Mr. Stout, finding this

debate more enthralling than any he'd heard in Westminster in months.

" She was waiting by the bus stop to go to Pheasant Green, that is in the diametrically opposite direction from the cottage. When her friend came along in the car and said he'd give her a lift, he took her away from Pheasant Green and in the direction of Whipley Cross. But if she'd had the note and agreed—and if she hadn't she'd presumably have rung Mr. Burke—she'd have been waiting by the bus stop on the other side of the road."

There was another silence while they all digested that. Then Burke asked hoarsely, " What does that add up to ? "

" You can see for yourself," said Crook. " It's clear, ain't it, that she didn't have the note before she left the pub, because if she had she'd either have telephoned you and told you that if you thought she was goin' to walk a couple of miles on her shiny shoes you'd got wheels and if that was your idea of a joke you could damn well fetch her in your car, or, if she took the whole thing so seriously that she was prepared to agree even to that ridiculous suggestion, she wouldn't have been waiting where Mr. Posselthwaite found her."

Bairstowe said, " You're taking it for granted that his story's true ? " and Crook said in surprised tones, " Well, why not ? You don't believe he committed the murder, do you ? Because no jury will agree with you."

" Of course he didn't," said Burke in the same deadly voice. " Go on, Crook."

" Ergo," continued Crook, warming to his task a little, " she hadn't had that note."

" But it was found in her bag," urged Cotham.

" Sure it was found in her bag—because the murderer put it there after the crime."

" Taking a chance, wasn't he ? Right initials and all ? "

" He was banking on the fact that there were two R.B.s in the picture. You know, there's a lot to be said for keeping in the middle of the stage. The audience don't notice the chaps in the wings. No, that note gives the whole show away, if nothing else did."

Burke said, " Mrs. McKay muttered something about being nearly run down by a warden. I didn't think. . . . "

" If ever I'm in jug," said Bairstowe in a high unnatural voice, " I'll get you to act for me, Mr. Crook. You could persuade a jury that black was white. You've built up a very nice case. I don't suppose it matters a curse to you who swings so long as it's not your client. . . . "

"Well, that's what I'm being paid for," said Crook, who wondered whether anybody besides himself knew the meaning of logic. "To see my client don't swing, that is. Anyway, I'm not the last word. I just set down a few facts in my client's interest."

"Happen to remember where you were this afternoon?" asked Cotham grimly.

"Working—in my shop." Bairstowe sounded almost at the end of his tether.

"Anyone happen to come in?"

"It's early closing day, as you very well know. But I was doing some repairing in the back. No, of course no one came in."

"Still, your wife . . . "

"My wife's away for a few days."

"Too bad," Cotham condoled with him. "How about the day Bess was murdered?"

"I told you all at the time—I went over to Halton to see about some spares."

"I remember," said Burke. "You said you went in your car."

"You can't carry spares in a paper bag," exclaimed the goaded man.

"It all comes down to a question of timing," observed Crook, thoughtfully. "Time's the great factor in crime as in other things. Ask any chap on the stage. Now Posselthwaite said he and Miss Carter were waiting for the 4.10 and it was already late when the car arrived, and took Miss Carter away. So that brings it up to, say, 4.20 or 4.25. Of course, if you were at Halton then or around then and you could find someone who remembers seeing you, that would prove you couldn't have had a hand in it."

"As I've told various people already, my car broke down in the fog. And now ask me if someone remembers seeing me ditched by the road, and I'll remind you it was a black fog and no one came along, and after a bit I managed to patch her up and bring her back to Pullcheston."

"Too bad!" murmured Crook for the second time.

Burke started forward again, and again Stout put out his hand. "Take care!" he said. "You don't want to be run in for murder, do you?"

Burke muttered something about not giving a damn, but he stood back just the same.

"What's next?" Cotham asked. "The police?"

"There's still the hammer," said Crook. "It would help a lot if we could find the hammer."

" On my premises, you mean ? Well, I see you're prepared for anything. But if it comes to the hammer, I swear to you that several of you saw it after I did. I never set eyes on it after it was taken out of the tank and Bess made an offer for it."

" Well, I never saw it at all," said Burke. " Bairstowe made sure of that."

" I tell you . . . " began Bairstowe, and then threw up his hands as though realising the futility of speech.

" I didn't see it either," said Cotham in his gruff way.

" Why, Bess said she was buying it for you."

" I don't hold myself responsible for anything Bess may have said. I can only assure you she never showed it to me."

" We'd better take someone along who will recognise it," suggested Crook.

" First of all," said Mr. Stout, " we must get Mr. Bairstowe's permission to examine his premises. I won't be party to anything unconstitutional," an observation that would have caused any of his colleagues at the House of Commons to drop down in a fit.

" Oh, you can come if you like," said Bairstowe recklessly. " And Joe Bell, of the N.F.S., was there when we emptied the tank. I remember he said we have one zany among us anyhow, chucking away a good hammer like that. And someone else said most likely it was an evacuee, no local would be such a fool."

It was typical of Crook that in two brief visits he had already contrived to meet Mr. Bell and he now went off to telephone him, while Cotham observed that he'd have a word with Annie, warn her he had to go out for a quarter of an hour. The other three men stood uncomfortably avoiding one another's gaze, until Stout said, " I'm not satisfied that we're really within our rights pushing this thing."

" You're not in Westminster now," Burke reminded him. He, like the police, didn't approve of Members of Parliament pushing their way into crime. They weren't returned for that. Mr. Stout agreed more heartily than ever with the police. He wondered if he'd be called upon to explain himself at the Annual Meeting of the Malvoison Conservatives. If so, you could be sure of a packed hall.

" Besides," continued Burke in the same politely savage voice, " it would be a bit rough on Bairstowe if we didn't find the hammer, after all, and we'd dragged the police in. People talk so in a small place."

" Oh, have the whole force in," said Bairstowe. " Between you you've cooked up a very nice case against me, but if the courts pay any attention to your evidence it'll show there's nothing in British justice after all."

" They've been saying that from the beginning of time," said Crook, coming in like an actor on his cue. He didn't look any too happy, Stout thought, and put it down to the fact that he didn't like pulling in a man with whom he'd played darts. To his simple mind that was a perfectly adequate explanation of Crook's slightly apologetic attitude.

" I've got in touch with Bell," said Crook, " he'll meet us there. Ah, here's Cotham. Are we ready ? "

It was perfectly obvious that no one present intended to miss the last act. Cotham joined them at the side-door and they set out, Crook and Cotham walking with Bairstowe and Stout following with Burke. No one seemed inclined to speak, and indeed the walk was not a long one. At the door of the shop, which was locked, Bairstowe stopped and said, " Someone else better find the key. I might try and swallow it or something."

It was Cotham who stooped and took it from its hiding-place under a little mat before the entrance to the shop, that was built with a sort of little porch. They had just unlocked the door when Bell hurried up to join them, a big powerful fellow with curiosity written all over his face. Obviously he wanted to ask some questions but Crook put a stop to that. All he said was, " There's a rumour that the hammer no one can find might be on the premises, and in fairness to Mr. Bairstowe we've come *en bloc* to have a look."

Bairstowe said again, " You won't find it. I can promise you that." and the others glanced sideways at one another and then quickly away. Stout and Cotham both thought it possible they were going to be treated to an hysterical outburst, but Crook could have told them that hysteria never had a chance when he was around.

The men seemed rather awkward about beginning the search and Bairstowe taunted them.

" What's the matter with you ? " he said. " A hammer can't hurt you, can it, especially when it isn't there ? And there are plenty of you. Or do you think I'll have electrified it ? or got a pistol hidden somewhere with a string attached to the trigger, like they do in the penny dreadfuls ? "

Bell said stolidly, " Less of it," and then he looked again at Mr. Stout as who should say, " Well, you represent the Government here, so if you say so . . . "

Stout caught the glance and said, " Mr. Bairstowe has given us permission to look. If he hadn't, naturally, we couldn't be here."

126

The search began, Cotham and Bell doing the searching. Burke stood against the wall, with Stout beside him, and a little farther away Bairstowe was similarly guarded by Crook. Bell turned up a small hammer that he threw aside without comment, and then Cotham found a second, equally unlikely for the job. Bairstowe spoke. " That's the lot," he said. Neither man paid the smallest attention to him. After a few more minutes Cotham found a third hammer, and Burke remembered Bess's description of it. " It weighs half a hundredweight."

" That's more like," said Crook approvingly, as though what they'd been searching for had been hidden treasure instead of something that had killed a man.

Burke came forward and took the hammer in his hands. " That's it," he said. He turned it over. " There's the crack in the handle."

Stout and Bell came closer. " He's right," said Bell. " I remember that crack, too."

Crook glanced at the warden. His lips were moving but you couldn't hear anything he said. Stout was feeling that for once in a way he agreed with the local authority. Members of Parliament shouldn't get mixed up in this kind of thing.

He said in a tone in which relief and embarrassment were mingled, " Then that clears everything up, doesn't it ? "

" Well, there's just one thing I don't understand," said Crook. " Mr. Burke, how is it you knew there was a crack in the handle if you'd never seen the hammer before ? "

CHAPTER SIXTEEN

I

THE NEWS OF THE DAY had a tremendous scoop for its Sunday edition, no less than the exclusive story of the double Pullcheston Tragedy written by the murderer in his condemned cell, awaiting execution. Because at the last Burke had broken down. He'd fought a desperate battle, but it was no use. Crook could have told him that from the beginning ; and in his heart it was what he had feared. He remembered the evening when he sat in the bar and saw his reflection in the mirror and felt how strange it was that a man could be a murderer and still look like everyone else ; and he had had an inner conviction then that he wasn't going to win this fight. He might, after all, have allowed Bess to live. But right up to the last he had told himself there was no proof. But that was before he had heard all Crook had to say. For the lawyer was right. There's no future in murder. You may be lucky the first time, as he'd been, but you're still an amateur, and the fault of amateurs is that they don't know when to leave well alone. Anyway, Crook would probably have got him ; he'd have waited like a great red spider till the timorous fly crept to the edge of the web. And the fly had come, got itself entangled, tried to fight its way out, been embraced and crushed. . . .

It had been a sensation all right. The police hadn't liked it much, hadn't liked being reminded that they had the real criminal from the first and had let him go, to have him convicted by someone who was only an amateur to them. One paper had offered to pay all Burke's legal expenses if he'd give them an undertaking to write up his story for publication after the verdict. They weren't more bloodthirsty than any other paper that makes its living out of the ordinary man's love of sensation, but naturally it was much more of a scoop now that Burke had been found guilty and condemned. It was one of the few cases where no one attempted to get up a reprieve. You could be sorry for any chap who'd bumped Chigwell off, but Bess was another matter. And by the time the trial was over Burke knew he was lucky to have only another three weeks. A lifetime would be more than any man's sanity could endure.

2

This was Burke's statement.

Since this is my last chance of saying anything I'm going to set down the truth from the very beginning. And that goes back a long way. It goes back to the time that I was married to Muriel, and it's years since she left me. In a sense, it's her fault, though of course she won't admit that. Women don't. They clamour for equal rights and equal pay, but they burk the responsibility. Muriel left me because in her eyes I was a failure, couldn't write books people would read or paint pictures they would buy, so she cut her losses and went off. And that did something to me from which I've never recovered.

A man's got to have something to believe in, and if he can't believe in himself, and a steady round of failure saps any man's faith, then he's got to have someone who believes in him. Muriel didn't believe in me, and she didn't make any secret of the fact. After she left me I tried a number of things, but never with success. I got another book published, but it was obvious I wasn't going to make a living at that ; I tried painting, I even tried going on the stage. Some men are satisfied just to make a living. I wanted more than that, I wanted to make a name of some kind. And something always went wrong.

Then came the war. I thought that might be my chance. At first I couldn't get anything to do. Nobody wanted me, not the Services, not the authorities at home. But at last I managed to get into the Army and though I missed Dunkirk I eventually got sent overseas to the Middle East. I thought that might be my great chance. Of course, I went into the ranks like everyone else, but I thought that was only a beginning. After a time I applied for a commission. I could see at once that my C.O. wasn't sympathetic. I knew what it was. They never have much use for the man of forty. As though experience isn't worth at least as much as a slightly higher standard of fitness. Besides, I was fit. They passed me A1. At first he wouldn't recommend me, then I insisted on going before a Selection Board. They kept me waiting a quite unnecessarily long time for their decision and then I heard that they'd turned me down. They said I wasn't a suitable type for a commission. Of course I knew that was jealousy. It was obvious that with my experience of life and my general position I could have made an admirable officer. Besides, what about all this psychology we hear about ? The modern army is supposed to look at a man from every aspect. Couldn't they see what it would have meant to me ? They lost a good officer when they turned me down. I didn't take their decision without an argument, though. I know most advancement goes by favour, and it's always been my bad luck that I'd no one to pull strings for me. But I tried again before I was sent home after a year abroad. The other chaps were jealous. What's a year ? they said. A lot of them had been out longer than that, and they had wives and children. I hadn't been home long before I heard from the War Office that they didn't intend to make any further use of my services. No reason given. Just that I wasn't wanted any more—superfluous to army requirements in short, and that at a time when the Army all over the world was crying out for men, and keymen were being refused deferment. And here they have a good potential officer, and he's told he's superfluous to requirements.

I knew who I had to thank for that. My C.O. had never had a good word to say for me. I was pretty savage at first. Then I thought, Well, why should I worry ? It's their loss. Besides, the men at home were getting much the best of it. Wages were going up, as they always do in a war. The civilians had the whip-hand. I didn't have much difficulty finding a job, though it wasn't anything very striking. But then, as I've said already,

I hadn't anyone to pull strings. Still, it was a new beginning. I couldn't see why it shouldn't lead to something much better. I might marry again—I'd divorced Muriel years ago—have children, a wife who didn't think me a failure. I worked hard and things seemed to be going all right, only again my wretched luck let me down. My superior was a man called Edmonds, a typical civil servant type, always on the look-out for himself. I could have given him a lot of help, but he liked to work in a water-tight compartment. He wouldn't discuss things with me, practically told me I wasn't anyone, this was his Department, and this, mark you, at a time when the country was at war, when the man-power problem was getting desperate, and our only hope was a united effort. I tried to tell him that. And do you know what he said? My God, I can see why they didn't want you in the army. I never forgave him for that. However, I wasn't a fool. I knew he'd be glad enough to find an excuse to get rid of me, and I didn't mean to give him one. I just worked like a black, wouldn't let him quarrel with me. I had a feeling this was my last chance, and I meant to take it. Things went on like that for more than a year. I never liked Edmonds and he never pretended to like me, but he couldn't complain about my work, though he saw to it I never got a chance of showing what I could do. Still, I was cultivating patience and one day, sure enough, my chance came. I was working late that night, and there was a document I wanted that I thought might be on his desk. Well, it wasn't, but it occurred to me it might be in one of the drawers. He had a big desk with drawers to show he was the head of the Department, I suppose. Generally he kept the drawers locked, but for once he'd left them open. Mind you, I wasn't interested in anything but this particular paper, but while I was looking for it I came across something else, something very curious indeed.

This Department of the Ministry of Goods and Chattels where I was employed dealt largely with a certain essential war material in very short supply, short because we'd depended to a very great extent on the Far East for it, and naturally we weren't doing any trade with the Far East in 1943. In consequence the Government had made use of their policy of concentration, which meant that only a certain number of favoured firms were given contracts, and naturally all the firms in the trade scrambled to be on the official list. As I say, Edmonds never opened up much and I didn't know precisely how the authorities made their decision, why A should be on the list and B shouldn't. If I'd stopped to think I'd have imagined that there was a certain amount of influence, because

that's human nature, and here in Edmond's drawer I found
confirmation of my suspicions. Confirmation, did I say? I
found something much more damaging than that. I realised
that Edmonds had been doing deals on the side, wangling to
get certain firms on to the list, and of course taking a rake-off.
I suppose for a man in his position it wasn't too difficult.

My first thought was that I'd take my evidence to the C.O.
and see what he made of it, but when I'd thought about it a
bit longer I changed my mind. To begin with, Edmonds was a
popular sort of chap in his own way and he was in a position
to do favours, and as I've said he'd seen to it that I shouldn't be.
They couldn't altogether ignore the evidence I'd give them, but
it might be awkward. For instance, they'd want to know how
I got hold of the paper, and even try and make me the scapegoat.
So I hit on a better plan than that. I decided to have the whole
thing out with Edmonds himself.

This letter I'd found gave the game away completely. I took
it home with me and the next morning I found a chance of
getting five minutes alone with the man who was my chief.
He didn't make it easy for me, but for once I meant to stick to
my point and when my chance came I just put the position before
him. I never saw a man so furious. He called me every name
he could lay his tongue to but I let that pass. I could afford to.

" All right," I said to him, " I'm everything you say, but
let that go. The point is, what are you going to do about it ? "

He called me a few more names, but that was just waste of
breath and he knew it. At last he said, " Well, you so-and-so,
what are you going to do now ? "

I said, " I don't know a lot about the way the authorities
choose their firms, but I dare say you haven't really done much
harm. One firm's probably as good as another. All the same,
don't you think it might be a good thing if we were to work
a bit more closely together ? "

He was livid, but what could he do ? I realised, of course,
he might try and get me transferred, but I warned him what
would happen if he did that. I'd kept the original letter, you
see, and only offered him a copy, and if there was any trouble
I said I'd go straight to the fountain-head and put my facts
before them.

He said, " You've admitted yourself the net result's about the
same," and I said, " Well, not to you, I fancy."

I had him there, and he knew it. The upshot was he let me
in on it. Mind you, it wasn't the money I cared about so much,
as the fact that he couldn't treat me as a Grade II clerk any
more. In fact, after a bit I found I'd been recommended for

promotion. It wasn't much, but it was a beginning. I began to think my luck had changed. At that time I knew nothing about Chigwell. I hadn't even heard his name. How Chigwell knew what Edmonds' game was I don't know, but I suppose these men who make their living off other people the way *he* did have their spies everywhere. Well, for some months all went well. I was making more money than I'd ever done, and so far as I was concerned the war could go on for years. I didn't believe in that grand new world they were going to build ; at all events I knew there wouldn't be anything in it for me. My idea was to make hay while the sun shone, and the longer it shone the better pleased I'd be.

Then something happened I couldn't possibly have contemplated. Edmonds was found dead in his bed from an overdose of sleeping-mixture. A doctor said that he hadn't been sleeping well for some time and he'd given him tablets, and warned him to be careful about taking them. It was generally supposed that he'd made a mistake and taken too many, but I knew it wasn't that. Edmonds wasn't that sort of fellow.

I can tell you, it was a bit sickening to hear the way the high-ups spoke of him. A war casualty, they said, a man who'd done too much ever since he started this job, and now he'd paid the penalty. I don't think anyone suspected he might have done it on purpose. I could have told them quite a lot, but naturally I didn't. I did, however, wonder what it was going to mean for me. What it did mean was something else I hadn't contemplated. They gave me Edmonds' job. I tell you, I nearly cried when I heard that news. I swore I'd justify their faith in me. I thought I'd drop the game we'd been playing ; it was a bit dangerous anyhow. I'd make my Department the most damned efficient Department in the Ministry. I knew all I wanted was a bit of luck like this. My trouble was I'd never had a chance.

Well, everything went all right. The firms who'd been dealing on the quiet with Edmonds were a bit disappointed, I dare say, but they waited some time before putting out feelers to me, and, as I say, I meant to be careful. And I was careful. But there are some things no man can guard against. Chigwell was one of them. I'd had my Department for about three months when one night my telephone bell rang—in my flat, this was—and a voice I'd never heard before said, " Is that Mr. Burke ? My name's Chigwell. Did Edmonds ever speak of me ? " I thought a minute and then I said " No." I imagined, you see, he was something to do with one of the firms Edmonds had been—befriending.

"That's queer," said the voice. "We knew one another very well."

"I only knew Edmonds as a colleague," I told him, playing a safe game.

"That's why I thought he might have spoken of me," said Chigwell.

"Is there anything I can do for you?" I asked him, not meaning to lift a finger.

He said, "Well, perhaps we could get together sometime. How about you coming round here and having a little chat with me one evening?"

I was inclined to be on my high horse there. I supposed he was one of these rich chaps who think they've only got to crook a finger to get everything they want.

I said, "I'm a pretty busy man, you know," and he said, "Mr. Edmonds was a busy man, too, but he found time to come and see me."

For some reason I felt cold chills down my spine. And yet he said no more than that, said it in a quiet matter-of-fact voice. I think it was because he knew I was coming before I knew it myself, and he knew I'd come because I couldn't stay away. I didn't even then understand what it was all about.

"You'd better write to me," I said, but he replied, "Oh, no, I'm sure that would be very unwise. I see, though, that Mr. Edmonds hasn't confided in you."

I had been trying to place the fellow in my mind. Chigwell? The name meant nothing. I said, "What firm do you represent?" and he said, "James Chigwell. Just that." And then he added in a very soft drawling voice, "Then when may I expect you, Mr. Burke?"

I suggested he might come round to my office, make a date with my secretary, but he said, "When you understand the nature of my business I'm sure you'll agree it's best to transact it—privately."

I thought I knew what it was. I thought it was one of the firms Edmonds had—accommodated—coming back for more. Or even that it was some other firm who had found out about Edmonds and wanted similar favours. I'd made up my mind to say "No" to anyone. What Edmonds had done was his own affair, but I had my own code. I wasn't going to risk losing a good billet by doing anything out of the straight.

I went to see Chigwell the next day. I heard later that his nickname was "The Spider." It suited him. He was bloated with the flies he'd caught and scrunched. He soon made his business clear, and I began to understand why Edmonds had taken a short cut. It appeared he knew all about that business and my share in it. I told him he could go to my chief, if he liked. He had no proof. But he had. I didn't believe him at first, but Edmonds had sold me. I shall never know if it was because Chigwell dragged the truth out of him or whether it was his poor, pitiful way of getting his revenge. Whatever it was, it worked so far as Chigwell was concerned. I couldn't refuse. He said he'd go to the head of my section if I did, and I knew he meant it. He was clever, too, about protecting himself. He'd have seen to it he didn't suffer, would probably have impressed the authorities with a sense of his patriotism.

Of course, I never had a chance. I was forced back into the old ways. It's as though there's a curse on some men, whatever they do turns out wrong. My marriage, my writing, my army career and now my civilian job—I worked so desperately hard at all of them, and for all the good it was I might have slacked and lied my way through life like most men. I started the old secret game and I played it well. I hated it but I did it well. I didn't make much off it, because Chigwell was insatiable. If I made half-a-crown he wanted one-and-ninepence, and if I demurred he made it two shillings. Every now and again he forced his prices up. I was like a man bound hand and foot. Chigwell gave orders and I carried them out. If I'd refused he'd have put his threats into action and I should have not only lost my job but been faced with prosecution. And they would have prosecuted. The Government can't afford not to. They're answerable to the State, not to a private company.

So it went on, and all the time his demands were rising. I took risks Edmonds wouldn't have considered. It got so that I couldn't sleep, couldn't digest my food. I never knew what the next thing would be. And he used to taunt me.

" If you've developed a delicate conscience you know what to do," he'd say.

" If the terms are too high, stop playing. Only then, of course, you must take the consequences."

He almost invited his victims to murder him ; mind you, he never believed they would. That last minute before he died he half-lifted his head and my impression was one not of rage but of astonishment that at last someone had taken him at his word. He wasn't even afraid, there wasn't time. I'm sorry about that. I'd have liked him to suffer.

At last he went too far. He wanted me to take such chances I was almost bound to be discovered. It wasn't just money now, it was information he wanted. When I said it was out of the question he jeered at me.

" Turned very patriotic all of a sudden, haven't you ? " he said. " Or is it just funk ? "

Perhaps if he hadn't added those last five words I wouldn't have killed him.

I made my plans very carefully. Of course, the initials in the diary—I didn't know about the diary—were mine. I had an appointment for nine o'clock and I meant to keep it. But after he was found I had to persuade everyone that I hadn't been there at that time but later. Nine o'clock was a good time as a rule—of couse, I always made my visits at night ; most of his clients did ; none of us wanted to be recognised going into that dubious den—because most people put on the nine o'clock news if they don't listen to any other news programme during the day. And when a lot of wireless sets are turned on you're not so likely to be heard—always supposing something went wrong and he realised my intentions before I had time to strike.

I thought a lot about a weapon. Guns are no good ; they're too noisy and apt to act as boomerangs anyway. The police, and even the public, know far too much about firearms for them to be safe, and guns get traced to their owners, and bullets get traced to guns. Besides, I hadn't got a gun. I didn't mind about that. I didn't want to use anything that might later be traced to me. That meant I couldn't risk using a stick because it might be recognised, and if I tried to buy one specially the man who sold it might remember my face when he saw the news in the paper. I thought of a knife, but you need to know a good deal about anatomy to make sure the knife makes a fatal wound, and whatever I used had to be quick. Besides, the same objection attached to knives as to sticks. They can be traced—and you can't buy long, sharp carving-knives nowadays, or if you do they're so scarce no one could forget selling it to you. I wanted what I might describe as an anonymous weapon.

The best of all, as Crook would agree, are a man's hands. Everybody has hands, and hands don't leave fingerprints, but that was impracticable, too, because he was a bigger man than I was, an ape-like man really, and he had this particularly wide table between him and his visitors, so you'd never get a proper chance. That only left our old friend, the blunt instrument, since poison was out of the question, and my choice fell on a hammer. To begin with, I had a hammer that would do the job, and for another I didn't see why it should be traced to me, seeing I hadn't used it for ages and most likely nobody knew I had it. I wrapped it up in a bit of paper and put it in my overcoat pocket, and set out. My plan was nearly ruined at the start by a bit of bad luck—or so it seemed to me then—

135

in the shape of the air raid warden, Bairstowe. I was just going to ring Chigwell's bell when I heard voices on the other side of the door and then footsteps coming down the passage. I didn't want to be caught there that night of all nights, and if I went down I should almost certainly be seen and quite certainly heard. It was dark on the stairs, but most men carry a torch. However, the floor upstairs was deserted—they were all offices in that house and only Chigwell slept on the premises—so I slipped up as quietly as I could and waited. I heard Chigwell letting Bairstowe out and he had got a torch. I recognised him at once, and I heard Chigwell say, "Well, thanks for the warning. I'll see you don't have to call again." Then he went back and shut the door, and I went down and rang the bell. I had to wait till the man was off the premises, and that made me a minute or two late. Chigwell was in his most offensive mood ; he didn't open the door until I'd rung twice, and then he just turned the knob and asked if I thought I could afford to be so infernally casual about my appointments. I didn't answer that one. It didn't seem worth while. Besides, now that the moment had come, I was shaking and nervous. I couldn't afford to make a mistake. And with that fear was a sort of exaltation because I was going to have the last word, after all. All his money and his insolence couldn't save him. I put my hand on the newspaper-covered hammer and followed him into his room. I remembered those words of Sydney Carton on the scaffold : " It is a far, far better thing that I do than I have ever done." I don't mean to say I felt noble about a murder, but I felt in a way triumphant. He'd humiliated me for the last time. I let him have his say and stood by the wall in a downcast fashion. I knew exactly what I had to do, and I went over it in my mind while he was talking. I knew he'd sit down and keep me waiting because I'd dared to be a minute or two late. I didn't imagine that what he was doing was urgent, but he'd let me see that it was more important than his business with me. While his head was bent over the paper I'd strike—I didn't know if I'd need to strike more than once. I reminded myself I'd got to keep my head. You hear of murderers who go berserk with the first blow and then go on hammering their victim to bloody pulp. There mustn't be anything like that in my case. I'd have to be careful, too, about blood. It was lucky the table was so wide. As soon as he was dead I'd find my papers in the safe and take the really incriminating ones. Then I'd go out and hang about till ten o'clock. At ten o'clock I was coming back to put a note through the letter-box. In that note I was going to say that I had called at ten o'clock as arranged over the phone but could get no reply. This note I should push through the flap—to fall into the locked box inside. The fact that the box was locked would prove, I thought, that I had been outside the door when I wrote it. I didn't see why anyone should get into the flat between 9.15, when I should be leaving—though actually it was later; these things take longer than you anticipate—and 10 o'clock when I returned. But if the police did hear of the murder they wouldn't surely suspect a man who came openly up the stairs at ten o'clock. Well, I'd gone over and over that plan and I couldn't see any flaw in it. Of course, it would have been helpful if I could have produced an alibi to show that at nine o'clock I couldn't have been at Chigwell's flat, but I didn't see how it could be managed. I did even think of using Chigwell's phone and ringing up some friend or other, saying that I was speaking from my own flat. But I discarded that idea as being unnecessarily dangerous. Because it might come out that I wasn't at home—someone might have seen me in the street—someone might even have tried to ring me up at that time and not got a reply—and if I was caught out in one deception that would rouse suspicion, and that I couldn't afford. Crook never said anything truer than when he warned me that successful criminals commit their murders and then lie low. But it's a counsel of perfection, and in any case, no matter how logical you are, it's impossible to allow for every development.

All this flashed through my mind while I stood by Chigwell's desk. He had seated himself and was bending over the inevitable paper. After a minute or so he just glanced up and jerked his pen towards a chair.

" Sit down," he said. " I can't attend to you for a minute." With those words he really signed his own death-warrant, though I didn't intend him to live in any case. That gesture of contempt infuriated me. I saw him going carefully through those papers that were going to drag some other poor devil down as low as I was now, and I thought " Here at least is something at which I won't fail," and I tore the hammer out of my pocket and lunged at him. It must have been instinct that made him lift his head just as the hammer descended. It caught him fair and square, though ; I didn't know a skull would fracture like a china plate. I'd jumped clear of the blood, but I struck him a second blow to make quite sure. I couldn't really believe he was dead. I couldn't see how anything so powerful could be put out of existence so suddenly. I'm not going to pretend I liked murdering him, but I had to do it. It was his life or mine, and he'd had too much of mine as it was. For too long I'd been the defeated one. Now at last I'd taken the law in my own hands.

In my imagination I'd proceeded immediately with the next step, opened the safe, found my papers, but it wasn't quite so smooth as that. To begin with, I couldn't move right away. I was like a man with palsy. Then I remembered that he always kept the keys in his pocket, and I didn't see how I could search— that. But I did it. I've been defeated by my own feelings— squeamishness, if you like—too often, and now everything was at stake. I found the keys and opened the safe. There were more papers in it than I'd expected, and a sort of panic took hold of me. I couldn't find mine, I thought someone might come any minute, I'd be caught like a rat in a trap. I tore the papers out of the safe and dug my way through them. At last I found the ones I wanted. I didn't take them all away. That would have been too suspicious. You see, I wasn't going to pretend I'd never heard of Chigwell. The police aren't as easily taken in as some people think. Besides, I'd planned my ten o'clock visit. I left just enough to show that I was in his clutches, but nothing that would give the Ministry ground for a prosecution.

Then—I don't know why, instinct perhaps—I darted across the room and peeped out of the window. I can't explain what the atmosphere was like, that dead man and the silence and the rest of the house empty. I shivered when I thought of the number of stairs I'd got to negotiate. I thought someone might see me coming out. . . .

The first thing I noticed was that it was snowing, hard white flakes. I didn't mind that. I should get wet, of course, but then in a snowstorm no one notices his neighbour. He just puts his head down and goes for home like a horse going for his stable. I saw somebody coming up the street. I thought, I'll just watch and make sure which way he goes, and then my heart nearly stood still, because he turned in at the doorway of No. 32. I knew fear then all right, but it isn't true that it numbs you. It didn't numb me. I didn't stop to lock the safe or put things tidy. I didn't even think about fingerprints. I'd put on gloves before I opened the safe, so I didn't think there was any danger to be apprehended from that direction. I picked up the hammer and wrapped it in the newspaper. I didn't like putting it back in my pocket in the condition it was in now, but I couldn't leave it there and I didn't dare carry it. I might meet a policeman. I put it in the inside pocket of my overcoat—I always have a big one for papers—and threw a last look round. I'd got the papers out of the safe in my pocket, and I came out of the flat and heard the door close behind me. It had one of those self-closing doors that don't make a sound.

I dare say Chigwell had found that useful enough from time to time. As I waited an instant getting used to the dark I heard steps coming up the stairs and I knew I'd got to repeat my ruse of half an hour ago. Instead of going down I went up and crouched in the dark, waiting. I wondered what the new-comer would do when he found he couldn't get a reply. Call the police ? I didn't know. Most people don't want to advertise their whereabouts when they're visiting a man like Chigwell. All the same, it was murder. Still, I reflected, he wouldn't know that. Then I heard something I could hardly believe. A key scraped in a lock and then the door closed again with just the faintest click. I didn't know what to make of that. It hadn't occurred to me that Chigwell would have given anyone a key. That frightened me more than I'd ever been frightened in my life, because the best generalship in the world couldn't have foreseen that. Any minute now, I thought, the balloon will go up, the police will come. . . . I wondered if I could get out before they arrived, or if it would be wiser to wait and try to make a dash later. I waited. I had to. I'd got to know what was going to happen, what to expect. And nothing happened ! Inside the flat everything was perfectly still. I waited for the sound of wheels in the street, footsteps on the stairs. And nothing came. Then I realised that the man inside wasn't going to take the risk of calling the police. Probably, like the rest of us, he couldn't afford to be found in James Chigwell's flat at such an hour, and particularly not with James Chigwell lying dead in his study. I looked at the luminous watch on my wrist. The time was creeping on. Creeping ? It was racing. I felt hideously impatient. I wanted that chap to go, so that I could leave my note at the right time. I'd written it on a bit of paper torn from an old diary before I left the house. Oh, I thought of all the details. Then it occurred to me that it didn't matter if he still was on the premises. If he saw the note come through the letter-box, heard me on the stairs, it still didn't matter. He wouldn't dare open the door because he wouldn't dare show himself. I waited till my watch said ten o'clock and then down I came, moving as quietly as I could, and put the paper through the slot.

As everyone knows, things didn't work out as I'd anticipated, because of that 1000-to-1 chance of the note slipping between the letter-box and the door. Naturally that ruined my scheme because now there was nothing to show it hadn't been left from the inside. But at the time I'd no idea what had happened. I must admit I felt a bit feverish waiting to see the reaction of the police. But I never believed they'd arrest me. I was not only frightened, I was furious. It seemed to me to prove that there was some malign providence always working against me. Because that had been a good plan. It showed judgment and subtlety, it was the sort of plan that deserved to succeed. I'd considered every possibility, but how could anyone have foreseen the truth ? They say any number of murderers escape undetected each year, men who don't pay nearly so much attention to detail, men who don't even pretend to be artists. Yet they succeed where I—failed. When they shut me up in that cell I thought I should go mad. I'd no hope. They asked me about legal aid. I had no money to speak of, and I couldn't see what a lawyer could do to help me, but they sent a man called Anderson. I couldn't tell him the truth, but I repeated the story I'd planned. I forgot to say that on the way back I threw the hammer into the water tank. I cleaned it up as well as I could with the newspaper, and as soon as I got back I burnt the newspaper by holding it in a pair of pincers over a gas ring. Anderson didn't even pretend to be hopeful. He said I'd admitted I had an appointment and there was nothing to show it had been postponed, except my note, and there was nothing to show that that was sincere. He said they mightn't find the weapon but the weapon would be much less important than motive. He asked if I had an alibi for any part of that evening, but of course I hadn't, not the part that mattered. I couldn't tell him about the two men who, I knew, had also been on the premises that night because I wasn't supposed to be there when Bairstowe departed or when the second one arrived. I felt as good as hanged already.

And then the miracle happened. Young Jardine came forward with apparent proof of my innocence. It was a crazy thing to do, and I couldn't feel any sympathy for him, because a man like that doesn't deserve his luck. It was in a way proof of his innocence that he rushed in where any angel might be forgiven for fearing to tread.

You might have thought I'd be satisfied now to let well alone, thank my lucky stars that one man was fool enough to put his head into the noose in my place. But human nature's queer. I realised, of course, that Jardine would put up some sort of defence, and I had to know what that defence would be. I had to be prepared to counter every move made by the other side, know what his lawyer was going to say, find out if I should be asked to explain anything more and if so, what ? I had to have my answers pat. Lawyers aren't like other people. They've no compunction about stabbing you in the back. I thought that if I could find out their moves before they made them, then I should be prepared. It wouldn't be easy, of course. I'd got to find some good excuse. Otherwise I'd rouse suspicions. People always look askance at the man who wants to barge his way in. I made some enquiries about young Jardine. He didn't seem to have any relations or friends except this girl, Bess Carter. That in a way made it easier for me. I learned, too, that financially he wasn't very sound, and it seemed to me that this did give me a chance. To a girl like Bess, at all events, it wouldn't seem strange that the man whose life Jardine had saved should want to pay part of his debt. Because, without Jardine, I wouldn't have had a hope at all. I thought, too, that any reputable lawyer would be quite glad to discuss the matter with me, if Bess were the only alternative. She had the proverbial heart of gold, but lawyers usually prefer you to have a Kensingtonian accent. She knew her own limitations, too, which was lucky for me and she was mad enough about Jardine to accept any offer that might seem helpful. Of course, I know Crook's right, that the wise criminal is the unostentatious criminal. But huddling alone in the dark and hearing other people move about in the light beyond your cave is too much for most of us. Besides, I'd got to know if suspicion ever pointed again in my direction. I'd got to know. It was worth any risk.

I said at the beginning that I never really had a chance, and it's true. Every star in its course was against me. I don't know how many hundreds or thousands of lawyers there are in the country, but Bess had to get in touch with Arthur Crook. Now he was the one man who wouldn't be satisfied with a " Not Proven " verdict. He'd see beyond the acquittal and realise that " Not Proven " doesn't do a man much good ; in fact, he's often luckier if he swings. No, Crook had his reputation to maintain and he'd feel he owed it to that reputation to find the real criminal. Here again I'd be unlucky. Other men might stumble on to someone else, but not Crook. Crook would go on till he'd unbuilt all that careful painstaking edifice I'd erected. My only hope was to give him someone else in my place, someone against whom he could bring a foolproof case— and that was harder than the murder itself.

There wasn't very much choice. As Crook said later, we were bound by the time factor. We had evidence that Chigwell was alive at nine when Bairstowe called and dead at nine-thirty when Jardine arrived—that, at all events, would be Crook's case. It was going to be difficult to discover anyone who could have arrived between Bairstowe's departure at nine and Jardine's arrival half an hour later, who could have got in, murdered

Chigwell, ransacked the safe and got away again without being seen. And in any case you can't in real life build up a case round a non-existent man. Then I saw my opportunity, saw what Crook saw, that at last the luck had turned if only for a minute in my direction. Here was a man who was admittedly on the scenes within a few minutes of the murder, a man whose initials were the same as mine. It seemed to me it might be possible, by not letting up for an instant, by paving the way, by faking evidence that could easily be genuine, to build up a case against Bairstowe.

Since it won't matter to me now what anyone thinks, I'll be frank and say I didn't have a qualm about trying to get an innocent man taken for my crime. Self-preservation's the first law and the instinct's never so strong as when one is in great danger. Of course, I had to be, as it were, inside the shop rather than just staring through the window to make sure what was going on. If I made one false step I was lost, and unless I was keeping up with the defence I was bound to go wrong. The first thing I had to do was to win Bess's confidence and that wasn't hard. She didn't think it strange that I should want to help. A woman as infatuated as she was has no sense of humour, she doesn't work by logic. She wouldn't sit down and ask herself why, having escaped the gallows, I should want to come back into the field ; it wouldn't seem to her odd that anyone should want to help Jardine to get off. So she accepted my offer of money without a grain of hesitation. Crook, of course, was a different matter. He probably thought it a bit fishy from the start. I had to give him the impression that I was after Bess myself, though whether such a cynic believed that any man would put down good money to save a rival I don't know. Still, that was one of the chances I had to take.

Crook, of course, would say that was my first blunder—if you discount the murder, that is, and all that led up to it. The trouble about making mistakes is they're like stitches on a knitting needle. One follows the other, you can't help yourself. That's why I began my story with my unfortunate marriage years and years ago. I knew I'd have to be patient. It wouldn't do to try and worm too much out of Crook. I'd have to work through Bess, who could be trusted to tell me anything she knew. So I waited to see which way the cat would jump. And that was where Crook was so infernally clever. He didn't jump at all. He did nothing. In fact, he was so infernally sure of himself that he gave me the advice he'd have given one of his own clients. He said, " The wise criminal's like Brer Rabbit. He lies low." Which was all very well, but how was

I to be sure that he didn't say that because it was part of his plan ? He might have suspected me already and be leading me up the garden, going behind my back and accumulating evidence and pretending he was waiting like a spider. . . . That great red face gives nothing away. He just said, " I shall expect the murderer to make the first move, and I shan't do anything till he does."

I tried to put out a feeler by asking if he wasn't afraid that the first blow might be against him, but he insinuated that even a criminal wouldn't be as crazy as that. He was someone, he was ; if anything happened to him the whole police force would be on the murderer's track. Anyway, it was too dangerous. Too many people have tried to put Arthur Crook out, and none of them with any success. I had to decide what to do next. I might have threatened Bess Carter with anonymous letters, but I couldn't see that she was any real source of danger—she'd done all the harm she could by dragging Crook into the affair. Or so I thought at the time. I couldn't guess she'd lay hands on the hammer. Solomon himself couldn't have foreseen that. So the only person left was myself. I had to play on the financial motive. That and personal danger. Keep out, withdraw your offer or it'll be the worse for you. It wasn't a very trump card, but it was the best I held in my hand.

I thought even Crook wouldn't imagine I should send myself anonymous letters, and if I was going to implicate Bairstowe I had to have something tangible to go on. The first letter I wrote on part of a bill I'd had for wireless repairs. I thought that was rather subtle, and I knew Crook wasn't the man to miss that clue. I posted that first letter, so that it would show that the criminal came from our part of the world, but the second one I wrote and left sealed and stamped (in an already used envelope) in my own letter-box. I put it there before I left for London. I knew Mrs. McKay, who " does " for me in a more sketchy way than she'd admit, wouldn't come up till about ten, by which time there were certain to be other letters waiting for me. In fact, I arranged that there should be. No one can say I didn't consider every detail, but no man can fight a persistent round of bad luck. I guessed that Crook would notice there wasn't a second postmark, but that would strengthen the conviction that the murderer was a local man.

Crook reacted as I'd anticipated, and I waited to hear what he proposed to do before I took the next step. But he didn't give himself away, and even if he had formulated a plan he had no time to put it into action, because when I got back I found that Bess had pounced on the hammer and intended to drag that into the case. That was something I'd never thought of. It was the sort of thing Crook would make capital out of. When I heard that I was in despair. What was the good of all my elaborate planning if sheer fortuitous evidence was going to defeat me ? That hammer had no right to be discovered until long after Jardine was dead and done for, and by that time people would have stopped talking about the case. That development nearly drove me frantic. I had only one thought in my head. Crook mustn't know about it. It was ridiculous to suppose that I could persuade Bess the hammer didn't matter. Even if I could have proved it to her she'd have taken her idea to Crook just the same, because she'd reached the desperate stage where logic and common sense meant nothing. She'd have put the last thing she had, including her own life, if necessary, on the slenderest chance of saving Jardine. And as it happened it was her own life she was risking.

Let me say here I never wanted to kill Bess, but I had no choice. I dare say a lot of the men at the Front don't really want to kill the enemy. They've no personal grudge against him but they have a job to do and they've got to push it through to the uttermost. It was like that with me. Either I had to throw in my hand or follow the thing through. And I decided to follow it through. It'll be obvious, therefore, that Bess had to die. I swear that if I could have found any other way out I'd have taken it, but there was none. What was more, I had to act quickly. Bess wouldn't wait. Even if I left it till the next morning she might telephone Crook and then, living or dead, she'd hang me. I had to get hold of that hammer and put it somewhere where it couldn't implicate me. I hadn't much time to make plans, and I didn't attempt to look further ahead than the next step. And the next step meant getting hold of the hammer and preventing Bess from talking about it. And there was only one way of doing that.

I've said I didn't want to kill Bess, but men in my position haven't much feeling to spare for anyone but themselves. Besides, I almost hated her for making me do this thing. Since I'm being honest, I'll add that what moved me most was the thought that it would precipitate me into yet more danger, and I couldn't see yet whether I could hang this crime on to Bairstowe. The rule of this mad world is slay or be slain, and I didn't mean to be the slain. I thought like lightning. I'd got to see Bess before she had a chance to talk to anyone else, I'd got to get the hammer and I'd got to silence her—for good. That was enough to be going on with.

You see, I'd got to do the practically impossible. I had to

see Bess and yet I had to show, when questions were asked, that I couldn't be implicated in her murder. I agreed to her suggestion to meet her at the tea-shop where I, at all events, wouldn't be known. But I knew I couldn't really go there. Because even if she wasn't recognised when she went in you only had to see her once to remember her, and someone might very well identify me as being her companion. No, I had to see her in some place where there would be no witnesses. So I laid my plan.

It was a good one. I was proud of it. I knew that Mrs. McKay always went out after lunch to do the shopping ; she used to come in about four, and I doubt if the end of the world or anything short of that would have stopped her. As soon as she came in she went to her own quarters and was invisible for the rest of the day. About a quarter to four, therefore, I went down to the front door, ostensibly to see how thick the fog was ; but while I was there I dropped on the mat the letter signed with Bess's initials addressed to me. I didn't know what Bess's writing was like, but that didn't matter as it was bound to be established that the letter was a forgery. I left it in the very middle of the mat. Knowing Mrs. McKay's insatiable curiosity I knew she'd bring it up herself. So I went back to the flat and waited. I got my coat and hat and was all ready to start, but of course I never meant to go out. As a matter of fact the fog very nearly spoilt my plan. I couldn't stay indoors much after four without exciting suspicion, and for once she was a bit behind time. But just when I was beginning to feel desperate up she came, with the letter in her hand. I was tempted to open it then and there, but I thought that might occasion comment later, as though I'd wanted a witness. You see, I thought of everything down to the last detail. It was sheer bad luck that defeated me all along the line. When she saw I wasn't going to open it she went away and I ripped open the envelope, and a minute later turned on the wireless. I put it on pretty loud so she was bound to hear it, and she'd argue, if she thought about it at all, that a man doesn't put on the radio if he intends to go out. I left it on when I left the flat, so that anyone passing would assume I was inside.

I'd left my car just along the road, and I didn't run into anyone as I made my way to it and got in. The fog was fairly thick now, and I was glad of that, because not only would I not be recognised, my car wouldn't be recognised either. I drove fairly slowly towards the bus stop. It was now about four-twenty ; I wasn't in the least afraid that Bess would have gone on, because the bus is never on time, and on a foggy day it might be as much as an hour late. When I reached the bus stop I could make out Bess standing on the other side of the road ; I didn't see anyone else there. It really was pretty thick now. I called out and she came across and I saw at once that she'd brought the hammer. I asked her if she'd mentioned her suspicion to anyone else, and she said " No," she even suspected the bottles of beer by this time. Crook had told her to keep her mouth shut if she had any suspicions, and she had the sort of faith in Crook heathens have in their idols. We talked about the hammer for a few minutes and I agreed that it might be what we were looking for. I said I'd take it up if she liked and show it to Crook, but she suggested that we might ask him to come down. I agreed to that, because it didn't matter. I'd made up my mind Crook wasn't going to know anything about it. If I had had any qualms before they vanished now. There was something about that solid obstinacy, that refusal to consider anyone except a comparatively worthless young man that roused my fury. Then something else happened that seemed to me indicative of the trivial nature of women. Bess discovered she'd lost a button off her coat. I wouldn't have made such a to-do about losing a fiver. Bess was really worried. She said you couldn't match up buttons like that any more. I said a bit sarcastically that it was too bad, but in a war. . . . She said, " I might look on the way back. I know I had it when I was waiting at the bus stop because I was twisting it while I was talking to the old man."

That was the first time I knew there had been anyone else there. I said sharply :

" Who was he ? "

She said, " Oh, you must know him. He's a museum piece. He lodges with Mrs. Lewis in Mowbray Crescent. I call him the toy soldier."

She went on to describe him, she took him off, not unkindly, but just for fun. A blind man could have identified Possel-thwaite after that. All this time my resolution was hardening. Mind you, I hated what I was going to do, and I was frightened. I was more frightened in a way than when I'd determined to kill Chigwell. Bess was so close, she was so alive, she had so many friends. No one except the police could mind Chigwell dying, but if it ever came out that I was responsible for Bess's death I knew I might quite well be burnt at the stake. I'd be glad then of the protection of the police. And all the time I couldn't really accept the fact that these things were happening to me. I didn't want to be a murderer. I wanted to be left alone to get my living and be like other people. I kept being

forced into things I hated. I said, apropos of the old man :
" Did you tell him where you were going ? "

She said, " I told him I was waiting for a friend."

I had to find out whether she'd mentioned my name. The
trouble was Bess was so slapdash she might have told him who
I was without remembering it. I couldn't face the thought of
a third murder, but it didn't make me wonder whether it
wouldn't be wiser to throw up the sponge now. I'd gone too
far. It's like gambling. Even if you know your next stake
means ruin if you lose you make the stake just the same. I'd
gone too far to turn back.

Well, I talked a bit more about the old boy, lightly so as not
to arouse her suspicions, but I was convinced after a bit she
hadn't told him who I was. She said she was remembering
what Crook had said to her, not to trust anyone. And then she
laughed.

" Not that my toy soldier could be any harm to anyone,"
she added.

She suggested that on the way back, if the fog had lifted,
we might stop the car and see if she had dropped the button on
the grass verge. If it wasn't there it would mean the old gentleman had picked it up and she could ask him. But she didn't
think he'd have it. He was probably as blind as a bat.

By this time we were getting near the cottage. She seemed to
realise it was a strange road and she said, " Where on earth are
we going ? "

I knew then the time had come. There was no sense pro-
longing the agony, and the sooner I got back to my flat the
better. I'd taken the receiver off the telephone, so if anyone rang
up they'd only get the engaged signal, but I hoped no one would,
because I might be asked who had telephoned me, and I should
have to say a wrong number, and that increased my danger.
I saw it all, you see, in terms of my danger. There's nothing in
that. Anybody would.

Bess turned her head and tried to look through the window
of the car. I think it was then that some suspicion dawned in
her mind. Her voice was different as she asked, " Mr. Burke,
where are we going ? What does it mean ? "

I was afraid she was going to shout, perhaps try to break the
window. It was zero hour for me and I didn't hesitate. She
was wearing a long blue scarf round her throat and I stopped
the car and caught the ends of the scarf and drew them tight.
She was a strong girl ; if she'd been prepared I don't believe
I could have done it, but I took her by surprise and it was a
minute before she got over the shock, and by then it was too

147

late. By the time she realised it was neither an accident nor a joke she'd no breath left to fight with. All the same, if I had to do it again I'd rather kill Chigwell than Bess. There was so little room in the car, and I was afraid I hadn't finished the job. In real life people don't die as easily and neatly as they do on films.

But presently I knew it was all over. Even then I couldn't let up. There was still so much to do. I had to get rid of Bess's body, I had to dispose of the hammer, and there was still the problem of the button. I kept telling myself I'd find that by the bus stop. And then I had to go on strengthening my own alibi. When they found Bess I was pretty sure I was the person they'd come to. I'd already telephoned Cotham to ask if she'd left the inn and to explain that I was expecting her and she hadn't arrived. I had to carry on with that. There was an A.A. telephone box quite close. I left the car near it and put through another call to " The Case Is Altered." It was now about five o'clock, and I hoped and anticipated that Cotham would assume I was still in my flat. I asked if he'd heard anything more from Bess and gave the impression I was really anxious. He was a bit short, and anyway I didn't want to linger. I came back to the car and drove it as near the cottage as I could.

The most ticklish part of the job was still in front of me. I had to get Bess's body from the car to the cottage. There was one thing, I wasn't likely to be seen. That road's pretty deserted at the best of times, and on a foggy afternoon I didn't think even the ardours of lovers would take them to such a spot. If you've never tried you've no notion how heavy a dead body can be. I had to leave her in the car while I reconnoitred and then I came back and opened the door and tried to lift her out. In the films the villain just picks up the body and dumps it as if it were a soft cushion. It's not like that in real life. I dragged and strained and tugged. I had to keep stopping to get my breath, with her dead weight lying against me. That was much worse than the killing. In a way perhaps I'm lucky I'm going to die. Even now I wake with the feeling of her in my arms, her hair brushing my cheek. Perhaps in time I'd have gone mad.

I was tempted to leave her among the bushes, but I had my own reasons for wanting her to be found at the cottage. I didn't think about her reputation or what people might say. Bess, living, had never cared what people said and now what difference could it make ? Half-dragging, half-carrying, I got her into the cottage. I put her on the settle, leaning against the wall, and tried to make her look as natural as possible. I remember how I pulled the red fishnet affair she wore over her hair and straightened the little red coat. Then I opened her bag and put the note in it. I forgot about the note at first and was almost back at the car when I remembered it. I had to force myself to go back, and even then I forgot about the mackintosh she'd been wearing round her shoulders, and that she'd pushed off in the car. I knew I ought to take that back, too, but I couldn't, I couldn't. I got rid of it eventually by loading the pockets with stones and dropping it down that disused quarry by Dead Man's Leap.

The fog was getting worse and worse ; I doubt if I'd have found the button even if I'd used a torch, even if it had been there. And I wanted to get back as quickly as possible. I had the hammer, of course. I'd got to plant that on Bairstowe. I wanted to stop and get rid of it at once, but I had to keep up the fiction that I hadn't left my house. I came back and telephoned Cotham again directly after the news. Then I rang up Bairstowe, but there wasn't any reply. That suited me all right. I knew about the key under the mat. All I had to do was choose my moment and put the hammer on the premises. First of all I'd thought of getting rid of the hammer as I got rid of the mackintosh, then I thought it might be useful as another nail in Bairstowe's coffin. I'd got to find someone to put in my place, you see. I'd got to.

You'd have thought all I'd been through would have been enough trouble for anyone. I was almost at the end of my tether. But I couldn't rest. I couldn't rest. My malign fate was still stalking me. There was the button. I went back the next morning, but it wasn't there. I didn't know what to do. If the old man had found it he might put in it his pocket and forget all about it, he might give it to the next urchin he met, he might pass it over to his landlady. It seemed to me I'd best do nothing till I saw if the button was going to be important. No one might notice it was missing. But, of course, they did. All the time I was playing the part of the anxious friend, going down to " The Case Is Altered," ringing up for news, even suggesting the police. Cotham was against that. At the time I understand it aroused some suspicion in some people's minds, but I could have told them he was much too hard-headed a business man to let anything happen to Bess if he could prevent it. I went to work as usual and kept waiting for the telephone to ring. Somehow I'd expected her to be found at once. The suspense was appalling. Another thing happened that I hadn't anticipated. People kept speaking to me with her voice. I suppose you might say that was a guilty conscience. I don't know. But I kept looking up and biting back her name. It was nervous exhaustion, I suppose.

I didn't really have to wait very long before they found the body. Mr. Stout found it, which was unexpected, though it didn't really make any difference. But the button immediately assumed considerable proportions. I could tell myself a hundred times that it had rolled down a drain or something, but I couldn't be sure. I managed to get into Posselthwaite's rooms and search thoroughly but the button wasn't there. I gave an excuse at the Ministry that I had to have special leave to attend to private affairs and I followed him round. If it wasn't in his room, I argued, he'd got it about him somewhere. If he'd given it to anyone else we should have heard about it.

I think I was beginning to lose grip by this time. I thought the whole world was in a conspiracy against me. If it's true that nothing succeeds like success nothing's so deleterious to the spirit as failure. And for all my efforts I hadn't succeeded. It's true I hadn't been arrested, but if the old man came forward with the button questions would be asked, and Bairstowe might be able to clear himself for that afternoon. He'd said he'd gone over to Halton for some spares. I thought if I could find the button and plant it on him that would strengthen my case. I see now it was overdoing it. Any man who found that button in his possession would have chucked it away—unless he was innocent and could make the police believe it.

I got rid of the hammer all right by letting myself into Bairstowe's shop one day when I knew he was on duty. Sunday morning that was. Nobody stirs very early at Pullcheston on Sundays, except the few ultra-religious who rise at dawn to attend early service. I didn't like keeping the hammer so long but it was my first chance. I breathed afresh after it was out of my care. But the relief was not for long. Other fears followed.

Let no man think a murderer knows any peace. There comes a stage quite early, I think, in most crimes when he asks himself, " Was it conceivably worth it ? Is life, any life, good enough to pay for these subterfuges, these terrors, these midnight sweats and daylong apprehensions ? Is it possible that happiness or even peace can return ? Am I to remain a prisoner for the rest of my days, prisoned not now by men but by my own knowledge ? "

The papers gave a good deal of publicity to the button. It was inconceivable to me that Posselthwaite could long remain in ignorance of the value of the clue that he, I was convinced, possessed. Desperation seized me afresh. Now I felt that to regain the button was not enough. I must ensure his silence, as I had ensured hers. This time I was resolved it should not be murder. Two murders were sufficient. One day I was driving down a lonely road when I saw him just ahead. Something whispered, " This is your chance. You'll never have a better. There are no witnesses. Road accidents happen every day of the week. And he is the last of them. When he is out of the way you will be safe." For this time there was to be no concealment. This time it was I who would report the death to the police. I might perhaps be censured by some officious coroner, but my licence was clean and old men are sometimes deaf. I could claim to have sounded my horn. To my annoyance he heard me coming and moved to the side of the road. I resolved he should not escape me so easily. It would be simple to say that I had swerved to avoid him and at the eleventh hour he had jumped backwards. But he was too quick for me. How was I to know he had been an acrobat and still retained some of the agility of his craft ? I drove past, my head well down. At the cross-roads I turned and came back. This time, I thought, I shall get him. There was now no thought in my mind of my own danger. I had reached a stage where one consideration and one only could occupy my attention of the moment. Now all that mattered was that he should be destroyed. The explanation I must offer I would leave until later. This time I was certain of success, but again he eluded me. I went past at a great pace to avoid recognition. I dared not make another attempt that day. But the next day I left my office on some excuse at the time that he was wont to take what he called his constitutional, and this time I used more guile. I overtook him, offered him a lift. He vouchsafed the information that he had evidence for the police, that he had been to see the Member. I coaxed him into the car. Now I knew no mercy. I would sooner, I thought, we both went over the edge together than that he should survive another day. I had put on a disguise after leaving the Ministry. Even my own colleagues might not have known me. My stage experience was useful here.

I shall never know whether he was deceived from the start and resolved in his pig-headed British way to risk his life in the interests of justice or whether realisation dawned on him after I had closed the door and we were driving along the road. He told me voluntarily about the button and I asked for it. And then he said he had lost it, must have left it at Bramham Manor. I helped him to search, I insisted on examining his pockets, but I never dreamed that all the while it was in my possession. He must have realised by that time that his own plight was desperate.

Perhaps he hoped fate would cause me to pull out the button in public and so avenge him. Could he guess that he would escape death ? And if I had clung to my original notion and squeezed the life out of him I might not be writing this now. After Bess, that young, vigorous woman, it would have been child's-play. But I had had enough of murder. This was to be accident. This was better than running him down in the road. When they found his body who was likely to link up Rupert Burke, the temporary civil servant, with an unfortunate accident ? And why should anyone wish to murder so inoffensive a creature ? Of course, there was the possibility that Mr. Stout would come forward, but even so the burden of proof would be with the police.

I saw him go pitching down that slope and I felt for him none of the distress that had irked me where Bess was concerned. I was glad he was dead, savagely, riotously glad. I peeled off my disguise, I turned the car, I stopped at a shop where I was known to buy tobacco. I thought at last my road was clear. Even the discovery of the button could not daunt me. Indeed, I saw in it a fresh opportunity to involve Bairstowe in the murders. I went down to " The Case Is Altered " that night. They were talking about Posselthwaite. I joined in, asking who he was, why he should disappear. Even the police, I thought, would not find him for several days ; he might even be white bones before the truth was known. During the evening I challenged Bairstowe to a competition at darts ; I found an opportunity to slip the button into his pocket.

Now let him find the explanation, I thought exultantly.

And all the time Crook was playing with me like a cat with a mouse. Crook knew, waited with that cynical, inhuman grin of his to see me sign my own death-warrant. Oh, it was clever, the way he allowed everyone to think he believed Bairstowe guilty. He tricked even me who believed I was prepared for him. When he spoke of retrieving the hammer I thought the case was almost done. What chance would Bairstowe have if Crook were his enemy ? And all the time he was baiting a last trap for me. Even so I might have saved myself if I'd kept my head, if I'd told them that Bess had spoken over the telephone of a crack in the handle. But probably they wouldn't have believed me. They'd have remembered that grinning fiend's motto.

Crook always gets his man !

EPILOGUE

MR. STOUT, crossing the public lobby of the House of Commons, was surprised to see a familiar figure in bright brown suitings and carrying a common brown billycock hat, standing near one of the statues of Britain's great departed. It was several weeks since the *News of the Day* had published Mr. Burke's dramatic confession and already the " Scarlet Button Case " was dusty history. Someone had found a woman's leg in a London sewer and the news was of greater interest to the vast B.P. than the prophesied European invasion. At all events for the time being.

" Why, Mr. Crook," said Stout. " What on earth brings you here ? "

Crook grinned amiably. " I always wanted to pay one visit to the British Museum before I passed on," he explained. " And I'll say it's worth it. Every dynasty and degree, haven't you ? I never saw a finer set of specimens."

He looked round him, beaming. On all hands Members of Parliament were lolling or plunging or meditating ; they went to the Post Office, the telephone booths, the Chamber, the Plan Room and the bar ; they interviewed constituents, they dictated to secretaries, they talked to one another or, if no other Member was available, to themselves. They bought railway tickets, stamps and cups of tea just like ordinary human beings. For all he—Crook—knew, any one of them might have murdered his grandmother that morning, provided there were sufficient centenarians left in the country. He grinned at them all. It was as good as the Earl's Court Exhibition of his heyday.

Mr. Stout, alarmed, as well he might be, by the amount of attention his companion was attracting, hurriedly suggested the bar and they went off together at a good pace.

" Tell me," said Mr. Stout, when they were comfortably settled, " when did you first start suspecting Burke ? "

" If ever you commit a murder there are two things you should bear in mind," said Crook, comfortably distending his waistcoat with some of the House of Commons excellent beer. " The first, of course, is to get me to frank you, and I don't mind telling you I'd put myself out for you. The second is to stick to the truth in details and keep your lies for the broad outline. Very few chaps have good enough memories to see the thing through. You've got to remember the things that haven't happened as well as the things that have, if you get me."

Mr. Stout said he wasn't at all sure that he did but probably it would all become clear by the time Mr. Crook had finished.

"Now, take the case of Burke. He said he'd originally had an appointment with Chigwell for nine o'clock, but he had to get the man to change it because he had a job of work to finish and couldn't get away from his flat in time. But the evidence showed that he'd left his flat soon after nine at latest. Y'see, we know the snow started at 9.20, and any man leaving his flat after that time would have taken a mackintosh or an umbrella, or both. Whereas Burke took neither. He said to the police, 'The snow took me by surprise,' which showed he must have left his flat by say nine-ten. Because if he'd been within two or three minutes of it he'd have gone back. That was his first slip-up. Then he said that, havin' failed to get any reply to his ringin' he went away but subsequently rang up without gettin' an answer. Now we know, though Burke didn't at that time, that young Jardine had removed the receiver, so anyone ringin' up would get the engaged signal and would assume that there was someone in the flat. Well, that was two whoppers and I began to ask myself, 'What for?'"

"And didn't have much difficulty in finding an answer?"

"Right first time," acknowledged Crook. "After that, of course, he simply served the case up to me with parsley round the dish."

Mr. Stout, keeping his head with some difficulty and reflecting that his colleagues would only imagine this was one of the more boisterous kinds of constituent, said intelligently," You mean, the anonymous letters?"

"Sure I mean the anonymous letters. Only one man could have written those and that man was the murderer."

"But I thought you said that whenever a murder was committed the country was running with fellows accusing themselves of the crime."

"So it is. But these fellows trip themselves up right away because they don't know the facts. But the chap who wrote these letters did know them, and there was only one man who could and that was Burke. Oh, the first two didn't mean anything, but then he tried to be clever. He sent a letter to Bruce. And I hadn't told anyone I was usin' Bruce except Mr. Rupert Burke."

"I suppose you told him on purpose," said Mr. Stout.

"No harm droppin' a hint or two. And then, mark you, it 'ud be rather too much of a coincidence for Chigwell to have two dates with two chaps with the initials R. B. on the same evenin'. I mean, I can swallow a lot," he looked meaningly at his tankard but Mr. Stout regrettably failed to take the hint,

" but that was a bit too much. And then, what was Chigwell likely to have on a fellow like Bairstowe, a part-time warden at about three pounds a week, with a little radio dump that hardly paid its way ? Why, he wouldn't repay stamp duty."

" Personally," suggested Mr. Stout, " I couldn't believe that if Bairstowe were guilty he'd come forward and draw attention to the fact that he'd been on the premises at approximately the crucial hour."

" He'd have been a damned sight more intelligent than most murderers are if he had," acknowledged Crook heartily. " The essence of successful murder, for what it's worth to you," he looked thoughtfully round the occupants of the bar, " is, ' Don't take any unnecessary chances.' There was a 1000-to-1 chance that someone did see him coming out of the house. Someone might have been passing or standin' in the doorway opposite. . . . "

" Would you have recognised anyone in a storm and at that hour of the evening ? "

" Might have recognised the warden's dress. Might have met him at the end of the street. But if he said of his own free will that he'd been puttin' Chigwell on the carpet over a light offence no one had anything on him. No, Burke was my man from the start. I said these criminals never know when to lie low. He had the sort of luck most murderers pray for when young Jardine came forward and he should have copied Brer Rabbit. Then I wouldn't have had anything on him. But he couldn't do it—they never can. When he knew Bess Carter was goin' about like a lioness with a wounded cub he thought he saw his chance. He wanted to know what I was goin' to do, and he thought he could persuade me to put my cards on the table."

" And you did," said Mr. Stout slowly.

" Yes, but not the trumps. His trouble was he didn't know which were trumps, so he didn't know which were my valuable cards. I told him the bit about Bruce on purpose. And then— that letter he sent himself the day Bess Carter was murdered. A real killer—one from outside, I mean—wouldn't have risked leavin' it on the mat. It was a foggy day, a chap going out in a hurry mightn't have noticed it. The man who put that letter where Mrs. McKay found it knew it was goin' to be found. An outsider would have come up and dropped it into the letter-box. He'd have had plenty of time to get out of sight just by goin' on up to the next floor before Burke had opened the envelope and started lookin' for the messenger. You'll have noticed, too, that chaps always plunge downstairs when they're lookin' for someone, so it's generally safe to go up and then he could have come saunterin' down at his leisure. If anyone did see him on the stairs in a block that size he'd simply be taken for a tenant or an evacuee or somethin' harmless. There was one other detail, too," he added, his voice flagging a bit from acute thirst, " and that was that Cotham said when Burke rang him at six he could hear a dance band playin' on the radio, but he didn't remember hearin' anything at five. Well, of course he wouldn't. Because at five Burke wasn't ringin' up from his flat but from a call-box and they don't give you the radio there—not yet."

Mr. Stout sighed. " There isn't a single big outstanding fact in the lot," he said, " Just trifles. . . . "

" Many a mickle makes a muckle," returned Crook, rather indignantly. " The squirrel is a saver—are you ? No, I had to get him to give himself away for good and all, and the hammer was my chance. Y'see, for once he was off his guard. He thought I'd swallowed his plot, hook, line and sinker. I had to let him think that, though it was tough on Bairstowe, because I had to make him destroy himself. When he thought he'd thrown dust in my eyes he let himself go. It's like what they tell you in the Bible—all is vanity. It's man's undoing at the last."

Mr. Stout nodded. " I see," he said. " I wondered."

Mr. Crook wondered too, along different lines, but it was a clear case of parallels not meeting. When Mr. Stout spoke again he didn't say, as Crook had hoped, " What's yours ? " but, " See about young Jardine ? "

Crook hadn't. His clients ceased to exist for him once he'd got them off.

" Posthumous V.C.," said Mr. Stout. " They took him back in some capacity or other and he got himself finished dragging some pilot out of a blazing plane. He doesn't seem to have got much out of life one way and another."

He sighed. Mr. Crook reflected sympathetically that he was obviously born to a political career. He took life so hard.

" Cheer up ! " he said. " It was a lot better than swinging for murder. And don't look so blue. After all, you and me are still battin' for the Home Side. It's still got a chance."

And then, because he liked to boast that he wasn't afraid of risks, he said heartily, " Do they let me buy drinks in this joint or do I slip you the money under the table ? "

When Mr. Stout, startled and affronted, said that in Westminster they kept the laws they framed with so much care, he nearly passed out.

" Make it a double for me," said Mr. Crook.

>>> If you've enjoyed this book and would like to discover more great vintage crime and thriller titles, as well as the most exciting crime and thriller authors writing today, visit: >>>

The Murder Room
Where Criminal Minds Meet

themurderroom.com

9 781471 909801